Cassidy Jones and the Seventh Attendant

"I have never had such a physically visceral reaction to any other story I've read. I felt an ache when Cassidy was hurt, fear when her life was in jeopardy, and happiness when she made it through another day. A solid five star adventure." —Lindsey Gray, Author of The Redemption Series

"Rarely ever have I come across a story that was such a complete and utter joy to read...Cassidy Jones Adventures is, hands down, the best series I've had the pleasure of absorbing." —Javier A. Robayo, Author of *The Gaze*

Cassidy Jones and the Luminous

"I said it once, and I'll say it again: CASSIDY JONES ROCKS!...Ms. Stokes writes on-the-edge-of-your-seat adventures that are appropriate for kids and adults. I am a huge fan..." —Erik, This Kid Reviews Books

"Cassidy Jones is a spunky heroine who hooks you with her charm and vulnerability right before hitting the fast forward button on a rocket ride of an adventure. You won't be able to put this down until the very last zinger! Enjoy the ride." —Tara Fairfield, Author of *Makai Queen* and *Makai King*

Cassidy Jones and the Eternal Flame

"I absolutely LOVED reading *Eternal Flame*... heart-pounding action, tugging at the heartstrings — this book has a LOT of heart. The whole series continues to grow in complexity and the stakes are raised ever higher. It's a great adventure and a worthwhile read." — Karie, The Dragon's Nook

"Stokes gives us another edge of your seat adventure with one of the most amazing super-heroines I've ever read about." —Erik, This Kid Reviews Books

ELISE STOKES

CASSIDY JONES
AND THE SECRET FORMULA

BOOK ONE

Publishing LLC.

Name, characters, places, and incidences portrayed in this book are fictitious. Similarities to a real person, alive or deceased, locales, establishments, or events are coincidental and not intended by the author.

info@cassidyjonesadventures.com

Edited by William Greenleaf, Greenleaf Literary Services

Cover design by Twin Art Design

ISBN 978-0-615-37713-1

Publishing LLC.

Printed In The United States Of America

For Julia, Audrey, Catherine, and Ethan

Contents

Prologue

Serena Phillips was in the midst of recording her discoveries of the day when the door to her laboratory swung open.

Not even a knock, she thought to herself, ignoring the intruder while continuing to write. The data she noted was more crucial than anything this person could possibly want. These discoveries could lead to her atonement for past work, work meant to destroy life.

Serena was only inches away from a breakthrough, inches away from changing the world.

The intruder cleared his throat. "*Aw-hem!* Not real hospitable, are ya, Professor?"

Serena looked up at the intruder and started.

In the doorway stood the most ridiculous man she had ever seen. No more than five feet tall, he wore a blue and red checkered suit, a turquoise shirt with a neon-green tie cinched at the collar, and polished red leather dress shoes.

Who would create such a thing? she wondered, staring in awe at the shoes. Her gaze then traveled to the man's companion, who now stepped into view. Her breath caught at the sight of the imposing figure outfitted in black leather. Icy fear crept into her stomach as she observed his stony expression and empty eyes.

The silent companion stepped out of the room and robotically pulled the door shut. Through the frosted

1

glass, she saw him station himself beside the door, motionless as a statue.

Serena slowly rose to her feet, her gaze riveted on the little man as he strolled through her lab, hands behind his back, looking around appreciatively as if taking in the sights of Paris.

"Your reputation precedes you, Professor," said the little man, swatting like a playful kitten at a pair of trousers Serena had hung to dry on the clothesline extending across the room. "A little *cuckoo,* wouldn't you say?" he added, whirling a stubby finger at his temple as he continued to move around restlessly.

Serena found her voice. "Who are you?"

With his back to her, the man stood before the coffeepot, tipping it towards him. Peering into the glass pot, he snorted a laugh. "Don't tell me you drink this stuff! I'd think a *brilliant* geneticist such as yourself would have higher standards." He shoved the pot back in place and then stepped left to the beakers simmering on a set of Bunsen burners.

"Get away from those," Serena demanded, hearing panic in her voice.

The little man heard it, too.

Leaning over the steam rising from the beakers, he inhaled deeply, closed his eyes, and smiled to himself. "Mmmm. Tantalizing. Animal DNA with a little touch of—"

He abruptly turned to Serena, and it was then that she saw the similarity. Those were the same steely gray eyes, eyes she had prayed never to see again. The shock of recognition caused her knees to buckle, and she fell into her chair.

2

The man's lips twisted into a sadistic smile. "...Some*thing,*" he finished, sidling toward her desk. "I can see by the blood draining from your face that you've noticed the family resemblance."

He paused in his progress to snort another laugh, slapping a hand against his thigh. "You should see yourself, Professor! It's like you've seen a ghost." Imitating her expression, he waved his stubby fingers in the air like spider legs, adding, "Mwa-ha-ha-ha."

"What does he know of my recent research?" Serena managed, the "some-*thing*" ringing through her head.

The man stopped before her desk. "Oh, come on, Professor. Let's cut to the chase already. What *don't* we know about Formula 10X?"

Hearing the classified name of her secret formula come from his mouth drove the air from Serena's lungs. *What other intelligence has he gathered? Does he know of the accelerant?*

"What don't we know about...you?" He shoved stacks of folders aside and heaved himself onto her desk, dangling his legs off the side. "You really need an extra chair, Professor, but then you're not so savvy about social etiquette, are ya?" The little man sighed, quoting, "'Serena has her head in the clouds,' he always says."

"What does he want?"

The gaudy man went on as if she hadn't spoken, his gaze bouncing around the room. "Phillips is a household name for us. The magnificent Phillips family! Serena Phillips...Gavin Phillips...and, drum roll, please!" His hands drummed the desktop; his steely eyes bore into hers. "Emery Phillips."

Oh, God in heaven, no!

3

Her eyes dropped to her notebook, staring unseeing at the data. "What does he want?" she repeated, knowing the answer full well.

"I'll tell it to you in one word, babe…Assassin."

One

Any Normal Day

"Robin! Robin! Robin!" the adoring crowd shouted.

Actually, the adoring crowd consisted of three members of Robin Newton's girl squad, or the "remoras," as I liked to call them, and a few infatuated ninth-grade boys who had decided there was safety in numbers to show their admiration for our school's shining star.

The rest of us in seventh-period P.E. silently watched her pull herself up the rope like a monkey. Not that she looked anything like a monkey, because monkeys aren't tall, blond, and beautiful.

The first thing I thought while watching her move up the rope was, *Why does someone so mean have to be so knock-out gorgeous and good at everything?* The second thing was, *Why do I have to be next?*

When she reached the top of the rope, Robin lazily tapped the ceiling. Sliding back down, she looked at us below with a bored expression. About three feet from the floor, she released the rope, landing easily on her feet.

I'd be lucky if my scrawny arms could pull me up three feet.

Robin didn't look at me as she walked past. It wasn't an intentional snub. I literally don't think she saw me. Honestly, I'm not even sure if she knew my name. I wasn't the type of girl whose presence registered with her, being neither a threat nor completely pathetic.

Wishing I had some monkey in me, I stepped up to the rope. No cheers came for "Cassidy." We all knew what to expect.

But no one can say I didn't try.

Gripping the rope high, I pulled with all my might. I attempted to look bored like Robin had because I didn't want anyone to think I actually cared about any of this. That alone would have been humiliating. No one was fooled, I'm sure. They all knew I was giving it all I had, and they all knew that I cared what they thought.

I pulled myself off the floor. *Yes!*

My arms started shaking. *No!*

I quickly reached further up the rope and wiggled a few inches up. It was progress, but all the progress my measly muscles were willing to make. For seconds, I fought to squirm a couple of more inches before drop- ping the whole two feet I'd crawled up.

Mr. Saunders blew his whistle. "Lockers," he shouted.

Turning from the rope, I met the relieved faces of my friends, who had been silently waiting their humiliating turn. My sad rope-climbing abilities weren't uncommon among girls my age. Robin's were, and if she hadn't been so good and so fast skirting up that rope, the whistle would have saved me, too. Too bad my stellar performance ended the whole miserable period.

Five minutes later, when the final bell rang, we rushed through the gym doors. This rush of bodies always felt like getting swept up in a wave. We poured into the halls and let the tide of fellow students carry us to our lockers.

Pulling in close to my locker, I let the roaring current flow by. On autopilot, my fingers quickly dialed the locker combination. Yanking the door open, I unhooked my backpack and stuffed in the gym clothes, saturated with five days of stinky sweat. Slamming the locker door, I streamed back in.

While flowing with the current, I thought more about this sea imagery. If we were like the sea, then we were also like the creatures that lived in the sea. Most of us were just trying to survive in an unpredictable, sometimes cruel ocean. There were definitely predators out here, such as the shark. Those who didn't want to be potential shark prey became remoras, suctioning themselves to the cold-blooded fish. Being a remora didn't appeal to me, so, to avoid the sharks' radar, I adopted the strategy of being a sardine. A sardine wasn't exciting, but it was safe.

As I drifted along, I thought of what creatures my best friends resembled. My playful, mischievous friend and neighbor, Miriam Cohen, resembled an otter. Carli Cooper, the cheerful friend, reminded me of a dolphin, and a barracuda best reflected the tiny but mighty Bren Dawsen.

"Cassidy."

Speaking of the otter...

Going against the flow, I stopped and turned toward her. A few heavy backpacks tossed me about while rolling by. "Hey, Miriam," I called.

Beaming, she bobbed toward me with bouncing black curls and sparkling cobalt blue eyes. Her pretty features looked especially dazzling because they were always so alive and animated.

A boy in my freshman class flowing next to me attempted the same maneuver I had made, turning against the current of bodies. Unfortunately, he made this move in front of Dixon Pilchowski.

"Get out of my way, idiot!" Dixon yelled at the boy, viciously shoving him into the lockers.

Flanking Dixon's sides were his toadies, Toby Crocker and Rodrigo Perez. When the boy slipped to the floor after the locker impact, the toadies obediently laughed at him.

A spontaneous crowd of gawkers formed around Dixon and the boy.

Scrambling to his feet, the wide-eyed boy mumbled, "Sorry."

His apparent terror and embarrassment probably would have been enough to appease Dixon; his mood seemed generous. Unfortunately for them both, Miriam witnessed the event.

"Dixon, you are such a jerk," she said loudly.

His menacing eyes whipped to her. "Did you say something to me, Big Mouth?"

Miriam, of course, rose to the challenge. "You're a jerk, Dixon."

Dixon glared down at her in seething hatred, while she smiled up at him victoriously. As far as Miriam was concerned, she'd already won.

A pit always formed in my stomach during their confrontations. So far, Dixon hadn't crossed the line by sticking his fist in her mouth that he so obviously detested, but how far could a guy like Dixon be pushed? Miriam definitely tested the limits of his self-control.

Pushing further, Miriam motioned to the boy who looked like he wanted to run. "Shouldn't you apologize?"

Dixon appeared ready to implode. Smart gawkers stepped back. Attempting to intervene, I tugged at Miriam's arm, urging her away. She ignored me, holding her position.

Dropping his face close to hers, Dixon bellowed, "Will you just shut up!"

When Miriam didn't flinch, he proceeded to call her a string of swear words. With each profane word spewed,

Miriam appeared more powerful. Her satisfied grin spread from ear to ear.

Noticing Dixon's hands clenching and unclenching, I scanned the faces around us, searching for a hero. There were none. No one was stupid or brave enough to step between the biggest bully in school and the silly, bold girl who decided to take him on. However, someone had to intervene, and that someone would have to be me.

Sucking in a breath, I asked, "What, Dixon? Are you bullying girls now?" This question was super lame, because Dixon would bully his own grandma.

He cut me a look, and I felt my legs wobble. "You're both losers," he snarled.

To my horror, Miriam began to laugh hysterically. She wasn't mocking him. He genuinely made her laugh.

Jaw tight and face red from the building pressure, Dixon turned from her before his clenched fist could plow into her face. I was amazed he could resist. With toadies in tow, he stomped down the hall.

The gawkers, as always, gaped at Miriam. Though she didn't purposely seek it out, attention never bothered her when she did get it. A couple of gawkers cautiously joined her laughter when Dixon was out of earshot.

Without a spectacle to observe, the crowd disbanded. At this point, Miriam's laughter had reduced to giggling.

I gave her a disapproving look. "Only you would think that was funny."

My reaction produced a new spurt of giggles. "Cass, I can't help it. He's *soooo* pathetic."

"At some point, he'll become more than pathetic," I warned.

This made her laugh, too, as we returned to the current.

Surging out of the brick building, I felt the energizing rush of cool October air, settling the nerves Miriam's confrontation had put on edge. We were having one of those rare sunny days in Seattle. When the gray that usually blanketed the area lifted, I was always surprised to see how big and blue the sky really was. Sometimes, it seemed too big, and I would wish for the gray blanket to cover us again, making everything cozy.

Miriam prattled the entire half-mile walk to our homes. Every so often, I grunted in response to something she said so it felt like we were having a conversation. When she was like this, she really didn't need my participation, anyway. Knowing Miriam was self- entertained, I decided to lose myself in thoughts about Jared Wells.

I was secretly, and hopelessly, in love with Jared, and it wasn't one of those crushes where the guy doesn't know the girl exists. At one time, Jared very much knew I existed. In fact, from what I understood, he felt very much the way I did now. However, I had missed that boat, so to speak, and now that it had sailed off, all I had were silly daydreams. Daydreams were better than nothing, though.

While Jared formed a pleasant thought in my head, Miriam's voice formed a pleasant hum in my ear. Suddenly, the hum hit an irritating pitch.

"You're not listening, Cassidy Jones," Miriam accused.

"I'm listening." I did hear the hum, after all.

"Sure you were. I could tell by the spaced-out look that you were taking it all in." She gave me a naughty smile. "Okay, now, tell me who you were thinking about."

I couldn't help but blush.

Miriam laughed. "Okay, I'll guess," she teased.

Like I said, my crush was a secret. No one knew how I felt about Jared, not even Miriam. Unlike Miriam, who held her torches up high, I kept mine safely to myself. If, by chance, Jared's name made it on the list she was preparing to antagonize me with, I knew I wasn't enough of a poker face not to get caught.

When I scowled, she smiled.

"Really, Cassidy," she said with a sigh. "You give me no choice." Her eyes mischievously sparkled as her lips formed the first name. It began with a "W." Before she could get it out, I found a distraction.

"No way! They just moved in," I exclaimed, nodding to a moving truck parked across the street from my house. This was a weak attempt to throw Miriam's mind off-track, but she was easily distracted.

Her gaze followed mine. "That house is like a revolving door," she said, squinting her eyes. "It must be a total dump, or else the rent is outrageous." Pausing in thought, she grinned, elbowing me. "Maybe cute boys are moving in. Twins. One for me, one for you. I'll even give you first dibs," she generously offered.

No matter how many tracks her quick mind jumped to, it always seemed to return to the same one.

"Oh, geez, thanks," I joked. "Knowing our luck, though, if there are twin boys, they'll be snot-nosed, three-year-old terrors that we'll be asked to babysit."

"That's *your* luck, Cassidy, not mine," she pointed out with a laugh, stopping at her front gate. "Want to hang out while I pack for Portland?"

"Can't. I don't know when my dad is picking me up."

"Oh, that's right. You're going on that boring interview today."

I couldn't really argue with her, because I also expected the interview to be as exciting as watching grass grow. My dad had been a news anchorman up until two years ago, when he'd decided he would rather spend more time with his family than keep his prestigious position. He had proposed to the local news station that he develop a human-interest segment to be aired at the end of the weeknight broadcasts. Eager to keep their anchor airing, the station agreed.

Everyone loved Drake Jones and his human-interest segment. When I say everyone enjoyed Dad's segment, I'm referring to anyone above the age of eighteen. Most of the people Dad interviewed were a little dry for my taste, and for anyone else my age. He usually interviewed local "movers and shakers," never anyone cool. Today's interviewee, who was some kind of scientist at Wallingford University, promised to be really bland, but being bored to tears was worth it if it meant hanging out with my dad.

"Yep, that boring interview," I said.

Miriam grinned. "Well, have a good time," she wished, teasing, of course.

"You, too." My wish was sincere. "Say hi to your grandma for me. See ya Monday."

I walked two doors down to our English Tudor home and went inside.

Two

My Wonderful Family

Entering the kitchen, I had to shield my eyes—not because my sun-deprived eyes were being blinded by the light pouring in through the room's large window, but because of the glare the light created in this completely white space.

From the cabinetry to the marble countertops to the grout between the limestone tiles, everything was white, or a variation of it. Three years ago, during our historic home's renovation, the designer had warned my mom against light colors and three kids. But my mom, who had always dreamed of a pristine kitchen, could not be persuaded otherwise. Of course, the designer had been right. There was no hiding peanut butter fingerprints on white cabinets, and mud dragged in from the back yard didn't camouflage well on creamy limestone. However, Elizabeth Jones wasn't easily defeated. Much of her time was spent scrubbing her kitchen until it shined, and she expected the same enthusiasm from the mess perpetrators. Being one of those perpetrators, I had come to resent white and kitchens altogether.

"Hi, Cass. How was school?" Mom asked, while scrubbing the porcelain farmhouse sink.

"Fine." What more could I say? Nothing much ever happened to someone whose entire goal was not to attract attention.

My five-year-old brother, Chazz, sat at the kitchen's island, dipping graham crackers in a glass of milk. Chazz

13

lived and breathed superheroes. If his nose wasn't stuck in a comic book, he was improvising a costume. Today, he wore a green sweatshirt, lime-green sweatpants with holes in the knees, and a pair of Dad's boxers pulled over those. I really hoped he hadn't gone to kindergarten in that getup.

Easing myself onto the stool next to him, I decided to ask. "Hey, Chazzy, I like the outfit. Did you wear it to school?"

"Nope." He shook his head proudly. "I just made it up when I got home…Guess who I am?"

Green, green…Who wore green? "The Green Goblin?" I guessed.

He looked horrified. "That's a bad guy." His bottom lip jutted out.

"Come on, Chazzy, you know I don't know anything about superheroes."

"I know you're not real smart about them," he agreed graciously. "I'm the Hulk, the *Incredible* Hulk."

"Oh, yeah. He's green."

Though disappointed, Chazz forgave my ignorance. "Want one?" he asked, pushing the graham cracker package toward me.

"Thanks, buddy." I slid a cracker from the plastic.

Taking a nibble, I glanced out the window at our classic Seattle view of the Space Needle. On a clear day like today, Mount Rainier, a humungous, dormant volcano, partially framed the city.

"You're here, but Miriam's not."

I turned my head to look at my twin, Nate, who stood at the kitchen entry. "Great observation, Sherlock," I came back. "Why would she be here?"

Walking to the island, he grinned at my sarcasm. "Because she always is. Hi, Mom."

"Hello, Nate. How was your day?"

"The usual," he answered, then looked at Chazz. "Hey, Hulk."

Thrilled to be recognized, Chazz growled in response.

Swiping the cracker from my hand, Nate asked, "So where is she?"

Grabbing the cracker back, I answered, "You'll be glad to know that *she* will be at her grandma's all weekend."

"Good. My ears could use the break."

Miriam generally had two effects on boys. They either thought the sun rose and set on her pretty face, or they avoided her like the plague. Nate fell into the second category.

"I heard she and Pilchowski got into it today."

My jaw dropped. "Today? That happened, like, twenty minutes ago."

Nate shrugged. "News travels fast." His tone turned advisory. "She'd better watch it, though. Pilchowski is a ticking time bomb. He won't care that she's a girl."

"I know. So does she, but you know Miriam."

"That's why it's only a matter of time."

Mom moved to the island, armed with a sponge. "What's this all about? Did someone threaten Miriam?"

"No threat, Mom," I said quickly. "Everything is fine. Dixon got a little intense but walked off. No big deal."

"There's always some problem with that boy." Mom frowned, wiping up cracker crumbs. "Be sure to tell me if this progresses."

Mom was like Miriam. They both liked justice and had no problem enforcing it.

"Sure," I answered to appease her, admiring her dark red hair in the sunlight.

All of us kids had inherited her hair color, as well as her wide-set green eyes and fair complexion. Though we were fair, our complexions were not interrupted by freckles, except for a light splash across our noses. I hated that splash. Dad was the odd one out in the family, with his crystal blue eyes and blond hair, though there was hardly anything odd-looking about my dad. What can I say? It wasn't only the public that loved Dad; so did the camera. All around, my dad didn't have a bad angle.

Dad strolled into the kitchen, making a round of hugs. To Chazz, he said, "How did you get in here, Hulk?"

Chazz growled an unintelligible explanation.

Ruffling the Hulk's hair, Dad turned to me. "We've got to shake a leg, Cass. Professor Phillips was reluctant about this interview. I don't want to give her the chance to back out."

"I've been waiting for you," I said, hopping down from the stool.

Dad pecked Mom's cheek. "We shouldn't be more than three hours. Do you mind if I invite Ben for dinner afterward?"

"Not at all. I'll put another chicken in the oven," she teased.

Mom loved Dad's cameraman, Ben Johnson, as much as we all did. Dad had taken a chance hiring Ben two years ago. Though a natural talent, he was only twenty- one when Dad hired him, but he didn't disappoint. The other thing Ben was natural at was being himself, and there weren't too many Bens out there. Wherever he went, his good nature and easy humor put everyone at ease. He truly was one of my most favorite people.

~~~

"Hey, Cassy Girl. How are ya?" Ben greeted me as I climbed into the back of Dad's black Volvo. Turning around, he gave me a toothy smile.

"Fine, Ben." I flopped into the backseat. "How are you?"

"Good." When he nodded, his wild, corkscrew hair came alive. "Real good."

Ben's four passions in life were filming, X Games, conspiracy theories, and food, and not necessarily in that order. One of his passions always produced interesting conversation or entertainment.

His first passion to come up, which I could have predicted because of the time of day, was food. Ben's endless quest was to keep his stomach full, though it appeared to be bottomless. The guy did burn a lot of calories with all the extreme sports he participated in.

Ben glanced at Dad's profile. "Deluxe is up ahead. Mind going through, Drake?"

Inwardly, I groaned.

I despised the saucy, greasy burgers that were considered by many, including Ben, to be Seattle's best. Even smelling a Deluxe burger made me want to hurl. The only relatively tolerable item on the entire burger joint's menu was the fries. They were laden with grease, but fries are supposed to be.

At the drive-thru window, Ben ordered enough food for all of us, though he was the only one eating. Thoughtfully, he ordered extra fries for me. As he offered them to me, I shook my head.

"No, thanks, I'm not hungry." Today, I didn't think I could stomach the grease.

Ben stared at me in disbelief. "No fries? But you're a growing girl."

He would consider grease essential to growth. He claimed ketchup was a vegetable.

Back on the road, I eyed Ben's teeth sinking into the soppy Double Deluxe, which was double the grease. It probably made him feel like a health nut.

The bite went down in one gulp. "Best burger ever," he claimed, rolling his eyes.

Grimacing, I glanced out the window.

"Cassidy," Dad spoke up.

I turned to look at him. "Yeah."

"Do you know what DNA is?" he asked.

The question would have seemed out of the blue if I didn't know where we were headed. Dad always attempted to build intrigue in us kids when we accompanied him on an interview. Today, my goal was only to stay awake, though I didn't share my lack of enthusiasm with him. Instead, I gave the illusion of interest by imparting my DNA knowledge.

"Sure, Dad. It's what all living things are made up of. The blueprint of how we are designed," I said, quoting my biology teacher. "Our basic building blocks."

"Great visual," Dad complimented. "Now, have you heard of Professor Serena Phillips?"

I wasn't up-to-speed on nerdy scientists. "Nope. Is that who you're interviewing?"

He nodded. "Professor Phillips is a world-renowned geneticist. Wallingford recently announced that she's developing a gene therapy that will reverse the effects of many disabilities and diseases people suffer from. For example, her therapy may give a blind person sight or a paralyzed person the ability to walk. What's so cutting-edge about Professor Phillips's research is that she's using animal DNA to create a gene treatment for humans. If her treatment proves out, she will change the world as we know it."

"Oh, cool, Dad." My mind had started wandering at the word "geneticist."

"Wait just a second," Ben said, sticking an index finger in the air. "I know all about this gene therapy."

Dad groaned.

"Seriously, I know about this," Ben insisted. "Now don't start judging, Drake—just hear me out, okay?

"Awhile back, I was talking with this guy at a coffee shop. He told me about his cousin—no, wait—his uncle. Yeah, uncle. Anyway, this uncle is CIA—"

"Not Area 51?" Dad said teasingly.

According to Ben, Area 51 was a secret military base outside Las Vegas where the government hid alien spacecraft.

"No, not 51. It's the lab in North Dakota—Drake, now don't laugh. It's legit. Seriously, it's the same stuff this professor is doing, but with alien DNA—"

Dad's smile shifted to alarm. "Ben, please do not say that to the professor."

"Are you crazy, Drake? As far as I know, she's part of the cover-up."

The laugh I smothered slipped out.

Ben grinned at me. "Oh, come on, Cassy Girl, not you, too. Don't be like your old man. Be open-minded." Turning back to Dad, he continued, "Drake, think about all the crazy stuff going on all the time. Aliens make sense. Seriously, dig around a bit. I tell you, there *is* a story here—and an Emmy. If you're willing, I'll hook you up with the coffee shop guy."

"I'll tell you what, Ben. Give me evidence and legitimate sources, and I'll do your alien DNA story."

"Done." Ben slapped his leg. "I'll get you evidence. But, *you*, Drake, need to be open to the truth."

"I'm open, but none of your sources can be alien abductees or Roswell witnesses."

My laughter burst.

19

Glancing at me, Ben smiled a big, toothy smile. "You'll see, Cassy Girl." He playfully shook a finger at me. "You'll both see."

Three

Peculiar Professor Phillips

Once we had signed in at the front desk in the building's lobby, the security guard admitting us to Professor Phillips's lab directed us to a flight of stairs. Students and staff with badges rushing past us first noticed Ben's bulky camera. Their eyes then moved to Dad. That shocked look of recognition crossed their faces, but everyone was in too much of a hurry or too intimidated to inquire what Drake Jones was up to at Wallingford.

Watching Dad and Ben ascend the stairs, I observed how much they looked like polar opposites. My dad, with his clean-shaven, timeless good looks and million-dollar smile, looked like the guy in front of the camera, while Ben, in a Hawaiian shirt with a couple of missing buttons, board shorts, flip-flops, and untamed hair, most definitely looked like the guy behind the camera—or a guy who worked at Game Stop. Even their size and complexions were mismatched. Dad had the typical fair Nordic complexion, while Ben's skin was like a creamy café mocha. With a solid build, Dad stood at five-foot-ten, at least half a head shorter than Ben. Though athletic, Ben was lanky. He liked to joke that he had to run around the shower to get wet.

When we reached the third floor, a janitorial cart with a large trash bin hitched to it barreled into the hall from an open doorway, cutting us off. The custodian pushing the cart stared at us with some hostility, and then his lips turned up into a sneering smile, revealing a silver canine tooth.

"Pardon me, *por favor*," he said in a thick accent, eyeing Ben's camera and pulling the cart back.

As we walked away, I could feel his dark eyes burning a hole in my back.

At the end of the hall on the third floor, Dad tapped on the frosted glass of Professor Phillips's lab door. There was no answer.

Moving his fist over to the door's wood frame, he knocked firmly.

"Who is it?" a woman asked from inside the lab.

Relief washed over Dad's face. "Professor Phillips, it's Drake Jones from Channel Five News."

There was no response.

"We have an interview scheduled for four-thirty. I realize I'm early. I would be happy to come back then if it's more—"

"No, no. Now is fine," the professor interrupted. A deadbolt turned.

How strange that she locks the door during the day, I thought.

"Please, come in, Mr. Jones," she said.

As Dad opened the door, the first thing that caught my eye was a clothesline stretched across the room with actual articles of clothing clipped to it.

Four long, white, laminate-top chemistry tables filled most of the small room's floor space. The tables piled high with stuff gave the feeling of a rummage sale rather than a famous geneticist's laboratory. Every table was heaped high with folders, notebooks, lab equipment, and open cardboard boxes with more stuff poking out the top. Between the clothesline and the boxes, I wondered if the professor had taken up residence in her lab.

A built-in cabinet, with its long, stainless-steel sink and counter space displaying lab equipment set up for use, suggested that something other than laundry was being done here. The burgundy-colored coffeemaker at one end of the counter, with dirty coffee mugs scattered in front of it, threw off the seriousness of the operation. But the five lit Bunsen burners with glass beakers simmering away on the counter gave the impression that maybe something science-oriented took place here— nothing too lethal, though, with a half-eaten bagel lying on a crinkly napkin next to the burners.

After soaking in the environment, I took in the petite woman responsible for the chaos. She didn't differ too much from her surroundings. Straight brown hair hung limply around her heart-shaped face. Her skin, creamy and smooth, gave her a childlike appearance, though she had to be at least forty. The crumpled lab coat she wore probably had been line-dried. It definitely had never made it into a dryer, considering how wrinkled it was. Most disturbing—or perhaps stunning, I'm not sure which—were the professor's brown eyes. Round and dewy, like a doe's, at this moment they looked shocked, as if she had just been caught in headlights.

Dad and Ben looked similarly taken aback by the room and the professor. Dad hid it a little better than Ben did. Slack-jawed, Ben stared, his eyes bouncing around the room.

Quickly stepping forward, Dad extended his hand. "Professor Phillips, I'm Drake Jones. Thank you for agreeing to this interview. I know how busy you are, and I do appreciate the time you've given us today."

With a dazed expression, she took his hand. "It's nice to meet you, Mr. Jones."

"Please, call me Drake. Professor Phillips, I would like to introduce you to my cameraman, Ben Johnson."

The professor stared distractedly at Ben's hair, though I don't think his hair diverted her attention. I had the feeling it was something other than us.

Not deterred, Ben picked up her small hand, vigorously shaking it. "Good to meet you."

"You, too, Mr. Johnson," she responded mechanically.

"And this is my daughter, Cassidy," said Dad.

Her gaze moved to me, making me blush, for some reason.

"Nice to meet you, Professor Phillips," I said awkwardly, painfully aware of my burning cheeks. How embarrassing to be so embarrassed.

Losing the dazed look, her expression became kind. "It is very nice to meet you, Cassidy." Fully engaged now, she turned to Dad and smiled. "Forgive me, Drake, if I appeared reluctant. I admit I have been so caught up in my work that I neglected to observe the time. I am prepared for this interview, and I know you, too, are busy. I do appreciate your interest in my research and your desire to better inform the public about it. Now, where would you like to conduct the interview?"

Dad's professional eye scanned the room, settling on a desk area in one corner. "Would your desk be all right?"

"Perfectly."

As she turned to lead the way, I was startled to see the back of her head. From the front, her hair had been flat and smooth, but the hair in the back was a knotted, tangled mess. *Maybe she only brushes what she can see,* I thought.

Moving quickly, she weaved through the narrow path between the tables and clutter. We followed single-file, ducking the clothesline. As Ben crouched under the thin cord, his camera snagged a pair of pantyhose, of all things. Rapidly untangling the nylons, he threw them back over the line.

24

With a dinged metal file cabinet and a disorganized bookshelf behind it, her wood desk didn't make an impressive platform for an interview. At least the thick books on the shelves, with titles I couldn't pronounce, looked scientific. Dad and Ben staged the area as best they could, gingerly asking permission to clear files from the desk and stack the clutter of books. Dad found a single folding chair from which to conduct the interview, while Ben stared at the clothesline. With a furrowed brow, he was likely mentally debating whether to ask if he could take it down. Finally shrugging, he tried different camera angles to keep the low line out of the frame, instead of risking a blunder.

As they prepared for the interview, the professor silently observed me, while I pretended not to notice. After a few minutes of this, she asked, "Cassidy, are you fourteen?"

"Yes, I am, Professor Phillips."

She smiled. "My son, Emery, turned fifteen this last August."

Not knowing what else to say, I disclosed, "I'll be fifteen in February."

She scrutinized my face, making me feel like I was in a petri dish. "You're quite lovely. Your hair is an extraordinary color."

The remark flabbergasted me. After saying this, she curiously watched my cheeks turn crimson.

Though I hated receiving compliments, I attempted to handle this one graciously. "Thank you. All of us kids have the same color hair. We got it from our mom." Patting my cheeks, I attempted to calm them down. She seemed to find this interesting, too.

Dad broke the spell. "We're ready, Professor Phillips."

Breathing a sigh of relief, I watched her move to the desk and sit in the chair Dad pulled out for her. Then he looked at me. "Cass, why don't you take a seat?"

He glanced down at a notepad in his hands, without first suggesting where I should take this seat. Obviously, he had some idea, or he wouldn't have suggested it. Scanning, the only likely candidate I could see was a wooden stool next to the coffeemaker.

It was silly, but as I crossed the room to the stool, I felt like I was walking to the electric chair. Feeling panicky, I told myself, *This weird room and the weird professor has weirded you out. So just chill, and don't make something out of nothing.* Taking my sound advice, my heart slowed to a reasonable pace.

The stool tottered as I climbed up on it. Carefully, I centered my backside over it. The rickety thing felt like it would topple with the slightest move. *How can Professor Phillips work from this without nose-diving into a microscope?* I wondered.

As I held still, my eyes moved to the steam rising from the beakers. The boiling liquids were a tawny, burnished color and smelled like chicken broth. *Is this her way of heating up soup?* I asked myself.

Shifting my gaze from the cooking project to the interview scene, I met Professor Phillips's anxious eyes. Her expression was conflicted.

"Are you ready, Professor Phillips?" Dad asked.

"Yes, we shouldn't delay this any further."

I thought the comment rude, but Dad took no notice of it as he presented her with his first question.

One thing I had predicted about the interview proved to be spot-on. Listening to the professor explain her gene therapy was like watching grass grow. Bored by her lengthy responses and foreign words, my mind picked up where it had left off in the daydream Miriam had interrupted.

Jared and I are walking along a sandy beach, cool waves lapping at our feet. Suddenly, the sand trembles beneath them. Earthquake?

Snapping out of the daydream, I realized the stool was giving way beneath me. Before any reflex could kick in, I fell towards the coffeemaker and dirty mugs. Before I could smash into them face-first, my hands came to life. Frantically waving while I plunged, I knocked the beakers off the burners. Catching the edge of the counter, I had a close-up view of the strange occurrence on top.

It's difficult to describe what happened in that fraction of a second as the hot liquids ran together. The best description I can come up with is "Poof!" The liquids instantaneously vaporized, forming a white cloud. At the same instance, I took a fateful breath, sucking in the cloud puff. In the cloud, my eyes felt like acid had been thrown into them, and my lungs seemed to collapse.

As I gasped for air, my heart burned as if on fire, pumping the inferno into my body. The blood flowing through my veins became flaming rivers, carrying the fire throughout. When the fire circulated through every part of me, a jolt shook my brain like I'd been struck by lightning. The inferno turned cold, and blackness engulfed me.

Impenetrable black surrounded me. My ears detected no sound. Because I felt nothing beneath me, I thought I could be floating, though I didn't seem to be in motion. Cognitively, I was aware of my limbs, though they were unresponsive when instructed to move. My skin felt thick and numb.

Assuming my nerve endings had been fried in the blaze, I thought perhaps I was dead. But I could breathe. Besides my mind, my lungs were functioning. Inhaling, I detected no odor or fragrances in this dark place. Never had I been aware before of how many subtle scents I would take in with each breath, until they were gone—completely gone.

The senses I had lost were threads that attached me to the world. With those threads clipped, I drifted into nothingness.

I felt a soft thud against my eardrum. The thud grew stronger, becoming a vibration. The vibration turned into distinguishable sound. Voices. I could hear the murmur of voices. The voices were far away, but with each elapsing second, they moved closer. They were familiar, especially one. I recognized it as Dad's. For a moment, I listened to the tone of his voice. He sounded urgent, upset. My mind pushed further to decipher the utterances that flowed together, until those sounds came together into words.

"Cassy, come on, open your eyes. Talk to me." Something thumped against my cheek. It was persistent and annoying. Something else warm trickled over my temples. The source of the warmth welled up in the center of my forehead.

"Drake, here. This is clean," a woman said, her voice full of concern.

Something soft pressed against the oozing well. The trickling stopped, but pain sharply ripped through the well. A scream thundered in my ears.

"Cassy, it's okay. I know it hurts, but please, don't struggle. You have a gash in your forehead. Please, calm down."

Aware now of my flailing limbs, I stilled them.

"Good, Cassidy, just rest. I'm taking care of you."

Comforted, I sighed, slowly opening my eyes. The brightness was shocking. Through the glare, I made out subtle outlines. The outlines came into focus.

"Dad," I forced through my parched throat.

Dad smiled down at me in relief. "Hello, sweetheart. That was quite a fall."

My gaze drifted beyond him to Ben. His lips turned up into a worried smile. "Cassy Girl, you scared me there for a minute, but you're going to be okay," he assured in a soothing voice.

Only a minute? I thought.

My eyes drifted left, where I found Professor Phillips. Her face looked distressed as she examined the countertop. She ran her fingers along it. Flipping her palm over, she rubbed her thumb along her fingertips. Bringing her hand to her nose, she sniffed her fingers, tasting them with the tip of her tongue.

I watched her lips form a word that she spoke to herself in a whisper: "Evaporated."

Her eyes sharpened, darting down to me and searching my face briefly. Turning abruptly back to the counter, she examined something on top. *What is she looking at?* I wondered. Wanting to see, I lifted my head and shoulders off the floor.

"Whoa, where do you think you're going?" Gently, Dad pushed my shoulders back down to the floor with one hand, while the other pressed the soft thing against my forehead. "Take it easy until the bleeding slows down."

As he said this, Professor Phillips stared down at me.

Her face lit, like an idea had dawned on her. Suddenly, she moved from the counter, stepping toward me. Two steps later, she walked out of my line of sight.

As I twisted my neck to follow her, Dad pressed his hand more firmly to my forehead.

"That's too hard," I protested, pushing his hand.

Grabbing my hand with his free one, Dad explained, patiently, "Cass, the pressure slows the bleeding. Once it slows, we can get you up and to the hospital. You'll need a few stitches."

"And to get checked for a concussion," Ben added. "Drake, I'm going downstairs to make sure the cart's there." With that, he briskly walked away.

The door closed.

"Where's Ben going?" I asked.

"Security is sending over an electric cart to take us to the car," Dad answered, smiling warmly. "Ben is verifying the cart is there before we get you up."

Professor Phillips returned, bending down next to me. Her expression had changed again. Something looked different about her eyes. They appeared detached or focused elsewhere, though she looked directly at me. They also had a strange glow about them, like she was excited or intrigued.

"Cassidy, how are you feeling?" she asked in a clinical tone.

"My head hurts."

"Anything else besides pain? Do you remember anything that happened before you hit your head?"

"No," I lied, looking away from her.

Silently, she examined me. I could feel her eyes on my face.

"Here, Drake, a fresh towel. Give me the other one."

Towel? I turned back to her.

Taking the white hand towel she held to him, Dad carefully lifted the cushion on my forehead. The cushion was a white hand towel, saturated with my blood. Briefly inspecting my exposed forehead, Dad frowned. Quickly, he pressed the new towel against the wound.

"Thank you." Dad gratefully smiled at Professor Phillips, handing her the bloodied towel.

While Dad tended to me, she moved to the countertop. I watched her put the bloodied towel in a large Ziploc bag. Opening the cabinet door below, she put the bag inside.

"The cart's ready," Ben announced, walking back into the room.

"Let's get you up, sweetheart." Dad smiled, wrapping one arm below my lower back and cradling the back of my head with the other. "Here, Cass, hold the towel to your forehead while I pull you up... Good... Move slow. You're going to be lightheaded. "

While Dad pulled me up toward him, Ben bent behind me, lifting me under my arms. As I rose to my feet, I had a brief feeling of vertigo. Once it cleared, I felt stable.

"I'm fine," I said. "Let's go." I stepped forward. My sudden move alarmed them.

"Careful, Cassy," Dad warned, tightening his hold.

"You'll drop fast if you've got a concussion," Ben added.

"I don't feel dizzy," I insisted. "In fact, I think the bleeding stopped."

As I moved the towel from my forehead, Ben quickly pushed it back, holding his hand over mine. *"Keep that there."*

"Okay," I snapped, frowning profusely.

Removing his hand from mine, Ben's serious face softened into a grin. "Irritability. Definitely a concussion. Let's get your girl going, Drake."

Though I insisted all the way to the door I could walk on my own, Dad and Ben ignored me, each keeping a good grip.

Professor Phillips quietly stood at the door watching our ridiculously slow progression. I felt her ogling my face.

When we finally reached the door, she said to me, "My dear, it appears you're recovering beautifully. Perhaps the injury isn't as bad as we thought."

I dared to look at her, regretting it. The warm tone in her voice contradicted her clinical expression.

To Dad, she added, "I have your cell phone number, Drake. Would you mind if I checked up on Cassidy tomorrow?"

A pit formed in my stomach. I wanted to say, *Yes, Cassidy would mind very much, Dr. Jekyll and creepy Mr. Hyde.*

"Of course, Professor Phillips," said Dad. "Thank you."

The pit in my stomach miraculously closed up when the door with the frosted glass closed behind us.

The deadbolt turned.

Four

Not a Normal Day

M *mm… Someone is making pancakes…*
The delicious aroma of pancakes coaxed me out
of sleep. Coming to, I groaned. I had never been a morning
person, but my head didn't usually feel like a bowling ball.
Since dropping off to sleep the night before, I felt like I'd
been trapped in a loud, fast-moving, brightly colored anime
cartoon. My dreams had been insane, to say the least.

Dr. Randolph misdiagnosed me, I thought, pressing my
hands to my temples. *Having a heavy head and chaotic
dreams definitely indicates brain trauma. I don't need a
medical degree to figure that out.* This thought satisfied me.
Not that I wanted a swelling brain, but it sure would have
been nice to see the ER doctor's puffed-up head deflate.
Let's just say, his bedside manner wouldn't win any awards.

I had first taken offense to this Dr. Randolph when he
lifted the towel from my forehead and gave my dad an
exasperated look.

"Mr. Jones, this is only a surface wound," he said in a
scolding tone.

While Dad and Ben stared at my forehead, the doctor
wore a smug expression. I so wanted to wipe it off his face.

"I don't understand," Dad said, looking confused. "I
tended the wound myself, and it was deep."

"I saw the split, too, Doctor," Ben interjected. "And it
most definitely required stitches."

Dr. Randolph shrugged. "I can see from the towel that the
wound bled heavily. Sometimes even minor head wounds

will do this. The bleeding must have made it appear more serious to you both than it obviously is."

Translated: *You're both idiots.*

After slapping a butterfly bandage on my forehead and a square piece of gauze over that, the doctor checked me for signs of a concussion. When he found none, he told me to take Tylenol for pain and sent us home. I can only imagine the gossip he circulated in the doctors' lounge about Drake Jones.

I admit, I thought going to the ER was overkill at the time. No matter how much I had insisted I was fine in the car and in the ER waiting room, Dad and Ben would hear none of it. Now, it appeared they were right, and—*ha ha*—Dr. Randolph was wrong.

Shoving the doctor out of my head, I focused on the wonderful smell beckoning me. Bowling-ball head or not, I had to have those pancakes.

Flipping onto my back, I scooted my legs over the side of the bed, preparing to ease my way up. For a dramatic effect, I mentally counted down, *Three, two —*

Before getting to one, I stood upright. The freaky thing is, I had no idea how I got there. It was like I had lost seconds, though I did have a slight recollection of swift movement. *Is it possible to black out while being vertical?* I wondered, rubbing my head.

Dr. Randolph messed up big time, I added, taking a step toward my dresser. By the third step, I paused, freaked again. My steps felt oddly light, like I was walking across a spongy gymnastics mat. I realized, too, that my body felt good, with none of the morning stiffness I usually experienced when I woke up. My joints and muscles were loose, like I'd been up and moving for hours.

Attempting to ignore the strange sensation under my feet, I continued on to the dresser. Peering into the mirror over it, I looked at the square gauze on my forehead. Pinching a corner of the surgical tape that held the gauze in place, I lifted it, wincing in anticipation of what I would see.

With the gauze off, I stared at my forehead, not sure what to make of it. Besides the thin butterfly bandage and some crusty blood, my skin appeared normal. Yanking the butterfly bandage off, I moistened my fingertips with saliva. Leaning close to the mirror, I spit-shined my forehead, rubbing the dried blood away. Beneath the blood, my skin was smooth and healthy. There was no sign of even a surface scrape.

With my nose practically pressed to the glass, I gaped at my forehead. To say I was stunned is an understatement. In shock, my eyes drifted down to my nose. My upside-down world did another flip. The despised spray of freckles had vanished, completely disappeared. As if they were hiding, I roughly rubbed my nose. My skin turned red, but nothing reappeared. Trying to calm myself, I reasoned, *Mom always said the freckles were so light that only I noticed them. Maybe my bruised brain messed up my vision, making me farsighted.*

Narrowing my eyes on my nose, I attempted to focus better. Suddenly, a huge, porous surface appeared. After some confusion, I realized I was looking at my nose, but seeing what it would look like under a microscope.

Gasping, I sprang back from the mirror—literally— as if bouncing off a springboard. I landed on my feet, six feet from my dresser.

For several minutes, I stood wide-eyed and rooted to the floor. My mind desperately flipped the strange occurrences around, attempting to sift out a logical explanation. There was only one. *Misdiagnosis.*

Believing the next bed I slept in would be a hospital bed, I walked back to my dresser, reassuring myself, *None of this is real. You have an injured brain.* Though I wanted to run like a lunatic to my parents, I decided that wouldn't be prudent. Once my parents knew I was hallucinating, they'd toss me in the car in my PJs and rush me to the ER. Not wanting to risk that type of public humiliation, I decided to get dressed before running like a lunatic.

Strangely calm, I dug through my dresser drawers, choosing a good ER outfit. I went with faded jeans and a long-sleeved green T-shirt that brought out my eye color. Over the shirt, I pulled on my favorite hoodie. It was probably chilly outside, and in the panic, I might get tossed in the car without one. After brushing my hair, I placed the gauze bandage back over the wound I couldn't see but knew was there.

Opening my bedroom door, I got a fresh whiff of pancakes. Obviously, my parents were in the kitchen. Someone had to be flipping flapjacks. I decided not to stir up too much panic right off the bat. I wanted breakfast first. Hopefully, a concussion also heightened taste buds. This had the potential for being the most delicious stack of pancakes ever.

~~~

Stepping from the bottom step into the foyer, the only sound I heard was the television in the family room. There were no indications of breakfast preparation, but I had to check it out. I figured I'd find a plate of cooling pancakes on the counter. It wasn't completely unfathomable that I'd slept in and missed a family breakfast. I'd done it before.

The only thing on the kitchen counter was an open box of Cheerios and a couple of dirty bowls and spoons. The sight infuriated me. The scent of pancakes still hung heavily in the air. *Someone is going to pay,* I promised myself, fuming.

Stomping into the family room, I demanded, "Okay, where are they?"

Dressed in a T-shirt and PJ bottoms, Nate, lounging on the sectional, lazily looked up at me. "What?"

My fists balled at my sides. "You *know* what I'm talking about. Why didn't you save any for me?"

"Save what?"

"THE PANCAKES!" I bellowed.

In Batman pajamas, Chazz pulled himself upright on the sectional, gaping at me.

Nate looked at me like I was off my rocker. "What are you freakin' about? We didn't have any pancakes."

Glaring, I said through my teeth, "Stop messing with my head. I can smell them."

Both my brothers sniffed confusedly, infuriating me further.

"Cassy, I can't smell any," Chazz whispered timidly.

Instantly, I felt guilty. It wasn't his fault his sister needed a CAT scan.

"Never mind." I smiled at his cute, bewildered face. "It must just be my imagination."

As I turned to leave, Nate teased, "Good thing there's only one of you in this family."

Clenching my teeth, I stomped back to the kitchen. In the kitchen, I approached things more rationally. Except for the box of cereal and dirty bowls, the kitchen sparkled clean. Did I think my family made a pancake feast, devoured it, and cleaned up the evidence before I woke up? The coffeemaker wasn't even turned on, which meant my parents were probably still asleep. Obviously, there was no pancake deception going on in this kitchen, so why was the aroma strongest here? Glancing around more critically, I noticed the back door cracked open. One of the boys must have gone out this morning.

As I poked my nose out the door, the aroma grew stronger, clearing my family of all suspicion.

Throwing any ounce of rationality I possessed out the window, I decided my need to find out the source of the pancake aroma outweighed my need to be go to the ER. With my convoluted logic, I concluded that if I solved the pancake mystery, then the rest of the insanity I'd experienced since waking up would fall into place, too.

After tugging on my tennis shoes, I poked my head into the family room. "Guys, when Mom and Dad get up, tell them I went to the school."

"Now, why are you going there?" Nate asked impatiently.

Oh, he is really getting under my skin. "Because I need some fresh air," I answered, trying to maintain composure. "I'm going for a run around the track."

"You, run? I don't think so. What is this, some kind of secret rendezvous or something?" My twin impishly grinned.

"What's that?" Chazz asked.

Watching for my reaction, Nate's grin stretched from ear to ear. "That means Cassy has a boyfriend that she's sneaking off to meet."

Chazz gasped.

So much for composure. "You are such a moron, Nate. No, you are *beyond* a moron. I am going for a run, and that is all." Pausing, I forced a smile for my younger, sweet brother. "Be sure to tell them, Chazzy. I'm at the school, and I'll be back soon."

He nodded, terrified.

Grinning, Nate winked. "We'll be sure to tell them."

I drew in a deep, angry breath. Something foul filled my nasal cavity. "Oh, my gosh, Nate!" I exclaimed, crinkling my nose. "Your breath is so nasty."

Nate laughed, shaking his head. "Is that the best you can come up with? I'd be a little more convinced if you weren't like thirteen feet away."

I am like thirteen feet away, I realized, staring at my twin, stunned. *But I can smell his breath and I can smell... him.* I shot my eyes to Chazz; his eyes looked ready to pop out of the sockets. *I can smell him, too. I can smell everything!*

I've got to get out of here. "Brush your teeth, Nate," I screeched, pivoting away. He made loud kissing noises as I darted back into the kitchen. There I rationalized irrationally, inhaling the pancake aroma anew, *If I find the pancakes, this will all make sense. Time to hunt.*

On the tail of this last thought, a strange excitement stirred in my chest. *Time to hunt,* I mentally repeated, eagerly flinging the back door open.

Stepping out the door, I inhaled the crisp air deeply, breathing in an array of scents, each distinct and powerful. It was as if a glass bubble had been lifted off me, allowing me to smell the world for the first time. Something weird happened halfway through the breath. My mind became incredibly focused, searching through all the scents, pinpointing the desired one. Once it was pinpointed, I followed the trail, sniffing it out like a bloodhound. Every part of me was so intent on the hunt that I didn't care how crazy it all was or how crazy I'd look if someone noticed me. Tracking my target was all that mattered.

The quickest way to my target—or prey, by the way I was behaving—would be to climb over fences, because the aroma definitely drifted from the west, parallel to my back yard. Deciding that climbing over neighbors' fences wasn't such a great idea, I headed for the front of our house. Stepping out on the sidewalk, I turned left. Two doors down from mine, I stopped. The Crenshaws' house was the source of the aroma.

Standing in front of their house, I contemplated what to do next. *Mystery solved, right?* Wrong. I still had no answers. Knowing my odd behavior and experiences could be attributed to a bruised brain, that didn't deter me from wanting to confirm that the Crenshaws were indeed making pancakes. Though not rational, or even close to sane, I opened their white picket front gate.

With the aroma luring me, I moved up the walk toward the front porch. About six feet up, the Crenshaws' horrendous mutt dog, Princess, who had been hiding on the porch, lunged at me, baring her teeth. Startled, I jumped— not back, or in the air a few inches—but quite literally, I jumped up fifteen feet onto a thick tree limb that hung over the walkway. My reaction had been so quick and automatic that it took me a moment to comprehend that I was really up in a tree.

As I crouched on the branch like a cat, my mind raced, trying to place the pieces of this puzzle together. Princess barked manically below while I pondered. My brain swelling wouldn't have suddenly given me the ability to jump like a lemur or to smell pancakes cooking two houses away from mine.

It hit me then. My brain wasn't hurt in the fall, but perhaps it had been hurt. Visualizing the beakers, the puff of white vapor, the excruciating pain, the darkness, and Professor Phillips, I knew I had my answer—or, at least, who to get it from.

"Princess, come here."

Jason, the Crenshaws' twenty-five-year-old son, who had decided that he never wanted to grow up, stood in the front doorway, lazily gazing at the dog.

Ignoring her master, Princess continued to bark wildly below.

Before addressing his dog's disobedience, Jason took a long drag off the cigarette hanging out of his mouth. Exhaling, he yelled a string of cuss words at Princess.

Profanity worked. Though resentful, the dog submitted, skulking to the front door.

The front door closed.

Staring at the ground below, I asked myself, *Now what?* Quite unexplainably, I had gotten fifteen feet up in a tree, and now I had to get down. There were no branches below me, so climbing down wasn't an option.

Coming to the conclusion that my only way down would be reversing the way I had come up, I sprung from my crouched position. Strangely, the movement felt almost natural. My feet hit the ground together, solidly. I didn't even stumble forward.

Straightening up, I trotted down the Crenshaws' walkway, closing the gate behind me.

With so many thoughts racing through my head, going home and being distracted by my pesky twin wasn't appealing. I needed time to mull things over. I decided to follow through with running around the school track.

On my way to the school, I went through a mental analysis of everything that had happened at the lab. Thinking about the vapor cloud I had sucked into my lungs, I wondered if I'd been poisoned. *Maybe the poison damaged my brain, causing me to hallucinate, and it's slowing dissolving my brain. Gads, am I dying?* I gasped aloud. This thought alone made my heart pound, giving me the feeling I would keel over any second.

After deciding the pounding heart was a panic attack and not because my brain was melting, I really thought through how I physically felt. *I don't feel poisoned, sick, or like I'm on my deathbed. In fact, I feel good, really good. Healthy. Strong. Powerful.* Something stirred within that I couldn't quite identify...a sort of energy waiting to escape, like a racehorse at the starting gate.

~~~

Stepping on the school's track, I took off running, faster than a racehorse. I felt the wind rush by me, cool air licking my clothes and whipping my hair back. My feet flew, barely making contact with the ground. After four times around the track, my lungs experienced no burning, my muscles no cramping, no exhaustion. I felt unstoppable, like I could go forever.

The sixth time around, my ears picked up voices. Abruptly stopping, I looked around, breathing evenly. Scanning the school grounds, I didn't see anyone. As I listened more carefully, the murmur became clearer. Somewhere in the neighborhood behind the school, two women were having a conversation. I forced myself to listen even more closely, and their voices became audible, like I had tuned them in by turning a dial. I continued to move that mental dial, and their voices drew closer, as if the volume had been turned up. I felt like I was sitting with them, sipping coffee, and contributing to their gossip. They really were saying some horrible things about a woman named Blanche.

Thoroughly freaked now, I started on my short trek home. All the way, Ben's silly "alien DNA" comment rattled through my brain. The problem was, it didn't seem so silly anymore. I felt sure Ben would have agreed that what I was experiencing appeared extraterrestrial-ish.

Turning down our street, I saw Dad headed toward me. He didn't look very happy.

"Cassidy, where have you been?"

Sheepishly, I approached him. "Didn't Chazz tell you I was at the school?"

Dad's disturbed expression made me think Nate had shared his theory.

"Yes, he did. But since when have we allowed you to go to the school alone during non-school hours? It's not prudent in this day and age."

"Sorry, Dad. I didn't mean to worry you. I just needed to get out for a while."

"I understand, Cass. Just show more wisdom next time."

His face was still tense. "Dad, I promise I won't—"

"Cass, I know you're sorry. I'm not angry with you. I wasn't only on my way to check up on you. I have some disturbing news to share with you."

Disturbing news? Oh, he knows what happened. Professor Phillips must have followed through with the phone call. "Dad, I was on my way to tell you. I already—" I stopped short, realizing he wasn't listening. "Dad, what happened?"

"We need to leave now," he stated in a hollow tone.

"Why?" I gasped. "Is someone hurt? Not Chazz?"

Snapping out of his distraction, he assured me, "Chazz is fine. Oh, sweetheart, I'm sorry I worried you. This involves Professor Phillips, not our family. Apparently, after we left her lab last night, there was a fire."

My cheeks went numb, like I'd been slapped. "Is she dead?"

"I hope not. She is missing, though. I'll explain while we walk to the car."

As we walked, he continued, "My friend, Bob Conlin, is the detective working the case. He called and asked if we could come downtown to give our accounts of what took place while we were with the professor. Apparently, we were the last to see her. As I mentioned, not long after we left, there was a fire—"

"Did the fire start from the burner I knocked over?" I interrupted, with a speeding heart.

"No, Cass. I thought of that, too, but according to Bob, or Detective Conlin, her lab was ransacked. Her file cabinet was emptied, and the contents were intentionally set fire to."

This isn't possible, I thought, my breath shallow. *None of this is possible.* "So the police think she's been kidnapped?" I forced out.

Dad's face was solemn. "Right now, she's classified as a missing person."

"But you think she's been kidnapped?"

"I don't have enough information, but, in light of her recent research, it wouldn't surprise me if she's been abducted."

"Really? Is her gene therapy that important, that someone would kidnap her for it?"

He nodded. "Yes, it's that important."

Silent after this, we lost ourselves in our own thoughts. Guaranteed, they were different, though they surely revolved around the same missing person.

Feeling overwhelmed as we passed Miriam's house, I recalled her comment, *That's your luck, Cassidy.* Never had there been a more accurate statement uttered. My luck would be that the one person who could give me answers and possibly help me would turn up missing. A nagging feeling told me this was no coincidence. Our separate events were directly and terrifyingly connected. If she had been taken because of what happened to me, then I could possibly be the next to turn up missing.

One thing I knew, deep down in my agonized gut, was that I could tell no one about what had happened to me. Not my mom, my dad, Detective Conlin, no one, until we knew what happened to Professor Serena Phillips. Disclosing anything could literally be a matter of life or death—my own.

Five

The Mysterious Emery Phillips

As I walked by the coffee bar in the police squad room, a bouquet of sugary glaze, yeasty dough, and oil assaulted my nose. I inhaled deeply, the tantalizing scents reminding me and my stomach of how I never had gotten pancakes that morning, and how much I needed comfort. Donuts would be a welcome comfort.

Observing me eyeing the plate of donuts, Detective Conlin paused. "Hungry, Cassidy?" he asked.

Geez, he's a good detective. "Yes, Detective. I haven't eaten anything today."

He smiled broadly. "Why are you girls always skipping breakfast?"

"Detective Conlin has four teenage daughters," Dad explained, smiling at his friend.

"Yep! My household is a war zone, more or less." Conlin boisterously laughed.

Boisterous was a good way to describe this short, balding detective I had met five minutes ago. Though rough around the edges, Detective Conlin seemed like he would be a blast to hang out with. However, a prime suspect in an investigation likely wouldn't agree with me. I could see where his bold energy could be intimidating during an interrogation.

"Help yourself," Detective Conlin said to me, gesturing to the donuts.

"Thank you." I smiled appreciatively, quickly grabbing a small paper plate. I selected a chocolate donut with colorful sprinkles. My weak stomach felt reinforced already.

"Take another," he encouraged, winking at Dad. "I like to see a girl with a hearty appetite."

I really like this detective, I thought. Taking him up on the offer, I added a glazed old-fashioned to the plate.

While I made this second selection, Detective Conlin poured a glass of water and handed it to me. "Here. I don't want you choking on donut during the statement." He winked at Dad again.

"Thanks, Detective Conlin." *I bet the detective does a lot of doting in his war zone.*

With donuts in one hand and water in the other, I followed Dad and Detective Conlin to his office, on the other side of a wall of windows and miniblinds. Through the windows, I saw someone with black hair sitting in a chair facing the detective's desk.

The detective and Dad walked through the office door first. The person in the chair stood up.

"Emery—"

Emery! I peeked around Detective Conlin to get a look.

"I'd like you to meet Drake Jones."

While they shook hands, I observed the missing professor's son. Emery looked like a boy my age—or the way one would have looked fifty years ago. He wore a blue button-down shirt, khaki pants with a brown leather belt, brown leather loafers, and black-framed glasses. They reminded me of Clark Kent's. In fact, he reminded me of Clark Kent, the one from the original black-and-white Superman television show. Emery didn't look like he should be in color, either.

Looking beyond the Clark Kent glasses, I took in his face. He had nice features. His eyes were black, like two pieces of sparkling coal. There was also intelligence in them, which wasn't too surprising, considering who his mother was. Besides intelligence, he had inherited her complexion. His light complexion coupled with his black hair and eyes made him very striking. He wasn't Jared-gorgeous, but he definitely had the tall-dark-and- handsome thing going.

After taking note of his neatly combed hair, my eyes dropped back to his face, meeting those two pieces of sparkling coal. When I blushed, his expression became amused.

"Emery, this is Mr. Jones' daughter, Cassidy," Detective Conlin introduced me, stepping aside so I could be properly presented.

Emery extended his hand. "It's nice to meet you, Cassidy."

I would have gladly taken his hand if I'd had a free one. After glancing at the plate and glass in my hands, I stared at his helplessly.

Understanding my challenge, Emery smiled, lowering his hand.

Nice smile, I noted, almost making a horrifying blunder. "Nice sm—uh, nice to meet you, too, Emery." Though I caught the "smile" before it slipped, I still blushed at the close call.

His dark brows knitted as he studied my flushed face. I assumed he was scanning his mental dictionary for words that began with "sm." My blush lingered at the thought.

To the relief of my cheeks, Detective Conlin waved a detective in from the squad room, which drew Emery's attention from me to him.

"Emery, why don't you go with Detective Reed and get a donut and hot chocolate?" the detective suggested as the other detective entered the room.

Watching his eyes narrow on Conlin, I thought, *I don't think he's a donut-and-hot-chocolate kind of kid.* In fact, not much about him suggested *kid*. Intrigued, I watched his scrutiny deepen, like he was trying to read the detective's mind. I followed his intent gaze as it moved from the detective to Dad to Detective Reed. It settled on me. Staring into his black eyes, I fought to keep mine from widening. When his gaze moved up to the gauze bandage on my forehead, I quickly covered it with my hand.

He didn't play the donuts-and-hot-chocolate game when he answered the detective after his ten-second scrutiny. "Of course, Detective Conlin. I don't mind taking a seat outside." With a smile, he turned and left the room. Detective Reed followed him.

Surprised by his boldness, I watched him walk straight to Detective Reed's desk and sit in the chair pushed alongside it. He didn't even look in the direction of the coffee bar.

Closing the glass door, Detective Conlin remarked, "Poor kid. He's in a tough place." He motioned for us to sit.

Sitting in the chair Emery had been in, I set the donuts and water on the desk's edge.

"Why is he here, Bob?" Dad asked, settling in the chair next to mine.

"Emery is a minor with no relations or designated guardians," the detective explained, sitting heavily in the leather office chair behind his desk. "Besides his mother, his only other living relative is his father. Apparently, Mr. Phillips hasn't been local for a while. According to Emery, his father's absence is business-related, but he has no way of contacting him. Who knows about these sorts of situations, huh?" He shrugged with a look of distaste. "To answer your question, Drake, Emery is here at headquarters waiting for CPS to collect him. Child Protective will place him in temporary care."

The detective looked beyond us into the squad room and added, "Emery has been none too happy about being taken into our custody. Real independent. I've never met a kid like him."

48

Dad let out a long breath. "He's going through enough without adding a foster home to the mix."

"It's a shame, but there's no other option. Hopefully, the placement will only be temporary." From the top desk drawer, the detective pulled out a tape recorder.

"You're up first, Drake," he informed, placing the recorder in front of Dad and pressing the *record* button. He leaned back in his chair. "Drake, would you please explain why you were in Building Twelve at Wallingford University on October second, and what events took place between four-fifteen and five-twenty-three p.m. while you were there?"

Picking up the sprinkled donut, I munched as Dad talked. Of course, he articulated our time at the lab perfectly. Being a professional nitty-gritty guy, he left no detail out. While I worked on the old-fashioned donut, he began relating the most interesting portion of our time in the lab: my spill. The only part of the fall he witnessed was my head slamming into the table.

When Dad finished, the detective turned off the recorder. Glancing at my forehead, he commented, "It sounds like you had quite a fall, my dear. Drake, did you fill out an accident report for the university?"

"Security had me fill out a form."

The detective nodded approvingly. "Good, they followed protocol." Looking back at me, he added, "You're a lucky girl."

Nodding, I felt like *LIAR* was written across my forehead. Presuming my face to be a mask of guilt, I avoided eye contact with the detective, fixing my eyes on the recorder he moved in front of me.

"Your turn, kiddo." He hit *record*.

Let's just say my account wasn't quite as eloquent as Dad's, or as honest. Guilt caused me to stumble and stutter through most of it, and the lump in my throat made it difficult to push words out. I knew whatever "tells" liars displayed, I had them all, and was sure the detective read me like a book.

When I finished the account, Detective Conlin looked at me carefully. "Cassidy, is there anything you'd like to add?" he asked.

"I can't think of anything." I nervously twisted the ends of my hair.

He watched me twist my hair to the scalp. "What would you like to tell me about Professor Phillips?" he persisted.

I am an open book, I thought, dropping my hair. Though lying wasn't natural to me, it seemed my only option, and I had to improve my skill before Detective Conlin upped the ante and interrogated me under a hot light.

"Uh, um, there…there is something." My mind scrambled to figure out what that *something* would be.

The detective smiled encouragingly. "Go ahead, Cassidy."

The hair-twisting resumed. "Well, uh, she acted real, uh, nervous, like she was, uh, expecting someone. Yeah, she was real freaked about it, too."

"Please, explain in detail what you observed."

Feeling the donuts coming up, I quickly grabbed the glass of water. Detective Conlin patiently watched me gulp down the entire glass.

When I unsteadily placed the glass back on his desk, he smiled. "Better?"

I nodded.

"Tell me what you observed that made you conclude that Serena Phillips appeared frightened."

Did I say frightened? "Well, she locked the door."

"Anything else?"

I thought hard. She acted more creepy than frightened, but I couldn't tell him that. "Well, no, nothing else. It was more of, uh, a feeling. She was just weird."

50

Weird is true, I thought, relaxing a bit.

He looked at me hard. "I get the feeling you'd like to share more, Cassidy."

Geez, there is no getting around this man! Shaking my head, I dropped my eyes to my hands fidgeting in my lap. My palms were slick.

"Drake, did you observe any suspicious behavior?"

Grabbing my hand, Dad squeezed my sweaty palm. "No behavior I would consider out of character. Serena Phillips is a brilliant scientist. However, she does lack people skills. To a girl Cassy's age, her behavior would come across as strange and suspicious."

Detective Conlin turned off the recorder. "I've met a few people in my lifetime who lacked people skills, including yours truly." He laughed.

I held in a sigh of relief. *He was this close to breaking me,* I thought, pulling my index finger and thumb half an inch apart in my lap. Staring down at the gap my finger and thumb formed, my heart raced anew. As my lungs squeezed, I thought, *I've got to get out of here.*

"Uh, Detective Conlin, where is the restroom?"

~~~

When I walked out of the office, Emery immediately turned to me. Though his face was unreadable, I knew mine wasn't. Looking at the floor, I quickly walked through the squad room to the corridor where the detective had told me the restrooms were located.

Alone in the restroom, I paced back and forth like a caged animal. My nerves were jumbled. If I didn't find some way to untangle them, I would explode.

My eyes rested on the huge mirror bolted to the wall over the sink. Stepping close to the mirror, I slipped my fingernails in the lower corner gap between the mirror and the wall. I dug my fingers into the gap. Drywall crumbled into the sink as my fingers bulldozed through the wall. When my fingers were completely behind the mirror, I pulled them slightly toward me. The bolts that anchored the mirror gave way, and the side of the mirror I pulled came loose. Wide-eyed, I pushed the mirror back to the wall, pressing the screws with an index finger into the loose holes.

I felt like a lost child when I wandered back into the squad room. When I lifted my eyes, I met Emery's. This time I didn't look away. *If he can read minds, let him.*

"Hey, there, Cassy Girl."

At the sound of Ben's voice, the dark cloud hanging over me shifted, revealing the sun. Still looking at Emery, I smiled for Ben.

Noticing my response, Emery's gaze moved behind me to Ben before I pivoted around to meet my friend.

His ease put me at ease. "Hi, Ben."

"How's the noggin?" he asked, smiling broadly.

I smiled back. "It doesn't hurt a bit."

"That's good." Glancing at my forehead, his eyes squinted questioningly.

"Ben," Detective Conlin called, walking over to us. "Thanks for coming down. I know I caught you on your way out of town."

Ben grinned. "No worries, Bob. The surf will still be there tomorrow."

Detective Conlin gripped Dad's shoulder, shaking his hand. "Thanks a million, Drake. You're a lifesaver."

"Whatever I can do," Dad answered, glancing at Emery. "Ben, I'd like to introduce you to Serena Phillips's son before you go in with Bob."

Ben quickly turned to Emery. With a friendly smile, he lifted his hand to the boy. "Definitely, Drake. Introduce us."

"Cass, you should say good-bye to Emery," Dad suggested with a smile.

Frowning at him, I understood by his tone that this wasn't good-bye.

Six

The Unwelcome Guest

It wasn't like I hadn't seen this coming at police head-quarters. I knew my dad.

When the phone rang at home, I took the call. The caller asked to speak with "Mr. Jones" in a purposeful manner, and I understood the purpose immediately. Dad never could resist a hard-luck story.

After the phone call, I wrestled with how to view our anticipated guest. Honestly, the thought of having Emery under our roof stressed me out. The guy unnerved me. When he entered our house with suitcase in hand, his face was completely calm as he confidently received introductions. In his shoes, I would have been a basket case; any *normal* fifteen-year-old would be.

Maybe he is and hides it well, I thought. *I wonder what else hides beneath the surface.* The thought made me shiver, because my gut told me there was more, quite a bit more.

My natural instinct would have been to avoid Emery. Unfortunately, my present circumstances made avoiding impossible. He was my only link to uncovering what had happened to me. Not that I planned on becoming chummy. My plan was to have as little interaction as possible.

In short, I viewed our guest as an opportunity, one that I would keep at arm's length. Instead of friendly conversation, good old-fashioned eavesdropping became my chosen intelligence-gathering technique.

Mom asked the boys to take Emery upstairs so he could put his suitcase away in Nate's room. After making her request, she tossed me a reassuring smile. She assumed I felt shy. During intros, I had hung back, leaning against the wall next to Dad's office while my family gathered around our guests in the foyer. This was my arm's-length approach. When the boys turned to the stairs, I slipped into the office. Once inside, I realized I hadn't acknowledged Emery or the CPS caseworker, Miss Carmichael. No one noticed, except Mom, who had graciously let me off the hook.

Hiding out in Dad's office, I tuned in to the living room. Miss Carmichael wasted no time in getting down to business.

"Mr. and Mrs. Jones, I have a few things for you to sign. This is all a formality, because I have no hesitation about leaving Emery in your care. It's clear you will provide a safe and secure environment for him until a more long-term solution can be found."

"What do you mean by 'long-term,' Miss Carmichael?" Mom asked, concern in her voice.

"Unfortunately, Emery has no immediate or extended family. At this point, we are pursuing a foster situation for him."

"Detective Conlin mentioned there has been difficulty contacting his father," Dad said.

Miss Carmichael hesitated. "Yes, that is correct. Oddly, Emery has no contact information."

"Are the Phillipses estranged?" Mom asked.

I could hear Miss Carmichael squirming in the chair. "Forgive me, but I'm not at liberty to elaborate."

"This situation you can't elaborate on—does it put my family at risk?" Mom demanded, her voice rising in alarm.

"Oh, definitely not. I assure you, Mrs. Jones, Professor Phillips's disappearance is unrelated to the unavailability of her husband. If the police believed Emery was in danger, he would be in their custody. We certainly wouldn't involve your family if there were a threat."

"Now, Miss Carmichael, we have the same goal," Dad said, positioning himself, "and that is to provide a safe environment for Emery. You're entrusting us to provide this for him, and in order for us to do that, we need to understand the environment he is coming from. Please, give us all relevant information to better help Emery."

Miss Carmichael cleared her throat. "I respect your point of view, Mr. Jones. When I say I'm not at liberty to disclose information, well, what I mean is I don't have this information, either." Her voice dropped. "It's classified."

"Emery's father and his whereabouts are classified? By whom?" Dad asked, his tone curious.

"I'm prohibited from pursuing any more information than I've given you . . . Truthfully, Mr. and Mrs. Jones, this is all I know."

There was a long pause. I pictured Dad rubbing his chin as he often did when intrigued, while Mom frowned at the intrigue. Part of the silence, I knew, was because Mom had become undecided. Dad knew that, too. He was letting her make the decision she was comfortable with.

Confident in my mom's dislike of fishy situations, and her momma-cat protectiveness over our family, I sang in my head, *Miss Carmichael, you're going to be looking for another "suitable placement."*

My jaw nearly hit the floor when Mom broke the silence with her decision. "We will trust you, Miss Carmichael, that Emery and our family are not at risk, and please know we will do everything we can to make him comfortable. Please, hand me the pen."

Once again, my life turned upside-down. The only conclusion I could come to for why Mom wasn't graciously showing Miss Carmichael and her charge to the door was that her momma-cat instincts were being extended to the boy whose own mother was missing. Under normal circumstances, I would have applauded her; however, under these circumstances, I wanted to shake both my parents and tell them to wake up.

Well, if they're not watching out for this family, I will, I decided, slipping out of the office and springing up the stairs before I could be observed by the living room occupants.

~~~

Sitting on the hall floor next to my bedroom door, I tuned in to Nate's room across the hall. The boys were reading and discussing comic books. Apparently, Emery knew less about superheroes than I did, and my brothers had taken it upon themselves to get him up to speed.

"This is Johnny Storm, and he's the Human Torch," Chazz excitedly explained.

"And he's one of the Fantastic Four?" Emery asked.

"Uh-huh. His sister is Invisible Girl, and Mr. Fantastic is her husband."

"Does Mr. Fantastic lead this superhero team?"

"Yep. Oh, his best friend is Ben Grimm, The Thing, and he's the other member of the team."

"How did they get their powers?"

Nate jumped in. "Cosmic radiation flooded their spaceship, changing their bodies."

"Forever," Chazz added.

I could feel Emery smile. "Very interesting, though not plausible."

Yesterday, I would have agreed with him.

"I don't get how you've never heard of the Fantastic Four," Nate said. "Even if you're not into comics, there were the movies."

"These are the first comics I've ever read, and I've seen only a few movies." After a pause, Emery added, "I haven't spent much time with people my age."

Nate's voice was confused. "What do you mean? What about friends at school?"

"I've never been to an elementary or secondary school. I was tutored at home."

"Secondary school is high school, right?" Nate paused. "Do you mean, you're done with high school?"

"I've completed my high school equivalency."

"When?"

"A few years ago."

My jaw dropped, as I'm sure Nate's did.

"No offense, dude, but you're trippin' me. You're, like, my age. Did you go to college or something after that?"

Emery's voice was hesitant. "I received an undergrad degree from Wallingford last spring."

"In what?"

"Molecular biology with a genetics emphasis."

After a pause, Nate laughed. "No offense, Emery, but I have no idea what that is…This is crazy. If you're done with college, what are you doing now?"

"I've been helping my mom in the lab. This coming quarter, I'm continuing my studies at Stanford." He said this so matter-of-factly, like somehow this was all *so* normal.

"I can't relate, dude, but Stanford, cool."

I heard a vibrating sound like an electric razor and the rustling of clothes.

"Sweet, dude. A Droid."

Lucky, I couldn't help but think. I *so* wanted a cell phone.

"Excuse me," Emery mumbled, absently. "I need to check this text."

The room fell silent while he picked up the text message.

During this quiet, I mulled over my gathered intelligence, coming to this conclusion: The presence of this geeky-dressing, adult-talking fifteen-year-old college graduate and Droid owner, who had a missing mad-scientist mother, an absent "classified" father, and unnerving self-assurance, most definitely posed some kind of danger.

Who knows? He might even be dangerous himself.

Seven

Lost Love

F or the next half hour, I sat outside Nate's room, bored
out of my mind. Now I knew more about superheroes
and their many perils than I ever cared to know.

Fifteen minutes earlier, Miss Carmichael had left. In the
living room, Mom and Dad continued to discuss the
situation. Deciding their conversation deserved to be private,
I stayed tuned in to Nate's room.

The stairs creaked.

Springing to my feet, I moved left to my bedroom door.
When Dad reached the top of the stairs, I gave the
impression I was coming out of my room.

"Hi, Dad. What's up?"

"I wanted to see how everyone was getting along. How is
Emery?"

I shrugged. "Don't know. The boys have been shut up in
Nate's room."

Dad smiled, tapping on Nate's door. When told to come
in, he opened the door. He looked pleased by what he saw. I
peeked, too. The boys formed a triangle on the floor, comic
books scattered around them.

Stepping into the room, Dad picked up a comic book off
the floor. "It's been a long time since I read *Captain
America.*"

"Daddy, come in with us," Chazz said excitedly, scooting
closer to Emery. "Sit next to me."

"I'd love to." Dad plopped down next to my beaming brother.

Nate glanced at me in the hall. "Are you coming in or not?"

I kept my eyes on Nate but noticed Emery looking at me. Feeling flustered, I committed myself to something I normally avoided. "Well, you know how I *love* comic books, but I'll have to pass," I said with a nice bite of sarcasm. "I'm going to help Mom in the kitchen."

Nate gave me a suspicious look.

"She'd appreciate that, Cass," Dad said, impressed.

My heart jumped when Emery abruptly jumped to his feet. Stepping over the comics, he stood in the doorway, his eyes locked on mine. "Cassidy, I didn't have a chance to talk with you downstairs. It's nice to see you again."

I blushed. My awkwardness made me angry. "Thank you," I replied sharply. Pivoting, I walked away, feeling Emery's eyes on my back. Reaching the top of the stairs, I heard Nate say, "Don't take it personally. She's been an emotional roller coaster all day."

I bit my tongue to keep from shouting something that would prove Nate right, though he was right. I was not myself, in every which way.

Entering the kitchen, I reluctantly asked, "Would you like help, Mom?"

My voice startled her, causing her to splatter the tomato sauce she'd been stirring on the range top. Wiping the mess with a standby sponge, she smiled. "I'd love the help, Cassy. Why don't you grate the cheese for the lasagna? It's on the island." She continued stirring.

"Sure." I smiled in return, wanting to kick myself hard.

While rummaging through a lower cabinet for the grater, I glanced up at Mom's profile. Deep in thought, she had a resolute expression on her face. I had no doubt that whatever she wrestled with now would be resolved. Mom had grit. It would have been nice to have inherited some of it.

As I brooded over my frequent lack of courage, one glaring example of my cowardice came to mind: Jared.

One hundred and thirty-seven days earlier, I had made a mistake that now haunted me day and night. Before my pathetic error, Jared had been a regular fixture in our household. He and Nate were best friends. He had come from a broken family, so ours attracted him like a magnet. His dad seemed to drift in and out of his life, and his mom, struggling to make ends meet, was hardly at home. My parents, being who they were, had taken him under their wing. A welcome addition, Jared had become part of the family.

Though I didn't recognize it at the time, I had been given a privilege. Popular at school, Jared had the reputation of being nice but tough. He wasn't the kind of boy other boys messed around with—at least, smart ones didn't. Maybe because I was rather non-threatening or a deep thinker myself, Jared let me see that side of him. He was very observant, contemplative, and because he trusted me, he shared thoughts only privy to me. We were friends. Good friends. However, at some point, I'm not sure when, Jared's feelings had crossed the friendship boundary.

There was something I still didn't get. Why would Jared tell Sunny Chan, the biggest blabbermouth in school, that he liked me? He had to have known he was playing with fire. Maybe he believed that Sunny's desire to keep his teeth would outweigh his desire to talk. Jared had sorely overestimated Sunny's intelligence and sense of self-preservation.

Sunny's style was to wait for an audience opportunity before putting his target on the spot. He chose to corner me in science lab. At our group table of ten, Jared sat four seats away from me, which sweetened the confrontation for Sunny. I can still see his smug smile when he approached me.

"Cassidy, Jared likes you."

Every head at the table turned my way, including Jared's. His eyes narrowed on Sunny, but he didn't intervene.

Instantly full of resentment and mortified beyond belief, I decided to pretend not to hear Sunny. Lowering my face closer to the lab journal, I continued writing, like nothing had happened.

"Did you hear me? Jared is totally into you."

I couldn't imagine being in a worse school scenario. All eyes were on me, anticipating a response. I knew what they were all thinking: *Cassidy, really?* Every girl at that table would have killed to be in my shoes, which made me even more resentful.

Infuriated, I continued writing, unintelligibly now.

"Come on, Cassidy. Are you into Jared or not?"

The pressure was too much. I never did well with an audience. The humiliation and rage I felt became misdirected. Instead of aiming my fury at the boy who had put me in the hot seat, I fired at the boy who made me vulnerable to the attack.

Slowly, I lifted my face. My blazing eyes met Jared's. His were angry, too, but his anger had been properly directed. I'll never forget his expression when he realized he was my intended target. It is impossible to forget his expression, because it has been seared into memory.

"Not," I stated, tasting the acid in my tone.

The surrounding witnesses fell into a stunned silence. The unusual occurrence finally caught the attention of the teacher, who told Sunny to get back to his seat and the rest of us to work. Burying my face in the journal, I didn't look up until the bell rang.

When it rang, I braved a look in Jared's direction. For a brief moment, he met my gaze. His face was like stone, as were his eyes. Instead of humbling myself and apologizing, I glared before turning away. Since then, we have avoided eye contact altogether.

Jared wasn't the only one hurt by my cowardice. He and Nate had become more acquaintances than friends. Funny thing is, Nate never mentioned the event to me, but I was sure he thought it was funny that I'd never mentioned it to him. Sometimes, we kept our understood alliance silent, and this was one of those times. I do know that, at one point, Nate defended me, confronting backbiting friends. Miriam had picked this tidbit up from the gossip mill, as well as another. After school that day, Jared taught Sunny a valuable lesson in self-preservation.

Of course, the heart-twisting irony is that, after what I call "The Sunny Chan Incident," I discovered that my feelings had not only crossed the friendship boundary but well exceeded it. To say I missed my friend and my vanished privilege is a gross understatement.

Now, lost in my thoughts as I stood at the kitchen island, I began running the huge block of mozzarella over the metal grater. Cheese grating never thrilled me. It wasn't the worst food prep duty, but it was right up there. After dragging the block back and forth a few times, a delicious, naughty idea came into my head. Since I was presently inflicted with unnatural speed, why not make it work to my advantage? Why not speed along a lowly task?

I snuck a peek at Mom. She was in the midst of dumping lasagna noodles into boiling water. For the next couple of minutes, she would be preoccupied with the noodles, preventing them from sticking with a wooden spoon. My ears turned their attention to the second floor. The feverish comic book discussion continued. Peeking at Mom one more time, I let the mozzarella rip. Gripping the block, my hand

64

moved at lightning speed across the grater, whittling it down in seconds.

Clearing my throat, I casually informed her, "All done, Mom."

"Done?" she asked in surprise, turning to look at the pile of cheese. "You did that so fast."

I shrugged. "Mozzarella is soft."

"How about putting a salad together?"

To myself, I rolled my eyes. One thing about the kitchen, there is always another grueling task to replace the last. I decided to make the salad the old-fashioned way. I knew my luck wouldn't hold if I pushed it. Plus, I didn't want to lose a finger chopping vegetables.

During salad prep, Mom finished her mental deliberation, and we chatted lightly during the remainder of our duties. Together, we set the table. As she pulled the lasagna platter out of the oven, she asked me to get "the boys" for dinner.

~~~

Knocking first, I opened the door. "The boys" burst into laughter.

"What?" I demanded angrily.

"Don't be so paranoid," Nate said, trying to catch his breath. "It's not you. Emery just said something hilarious." He started laughing again.

Doubtful, I glanced at Emery. Slightly grinning, he watched Dad and Nate laugh. Though Chazz joined the laughter, he looked confused.

"What did he say?" I asked.

Emery turned his face to me. He appeared amused. Ignoring him, I looked at Dad, waiting for a response.

Dad smiled at me. "Honey, it's a guy thing."

A guy thing?

"Well, whatever," I said. "Mom wants you down for dinner." Without waiting for a response, I stomped off.

Frowning, I walked back into the kitchen. "They're coming," I announced, sitting in my chair. Crossing my arms, I glared at my place setting. For some reason, Emery being well-received, and hilarious on top of it, annoyed me. *So he's funny,* I pouted. *That doesn't change the fact that he's also dangerous.* This I was sure of.

"Feeling left out, Cass?" Mom asked, placing the lasagna on the table.

"Hardly." *You're the ones who are being left out,* I added silently. With this thought, annoyance turned to sadness. I had never felt sadness to this depth before.

I am alone, I realized, wanting to curl up in the chair and weep. *What am I going to do?*

~~~

"Mrs. Jones, this is delicious."

For the first time since he had sat across from me at the table, I looked up at Emery. I hadn't intentionally snubbed him. Brooding had absorbed all my attention.

Emery smiled at Mom appreciatively.

She smiled appreciatively back. "Thank you, Emery. Cassidy helped make it," she added graciously.

"I only grated the cheese," I clarified, not so graciously.

Emery fought back a grin.

Glad to provide entertainment, boy genius, I thought, scowling and stabbing a fork into the lasagna on my plate.

Dad winked at Mom. "Lizzie and Cassy, the lasagna is incredible. Thank you."

66

Feeling compelled, Nate and Chazz agreed and thanked us.

My quiet response was to spear another piece of lasagna.

"This is nice," Emery commented, looking around the table. "Do you always eat together?"

"We do," Mom answered, smiling at Dad.

Dad returned the smile.

"Where do you eat?" Chazz asked, looking at Emery curiously.

Smiling pleasantly, he answered, "It's usually only my mom and me, and neither of us cook, so we have most meals at the university cafeteria."

"Oh." Chazz thought for a moment. "Where does your dad eat?"

My fork paused midway to my mouth.

Alarmed, Dad and Mom glanced at one another.

Emery quickly took note of their reactions. "Really, I don't mind answering," he assured us, smiling. "My dad is away most of the time. I really don't know where he has his meals."

Oh, that is sooo sad, I thought, softening.

"Where is he?"

Dad cleared his throat. "Chazz, that is none of our business."

I was relieved when Emery said, "I really don't mind, Mr. Jones. Chazz, from what I understand, he's in China. He's working there."

From what he understands? I asked myself, staring hard at his placid face. *What the heck does that mean?*

The statement grabbed Dad's attention, too. He watched Emery intently.

"What's his job?" Chazz pressed on.

"My dad is an accountant. Most of his clients are overseas."

An accountant? Really? My danger assessment lost ground. How threatening could an accountant be?

Apparently, Mom agreed, smiling with satisfaction.

"What's that?" Chazz pressed.

Emery looked thoughtful. "Let me think how to explain. Basically, an accountant helps people manage their money better and cleans up their financial messes."

"Is your dad good at cleaning up messes?"

He smiled at Chazz like they shared an inside joke. "My dad is *very* good at cleaning up messes."

My eyes darted to Dad.

Staring at Emery, he rubbed his chin.

"Sorry about your mom," Chazz blurted, his round face sympathetic.

Coughing, I choked on the air I gulped in, cautiously glancing at Emery.

"Thank you," he answered evenly. Though his voice betrayed no emotion, I noticed, ever so slightly, the controlled calm leave his eyes. In its place I saw frustration, and then anger.

Dad noticed the change, too. I think he had been waiting for it. Leaning forward, squarely looking Emery in the eye, he said, "Emery, I want you to know I will do everything in my power to find your mother."

"Thank you, Mr. Jones," he replied with surprise.

As Dad smiled at Emery, we, his family, stared at him, understanding Dad's promise. His word was golden. He would do *everything* in his power to find Professor Phillips. I shivered considering this.

To lighten things, Mom began to tell a humorous story. Grateful for the subject change, the rest of the family engaged with her. They were ready for lightness.

While Mom talked, I looked up at Emery, meeting his gaze. He had been watching me. Curiosity overruled insecurity as I studied his black eyes, seeing the anger and frustration still smoldering.

Well, we have that in common, I thought. At that moment, an insight flashed through my mind, snuffing out apprehension. *We're both trapped alone in a nightmare, and maybe we don't have to be.* Suddenly, I saw not a threat but a potential ally in him.

Eight

Tears... Really?

N *o, not again...*

Pancakes lured me from sleep. While easing awake, I was sure this would be another scent trick. Tuning in to the kitchen, my kitchen, assured me this was no trick.

Pancakes are on the horizon, I thought, stretching and inhaling deeply. It occurred to me then smells seemed more intense, distinct, than they had yesterday. *Is it my imagination,* I wondered, *or am I getting worse?* Pushing down panic, I climbed out of bed.

While throwing on jeans and a T-shirt, I revisited the decision I had come to before dropping off to sleep last night. Today, I would take Emery into my confidence. Hopefully, he would have answers. Hopefully, he could help me.

I walked into the kitchen, trying to ignore the fact that I could smell more than pancakes.

"Good morning, sleepyhead," Dad greeted cheerfully, flipping pancakes at the range. "Pancakes always get you out of bed. Are you ready for these?" He offered me a plate with a couple of pancakes hot off the grill.

"Thanks." I took the plate, feeling saliva collect in my mouth. What Dad said was true, but pancakes didn't usually make me drool like a Saint Bernard.

What is happening to me?

At the table, I sort of grunted at the boys and grabbed the syrup. No rudeness intended; my strange pancake obsession

70

required full concentration. Stuffing a huge gooey piece in my mouth, I almost moaned. It was like every taste bud on my tongue sang. Chomping down on the delectable morsel, I looked up from my plate and into Emery's amused face.

"They're good, aren't they?" he asked, staring at my packed cheeks.

I swallowed hard. "Terrific."

"*Very* ladylike," Nate teased.

Cramming in another huge piece, I gave him a close-lipped smile, appreciating the harassment. It made me feel less crazed.

Nate nodded approvingly. "Nice." His comeback would have been similar.

"Cassidy, please pass the syrup," Chazz asked politely.

Apparently, he thought someone at the table had to show decorum. His salivating sister sure wasn't. However, his attempt would have been more effective if his face and pajama top weren't already drenched in syrup.

While handing him the bottle, I was careful not to make contact with his sticky hands.

"Thank you." He smiled, syrup dripping from his chin.

Mom carried four glasses to the table. "Orange juice?" she offered.

Setting the glasses down and taking a seat, Mom thoughtfully watched Emery sipping the juice. "Emery, I've been thinking about tomorrow—"

I tensed, knowing that tone.

"Nate and Cassidy will be at school," she continued. "It wouldn't be much fun for you to spend the day here with me. I thought maybe you'd like to be Nate's guest tomorrow."

My mouth dropped open. *Is she insane? He'd be a total laughingstock.* I glimpsed alarm cross Emery's face and interpreted the look to mean he wasn't so keen on the idea either. I felt compelled to intervene on his behalf.

"Mom, you can't just bring someone to school with you," I corrected, giving her a look that said, *Be reasonable.*

"Well, of course you can."

"Why would you think that? I've never known anyone to bring a guest to school."

She gave me a determined smile. "Don't worry. I'll work it out."

"Emery has already graduated," I blurted out. Mentally, I added a big *oops* at the end.

Of course, Nate caught the *oops*. He decided to answer Mom's questioning look. "Emery told us, *in my room…*" He briefly paused to let the emphasis sink in. "…that he has already graduated from high school."

Trying to appear innocent, I took a bite of pancake while Nate continued, "He's also graduated from college. Did you get that, too, Cassidy?" He grinned challengingly.

Grinning back, I took the challenge. "Yes, I did."

Nate laughed. "You have no pride."

I shrugged.

Mom and Dad were so surprised by Emery's academic achievements that they didn't catch my spying confession.

"Is this true, Emery?" Mom asked.

Emery summarized his accomplishments. He presented them carefully, weighing each word. He didn't appear embarrassed or self-conscious. I think he just regretted the subject had come up.

Mom and Dad were stunned. They understood the accomplishment better than we kids did.

"Amazing achievement, Emery," Dad said. "You are a determined young man."

"And real smart," Chazz added perceptively.

Though astonished, Mom wasn't distracted from her goal. "Regardless, you would still have fun going to school with Nate and Cassidy."

"Would you mind if I thought about it, Mrs. Jones?" Emery asked.

The way Emery said this gave me the feeling that he had no intention of being our "guest" at school or spending the day with my mom. *What you got planned, boy genius?* I wondered, studying his neutral expression.

"Of course. The decision is completely up to you." Mom smiled at him.

The doorbell rang.

"Chazz, would you let Ben in?" Dad asked.

As Chazz darted for the front door, I asked Dad, "Why is Ben here? I thought he was surfing today."

"He's planning on leaving after helping me with a few things."

"You're working today?" Nate asked in surprise.

Dad was usually a stickler about keeping Sundays "family time." Only a humungous story-worthy event would normally make him sacrifice Sunday.

I opened my mouth to ask what they were working on, and then snapped it shut, catching my first whiff of Ben. *Funny I didn't smell him yesterday at the police station,* I thought, feeling dread. *It isn't my imagination. I am getting worse.*

Ben walked into the kitchen, holding Chazz's hand. "Hi, all," he cheerfully greeted. "Cool, hotcakes."

"Help yourself, Ben." Mom smiled, getting up from the table.

With a towering stack, Ben flopped into the seat Mom had vacated. Thickly pouring on syrup, he took a generous bite. "Elizabeth, these are awesome."

Rinsing dishes, Mom called to him. "Thanks, Ben, but Drake's the chef today."

Teasing, he gave Dad an incredulous look. "What? No, come on. Don't tell me the guy can cook, too."

"He can, Ben," Chazz confirmed.

Ben grinned at him. "Well, Chazzy, if you say he can, he can. I know you'd never steer me wrong."

Chazz beamed.

"Well, finish up," Dad said to Ben. "We've got a lot to do."

"Sure thing, boss." Ben smiled, shoving pancake into his mouth.

"So what are you and Ben doing?" Nate asked.

Dad glanced at Emery. "We're checking up on some leads."

All of us kids looked at him, understanding he was fulfilling his *everything* promise, even on a Sunday.

"Thank you, Mr. Jones and Ben," Emery said, obviously touched. "Would you mind if I came along?"

My eyes moved from Dad to Emery. *What could he possibly do?* I wondered. *He's only a kid.*

Dad smiled. "I'm afraid not, Emery, but I will keep you updated."

Though Emery smiled back, he obviously regretted missing the opportunity, whatever it was.

Shoveling in the last bite of pancake, Ben pretended to get a piece caught in his throat. Bulging his eyes, he dramatically clutched his throat. "Dreeenk." He reached for Chazz's glass of juice.

Horrified, Chazz quickly handed him the glass.

Ben chugged the juice. Falling back in the chair, he smiled and sighed. "Chazzy, you always have my back." Messing up the top of Chazz's hair, he stood up.

"Will that tide you over?" Dad teased, standing up, too.

Ben patted his flat stomach. "That'll do me for the next hour or so."

~~~

After we cleaned the kitchen, Mom said, "I'm taking Chazz to a birthday party. Why don't the three of you go down to the park? It's a lovely day. I don't want you cooped up inside."

During cleanup, I had contemplated ways of getting Emery alone, eager to take him into my confidence. However, the park was not the place I envisioned doing this.

Knowing *who* I'd most likely run into at the park, I informed her, "Nate and Emery can go. *I'm* staying here."

Mom smiled at me impassively. "Fresh air will be good for *all* of you."

~~~

Apprehensively, I followed Emery and Nate down the stone stairs that connected our street above to what we called "Spinning Park." The playground at the bottom of the stairs had received this name because a good portion of the play equipment spun. We had spent years spinning wildly to the point of nausea and occasionally throwing up.

To the right of Spinning Park, a path weaved through a large wooded area, and to the left was a sports field. Nate and his friends spent a majority of their free time on this field. Right now, soccer seemed to be the rage. After school and on the weekends, these boys would meet to strut around and talk surly while chasing the black-and-white leather ball up and down the field. Before the Sunny Chan Incident, I would sometimes watch a game. It was fun listening to these boys razz each other and talk trash. There was definitely an art to it. Since Sunny Chan, I'd avoided the field because of one player's dedication to the game.

Walking through the playground, I kept my fingers crossed that Jared would be with his dad this weekend. Still, my heart leapt for joy when I spied him dashing across the field. Watching him, thoughts and concerns not relating to Jared abruptly faded from my consciousness, just as they had earlier when pancakes mentally absorbed me. For the moment, Jared Wells received my undivided attention.

As I looked at him, his face blurred due to distance, a thought popped into my head: *If I can't see him clearly, then he can't see me.* It occurred to me I had an advantage I didn't normally have. At this distance, I could ogle to my heart's content, and who would be the wiser?

Pulling Jared into my enhanced view, I took in his tousled dirty-blond hair, angular face, and beautiful eyes, thickly lashed and the color of milk chocolate. His lips slightly turned up in the corners as he called something out to a teammate, and his cheeks were an appealing ruddy against his olive skin tone, due to the cool air and physical exertion. It had been a long time since I'd had such a pleasing eyeful of Jared.

When admiring his perfection was no longer safe, I averted my eyes.

As we approached the field's sidelines, Bobby Neigh looked in our direction, yelling, "Times...Hi, Nate."

Nate smiled, shouting, "Hey, Bobby. Which side's short?"

"You can play on mine," Bobby said, walking toward us.

It surprised me that he was leaving his position. Following his lead, the other players moved our way, too.

76

This was strange. Usually, when a game was in progress, a new player would insert himself in. The game never just stopped.

Then I realized why. Walking over, they eyed Emery. They weren't approaching to welcome him, but to gawk. They wanted to check out the tall, "nerdy" kid.

As they drew closer, I moved closer to Emery. By the time all thirteen players had formed a semi-circle around us, I stood by his side, and Nate stood on his other side. "This is my friend, Emery," he introduced him.

They looked him up and down, their expressions unimpressed. Grunting greetings, they showed no enthusiasm. Some, I could tell, thought he had hardly been worth the effort of leaving the field. Others took the time to stare at the gauze square on my forehead. *Apparently, Emery isn't the only spectacle,* I thought, my blood boiling.

His friends' reactions didn't escape Nate. But instead of calling them on it, he decided to create a place for Emery. "Want to play?" he asked with a grin.

I glanced up at Emery's unperturbed face.

He smiled at Nate. "I don't know how. But you go ahead. I'll watch with Cassidy."

Peripherally, I noticed a head whip my way. Instinctively, my own head turned, and I looked directly into Jared's eyes. What I saw almost made me gasp. I had never seen his face so enraged or his eyes so piercing. They moved to Emery, sharpening.

"Are you sure?" Nate asked Emery.

"Yes. Cassidy and I will watch the game from the bleachers."

Emery made this assumption confidently, as if we had discussed it beforehand. Normally, presumption like this would require resistance from me. However, at the moment, resisting was something I was in no condition to do.

In a voice surprisingly calm, I encouraged, "Go ahead, Nate, play." Somehow, I added almost playfully, "I'll watch over Emery for you."

Turning abruptly away, Jared walked back out to the field. From the corner of my eye, I watched him. His shoulders were tense. The other players followed, taking this as *Show over, game back on.* Nate joined them.

I felt I would crumble.

"Should we sit down?" Emery asked.

"Sure, why not?" I mumbled.

As we headed toward the bleachers, my legs threatened to give way and sudden tears blurred my eyes. *What is this?* I asked myself, blinking back the tears. *I never cry!* Usually, I handled emotionally charged situations stoically, detaching myself before feeling pain. However, this pain shot through me like an arrow, preventing me from disconnecting. I would have to come up with another coping strategy. Picturing myself curled up on the ground, weeping inconsolably, I desperately drummed up a "bandage emotion." Scorn covered despair adequately.

Sticking on the "bandage," my mouth lifted in a sneer. Instantly, relief followed. Contempt felt easier to control than devastating grief.

As we sat on the bottom bench of the bleachers, I noticed Emery thoughtfully observing my profile. Silently, I scowled at the game in progress, struggling to maintain.

"I've never watched a soccer game before," Emery said lightly, leaning forward, placing his elbows on his knees and lacing his fingers together.

My response came out in a rude snort. "Don't judge soccer by what these morons are doing. No one out there is winning the World Cup."

Not intimidated, Emery replied, "No, but I'll learn the basics from this game."

"The basics are two teams, one ball, and each team trying to kick that stupid ball into those stupid goals," I snapped. "You don't need to be a genius to figure it out."

Oh, my gosh! What is wrong with me? Remorse tore the "bandage" off.

"I am so, so, so sorry, Emery." Tears welled. "You didn't deserve that, especially with what you're going through. I am *so* mean." My moistened eyes looked to the ground. "It's just that boy, Jared, the one who was trying to burn holes through you with his eyes—"

"Oh, I hadn't noticed."

As I looked up at him, he smiled, acknowledging that he had.

Returning the smile with a sad one, I dropped my eyes again. "Anyway, don't take it personally. It's me he hates." The word "hates" caught in my throat, making it impossible for more words to flow. The only thing flowing now were tears, so heavy I couldn't see the ground.

In my devastation, I felt a light pressure on my back. I realized the pressure was Emery's hand, attempting to comfort me. His voice soothed. "Cassidy, I wish I had a tissue handy—"

Holding up my forearm to show him I was covered, I wiped my wet cheeks with the hoodie sleeve. From the corner of my eye, I detected a small smile on his face. *He thinks meltdowns are the norm for me,* I realized, gasping breaths. *What else is he supposed to think? He's only known me as a basket case.*

"Your sleeve provides an adequate substitute," Emery agreed. "Forgive me, Cassidy, but I must contradict your last statement. That boy does not hate you."

"N-no. H-h-he does." Despair filled my every fiber. I was coming apart at the seams. I needed help. I needed Emery's help. "I-I have t-to t-t-tell you some—"

"Jared, what's your problem?"

Quickly looking up, I saw David Hsu bounding aggressively toward Jared.

Emery's hand slid off my back.

With a menacing expression, uncharacteristic for Jared, he held his ground. Picking up the ball trapped under his foot, he tossed it hard at the ground towards David.

Alarmed, David skidded to a stop.

"Fine. Your ball," Jared growled, tossing me a seething look.

Receiving the full impact of the intent, my heart convulsed. This proved to be the final, deadly blow. All at once, my heart broke, shattering into a million pieces. Letting out a long, ragged breath, I attempted to revive it, unsuccessfully.

"Let's go, Cassidy," Emery said, in a soft but firm tone.

Swiping my sleeve across my eyes, I nodded and bit my lip, forcing back new tears. Somehow, I managed to stand up, ready to follow wherever he led.

As we walked silently back to Spinning Park, I clamped down on the reeling emotions, pushing Jared into the recesses of my mind. Feeling somewhat rational again, I tried to sort out my breakdown. Jared broke my heart, but a broken heart did not take precedence over the more pressing matters at hand. I knew this, but in those emotionally gripping moments, I couldn't see the forest for the trees.

Emery, please have answers. Please help me.

Spinning Park was empty, except for a young couple swinging their squealing toddler. Enthralled with their child's delight, they took no notice of us when we entered.

Refocused, I took over leading. "Let's go over there," I said, pointing at an old-fashioned wood swing with two benches facing one another. I wasn't in the mood for anything spinning. My stomach was disturbed enough.

Nine

A New Friend

We sat on opposite benches, our knees a foot apart. Emery watched me curiously while I considered how to start. I resorted to small talk. "Uh, Emery, so where do you live?"

"We rent a condo near Wallingford," he answered patiently, making no attempt to elaborate.

"Oh." I touched my forehead. "Were you born in Seattle?"

"No, Washington, D.C." Placing his forearms on his knees, he leaned forward. "How did you hurt your forehead?"

I dropped my hand. "Funny. That's what I want to talk to you about."

Intently looking at my face, he waited for me to continue.

I touched my nose. "Before yesterday, I had freckles. They were light, but they were there."

Narrowing his eyes on my nose, he attempted to decipher.

Taking a deep breath, I continued, "Sorry, that didn't make any sense. Let me put it this way—I had freckles when I went to your mom's lab with my dad."

His expression became so intense, frightening almost, that I hesitated. My feelings about him were conflicted. He made me uneasy. Everything about him was so foreign.

Emery's voice took on a soothing tone. "I understand that you injured your head in my mom's lab. Please, tell me how. You can trust me. I want to help you."

I searched his eyes. It was difficult to penetrate through the blackness, adding to my unease. "I don't think you can."

Impulsively, or maybe intentionally, he grabbed my hand, holding it between his. "Please, tell me," he repeated.

I took another deep, tortured breath. "Your mom had something cooking in beakers on that Bunsen burner near the coffeemaker. While Dad interviewed her, I sat on a stool next to them. The stool collapsed and I fell, knocking everything over onto the table. When the liquids ran together, they formed this white cloud, and I breathed it in. It's difficult to explain exactly what happened. My whole body felt like it was on fire, melting from the inside, and then everything went black. I guess I passed out or something. Afterward, I was…changed."

"What do you mean by 'changed'?" he asked, slowly and calmly, squeezing my hand.

Pulling my hand from his grip, I lifted it to my forehead. "When I passed out, I hit my head on the edge of the counter. My forehead split, or at least, that's what Dad and Ben said, and with all the blood, I don't think they were wrong." My fingers trembled against the gauze. "The doctor at the ER said it was only a surface wound. He thought Dad and Ben had been fooled by the blood, thinking it was worse than it really was. He put a bandage over it and this gauze."

Emery's gaze fixed on my unsteady fingers, watching as I pinched the surgical tape and hesitantly pulled the gauze away, exposing my forehead. His eyes filled with disbelief.

"How did this happen, Emery?"

Shaking his head, his gaze dropped to his hands in his lap.

Quiet minutes ticked by. With each passing one, I sank deeper into despair. When I couldn't take the silence anymore, I pleaded, "Please, Emery, say something."

"Be patient. I'm thinking."

"Well, think out loud."

Smiling slightly cock-eyed, he said, "Trust me, you don't want me to do that."

Does he think this is a joke? Furious, I slapped the gauze on my forehead. "Trust you? Apparently that was a mistake." Abruptly, I stood up, causing the swing to sway.

"Cassidy, sit down," Emery commanded calmly.

Glaring, I sat. I had nowhere else to go.

"Trusting me is the right thing to do. Aside from my mom, I'm the only other person who understands anything of depth about Formula 10X."

"Formula 10X?" I said with hope. "That's what was in the beakers?"

"Yes, or at least, a variation of it. I don't know for certain, because she kept her latest experimentation with the formula undisclosed."

"Why would she keep it a secret from you?" I asked, truly interested.

He smiled to himself. "That's the way she is. I assume she wanted to prove out her new theories before bringing me back in."

Strange, I thought. *He says this like he didn't ask her about it. Why wouldn't he ask?* "Well, she did it. It works. I'm living proof she succeeded."

"No, I don't think she did," he disagreed, sounding regretful. "How the formula has affected you would not have been her intention." Pausing, he looked thoughtful. "However, it's premature for me to come to that conclusion until I know precisely how you've been affected, or changed, as you put it. Tell me everything."

"Everything" poured out at once. I ended my twenty-seven-hour saga with this: "At the police station, I thought you'd figured it all out. The way you looked at me all intense, it seemed like you guessed everything that was going on."

Shaking his head, Emery smiled. "Though I admit I did find your behavior odd, I wouldn't have guessed this in a million years."

Despite the situation, I laughed. *He found my behavior odd?* I also thought the "million years" was an exaggeration. I had a feeling Emery wasn't in the dark about anything for long. "Okay, now you know everything. What do you think?"

Silence was his only response as he studied my face. His scrutiny reminded me of his mother's—clinical, detached— like he observed me under a microscope. This was disturbing, to say the least.

My brow furrowed. "Stop staring at me like that. I know I'm a freak."

"Cassidy, you are not a freak," he contradicted, his expression softening. "Don't ever say or think that. I certainly don't view you that way. I'm only astounded by how you've been affected. From a scientific perspective, it's impossible."

"It can't be." My eyes welled. "Look at me."

Alert to the coming despair, Emery placed a reassuring hand on my shoulder. "But that doesn't mean we won't find a solution. I promise you, we will."

Emery spoke with such earnest confidence that I couldn't help but believe him. Nodding agreement, I dabbed my wet eyes with my sleeve.

Dropping his hand from my shoulder, he said in a formal tone, "Allow me to tell you about Formula 10X. It's a type of gene therapy containing a variety of animal DNA, among many other components. My mom's goal is to find a way to manipulate these DNAs to benefit a human recipient by choosing genes that represent different strengths of the nonhuman and infusing those genes into the weakened cells and tissues of the human. For example, a human who is crippled would perhaps be infused with puma genes, since they are known for their agility and strength. The goal is not to make the human like the puma, but to restore the human's function and health within a normal range."

"Well, why am I like a puma, then?"

"I don't know exactly. Obviously, by your intense physical reaction when initially exposed, something in the formula overloaded your nervous system. Maybe 10X affected you so extremely because you're a young, healthy girl who received the formula in its entirety. What I mean is, you would have never been a 10X candidate, since you suffer none of the disabilities and ailments an appropriate candidate would. Also, the recipient would have been administered the formula in small doses, tailored to their needs. Your exposure was radical, and now you're experiencing the full potent effects of 10X. Do you understand?"

I nodded. "I think so. It's like a glass half filled with water, slowly having more added until it reaches the rim. I was already a full glass, and 10X was an entire pitcher poured into me at once." Dread brewed inside me as I continued. "And now that the water has spilled, there's no way to tell where it will go or what will happen to it."

"That's one way to look at it," Emery said, dismally looking at the woods. For several seconds he didn't speak, lost in thought.

During those quiet seconds, I stared at the ground, not thinking, only waiting. When I felt his eyes on my face, I looked up. His expression was determined.

"None of this makes sense, but obviously, it *isn't* impossible. As you pointed out, you're living proof. Since it isn't impossible, there is an answer and solution. Tell me again, in detail, what you experienced when the liquids converged."

Quickly, I explained again. Finishing the account, I held my breath expectantly.

Smiling slightly, he shrugged. "I have nothing."

My breath rushed out in an offended gust. "What? Do you think this is a game or something?"

"No," he quickly clarified. "I'm sorry, Cassidy, that came across as glib. I truly have nothing, and it frustrates me. I understand the compounds turned to a gas, but I have no idea why. And I have no idea what they formed or why your nervous system reacted so violently when you inhaled the gas. There has to be an unknown, a catalyst that pushed everything over the edge. What that catalyst is, again, I haven't a clue…Cassidy, are you listening to me?"

Actually, I wasn't. A black cat near the path leading to the woods had caught my eye. Low to the ground, it focused intensely on something in the tall grass. I recognized what it was doing because I had done it myself. The cat was hunting, stalking its prey. After commando-crawling toward its victim, it sank low in the grass, anticipating the kill. Opportunity arrived. Black fur gracefully glided through the air. The cat easily landed on the unfortunate victim: a brown field mouse.

I watched the cat excitedly toss the mouse in the air, remorselessly tormenting its victim. Dread slid through my stomach. "Emery, you mentioned pumas. Do you think there was cat DNA in that stuff I sucked in?"

Turning back to him, I saw that he had been watching the cat, too. He replied, "She experimented with feline DNA."

I took this as a yes. *Oh, geez.*

"There is another thing I've noticed different about me," I began hesitantly. Emery looked back at me, and I could feel my cheeks warm under his gaze. I really didn't want to bring this up, but thought I should after what he witnessed at the sports field. "I don't usually have meltdowns. I'm not one of those emotional girls… at least, I wasn't…I have no idea why I started bawling like that."

His response wasn't hesitant at all. "The changes you've experienced are not only physical, but chemical, so it stands to reason you will be more prone to mood swings and extreme reactions. And it will be more difficult—how should I say it?—to shove feelings down."

I stared at him in surprise. He had pegged me. I was the queen of shoving down unwanted feelings. "If you're right, Emery, poor me—poor everyone."

To this, he only smiled, and then said, "It's about time you showed me what you can do." Glancing across the sprawling lawn, his eyes settled on a couple lying together on the grass. They were far enough away that their facial features were indistinguishable. "Tell me about them."

Rising to the challenge, I adjusted the couple until they appeared a few feet away. On their stomachs, they turned their heads in so they were nose to nose.

"Okay, the guy has shoulder-length, brown—"

Emery interrupted, squinting his eyes. "You'll have to do better than that. Even I can see his hair."

"Well, can you see he has a silver hoop through the right side of his bushy, black unibrow? And there's a mole smack in the middle of his left cheek." I grimaced. "Geez, he should have that removed. Okay, his girlfriend has multiple piercings. She looks like a pin cushion. There are three small hoops through her left eyebrow. One. Two. Three. No, four diamond studs on the left side of her nose. Gross. A gold hoop hanging between her nostrils—"

With a look of distaste, Emery cut in. "You've convinced me with vision. All right, they appear to be talking. Can you hear what they're saying?"

"No prob." I smiled confidently, weeding through surrounding noise. After a moment, I tuned into the man's husky whispers. "Okay, got them. He's saying—" My jaw dropped. Immediately, I severed the connection, but not before turning bright red.

Emery laughed hysterically.

Still blushing, I watched him sternly. Every time he looked at me, he laughed harder. Child prodigy or not, ultimately, boys will be boys.

Taking a deep breath, he suddenly composed himself. "Sorry, Cassidy, but your expression was hysterical. You've convinced me that you heard them." He grinned.

In response, I scowled.

"Again, I apologize," he repeated with an amused grin. "All right, let's move on to another test." Scanning the park, his gaze settled behind me. "Don't turn around. Behind you, that toddler is now eating something."

Closing my eyes, I sniffed the air. There were so many competing scents. "Is it sweet?" I asked.

"Yes, it is."

Nodding, I took in a deep breath. Distinguishing scents, I pinpointed a sweet, edible one close by.

Opening my eyes, I grinned. "My, you're tricky, Emery. First of all, that isn't called eating. That's called *drinking*, and he's drinking apple juice."

Emery gave me an impressed look. "I can't see the juice box from here, so I'll take your word for it." Grabbing my hands, he stood up, pulling me to my feet. "Now, let's test strength."

"Are you asking me to toss you off here or break your fingers?" I teased, slightly squeezing them.

Grinning, he pulled his hands away. "Definitely not the fingers, and I think tossing me from this swing is too public, though I admit it would be a good show." He nodded to the woods. "We'll find something more discreet in there."

While following the path through the woods, Emery's eyes roamed for that something discreet. About a hundred feet in, he suggested, "Let's get off this main path. Over there." He pointed to a thinly trodden trail cutting through thick growth.

Following Emery, we pushed our way through the growth. Obviously, no one had come down this over- grown trail in a while. I got the brunt of the overgrowth as the branches Emery pushed forward sprung back at me. After getting slapped in the face with one, I was prepared to demand that I lead, when Emery said, "Yes, this will work."

Stepping into a clearing, he pointed to a fallen tree twenty feet ahead.

Smiling, I decided to show him leaping before strength. "Stand back," I warned, pushing him aside. Then, running forward, I leaped for the target. Leading with my right foot, my body glided easily through the air. The exhilaration I had felt while speeding around the school track returned, and that strange, pent-up feeling released. For whatever reason, this very unnatural thing felt as natural as walking to me, and incredibly freeing, as if I had been meant for this.

My right foot touched the top of the massive trunk, and my left pulled in next to it. The landing had been perfect, steady and strong, without even a hint of balance loss. Pivoting on the trunk to face Emery, I smiled smugly.

Walking toward me, he exclaimed, "That was incredible. You move like a cat."

His praise wiped the smile off my face. "Cat," I grumbled to myself. "What's up with the cat theme?" With a sigh, I hopped down next to him. "I suppose you want me to move this." I patted the thick tree trunk.

Emery examined the area around the tree. "It appears safe. I don't see any danger if you disturb it. First, make sure there isn't anyone nearby."

My ears quickly searched. "All clear," I announced, moving up to the trunk.

Emery stepped back, his face shining with anticipation.

Resting my palms against the trunk, I prepared to move the giant tree. Pulling in a breath, I pushed. The tree was heavy, but with exertion, the giant's resistance gave way. I

90

rolled the trunk up out of the indented ground. From underneath, something scurried up the trunk near my left hand. Squealing, I jumped back. The thick trunk rolled back into its resting place.

Emery grinned. "It was only a lizard."

"I *hate* lizards." I shuddered. "The nasty thing almost ran over my hand."

"Ironic. You can push fifteen hundred pounds, and you're scared of a little lizard."

I gasped. "One thousand five hundred pounds?"

Surveying the tree, he nodded thoughtfully. "At least."

The information stunned me. "Okay, then. What do you want me to do next?"

For the next couple of hours, Emery sought out all kinds of challenges, from moving boulders and leaping into trees, to distinguishing sounds and scents. He even had me describe in detail what tree bark looked like microscopically.

Something else took place during this time. My unease around Emery disappeared. In fact, it amazed me just how comfortable I felt around him. Though he was my age, he had none of the uncertainties we teens are usually plagued with. For the most part, I walked on eggshells around girls my age. Saying or doing the wrong thing could trigger an instant "girl war." Even though my friends weren't petty, instinctively, I was careful. The boys weren't as sensitive but were every bit as gossipy. So in general, I watched my back, never letting my guard down. It was exhausting. With Emery, I believed I could be myself, say the wrong thing, do the wrong thing, and he wouldn't hold it against me. He really was a breath of fresh air.

After testing senses, strength, and agility, Emery announced, "It's time for speed. Let's see how fast you can go through these woods."

Back at the main path, we parted ways. The plan was for Emery to go to one entrance and me to the other. After listening to be sure the coast was clear, I would tune in to him where he would be looping a countdown out loud. From my end of the path, I tuned in to the woods. All I heard was Emery's looping countdown. Positioning myself to run, I listened.

". . . Three, two, one—"

I took off at a mind-boggling speed. Within seconds, I stood before Emery. Wide-eyed, he stared at me like he'd seen a ghost.

"Unbelievable," he uttered above a whisper.

His reaction made me edgy. "How fast do you think I ran?" I asked, attempting to sound casual.

"My guess would be forty miles per hour. Imagine how fast you would be on a solid, straight surface. I've never witnessed anything like this." His mouth pulled down in the corners.

With an anxious feeling in my gut, I studied him. His face held no expression, as if he wore a mask to hide real emotions. The more I looked at him, the more I believed the emotion he hid was fear. *If he's terrified of me, everyone will be,* I anguished.

"What do you want me to do now?" I said sheepishly.

"Nothing," he answered, distracted. "Let's head out." He motioned for me to walk ahead.

With Emery following silently behind, I walked in a daze. I assumed he had me walk ahead to keep an eye on me. *I am the most dangerous thing out here,* I bitterly told myself. *I'd make me walk ahead, too, and—*

Something scratchy brushed my cheek, interrupting the thought. Reflex kicked in, and before a second passed, I was crouched on a tree branch, looking down at Emery. Smirking, he waved a dry tree branch in his hand.

"What's the big deal?" I snapped, hopping down.

Tossing the branch, he stated, untroubled, "I assumed you would react that way when startled. We'll have to work on those involuntary reflexes." With a grin, he added, "We can't have you jumping up in trees in public."

Glaring hard, I grumbled, "Nice. Real nice." With my shoulder, I shoved past him, stomping down the path.

"I couldn't have taken you off-guard if I warned you beforehand," he called after me. "For your protection, I needed to know how you would handle it."

I spun around. "For *my* protection? Don't you mean for yours or for the innocent public's?"

He grinned with understanding. "Oh, you think I'm afraid." Walking toward me, he continued, "Cassidy, I'm fascinated, hardly afraid. Not of you, at least. I am concerned about you being exposed, though." He stopped in front of me.

Glancing up at him, I asked, "So you think I should keep this a secret?"

Alarm washed over his face. Abruptly, he grabbed my upper arms. "Cassidy, you can tell *no one* about this. Absolutely no one." Bending close to me, he searched my eyes. "Do you understand? No one can know. Not your parents, not anyone. Keeping this a secret is not only for your safety, it's for your family's safety, too."

My eyes widened. "Why would my family be in danger?"

"Think, Cassidy. Whoever has my mom will want you. You are Formula 10X, and they would view you as a nonentity, something to be acquired. Your personal value and rights would mean absolutely nothing to them. You would become a lab rat. Imagine what they would do to you."

I tried not to.

"If they become aware of your existence, they'll do anything to get you. People like this have no boundaries. Everyone and everything becomes free game for them to get what they want. That includes Nate, Chazz—"

"Stop," I interrupted, shaking my head to dislodge the terrifying images. "I get it. I won't tell anyone."

After quick scrutiny, Emery released my arms. Calm replaced the alarm on his face. I believed this expression was his standard mask. For a moment, I studied the mask that showed no signs of strain or worry. As far as facades go, it was a solid one, but I wasn't fooled. I knew the turmoil that had to be going on underneath.

"Emery, I'm sorry about your mom," I said for the first time.

Tightening his lips, he nodded acknowledgment.

"Do you know who has her?"

He stared off into the woods. "No, but I know she's alive."

"Please forgive me, Emery." The words wanted to stick in my throat. It was wrong to ask, but I had to. "But how do you know?"

Looking back at me, he stated matter-of-factly, "She's too valuable to kill. They abducted her because she has something they want. The fact that I'm here talking with you means she must be cooperating to some degree. It's unfortunate."

It took me a moment to decode his meaning. "You don't want her to cooperate, even if it means she's protecting you? What is it they want from her?"

His smile was a mix of sadness and resentment. "I've already told you. They want *you*. Formula 10X. It is incredibly lucrative, and yes, I want her *not* to cooperate, no matter the sacrifice. In the wrong hands, 10X is detrimental to the world. Visualize an army of you."

"But they don't know about me."

"And I plan to keep them ignorant."

Staring up at him, I let his words sink in. *He plans to protect me. I'm not alone.* With this realization, I threw my arms around his neck, like he was a life preserver. "Thank you," I said in one grateful breath, tightening my arms.

Grabbing my biceps, he attempted to loosen the hold. "A little tight," he choked.

"Oh." Blushing, I released him.

Rubbing his neck, he smiled with ease. "You have quite a grip." Noting that my cheek shade deepened, he continued, "Please, don't feel embarrassed. I understand how scared you are. I promise you, though, everything will be all right. You will be all right."

"Thank you," I whispered, believing every word.

As he continued to smile, a curious glint appeared in his black eyes. "My mom will shed light on the situation when we get her back," he said in a casual tone.

Knitting my brow, I rewound his previous statements to figure out what I had missed.

Reading my expression, his smile broadened. "Oh, I didn't I tell you, did I? You and I are going to find her."

Ten

The Crime Scene

How are we going to find your mom?"

"I'm not sure." Emery's cell phone vibrated with a new message. "I'm not sure how to utilize you yet," he added distractedly, fishing his cell phone from his pants pocket.

"What the heck does that mean?" I asked, watching him read the text.

His mouth dipped into a frown. "I can reply to this text while we walk," he said, as though he hadn't heard me, and maybe he hadn't. Whoever sent the message clearly wasn't bearing good news.

He began walking, and I fell into step next to him. His long legs moved in big strides as his fingers quickly plucked at the Droid's keypad.

While he replied to the text, I thought over the fact that his cell phone was like Grand Central Station. This was his seventh text message since we entered the woods, and he hadn't mentioned who those were from, either. Judging by the frequency of the messages and his secretive reaction to them, I came to the most logical conclusion: "Is that your girlfriend texting?"

He let out a quick laugh and pushed *send*. I really wanted to know what was so funny.

"No, not my girlfriend," he said, not breaking stride. We were crossing Spinning Park, heading toward the stone steps. "I've been texting with a former classmate named Riley.

Riley has a very colorful past. She's been using her contacts to check into my mom's disappearance."

His explanation triggered ten more questions. I asked one. "Is Riley, like, a private detective or something?" We started up the stone steps.

"You could call her that." He smiled to himself, as if he found describing his former college mate this way humorous. "She is uniquely qualified in uncovering information."

I noodled on this momentarily. However, the information Riley had "uncovered" piqued my interest more. "The news didn't look so good that last text."

"It wasn't necessarily negative." He paused in his ascent and glanced at me. "I'm just disappointed. It was information we already had."

I circled my hand in a "keep going" gesture. "Okay? So?"

"So, Riley will keep digging," he said, climbing steps again. This wasn't what I was asking for, but apparently this was all Emery was willing to give. "I'll let you know when something crucial comes up."

This left a sour taste in my mouth. "Meaning when you figure out how to utilize me?"

"That was a poor word choice," he admitted. He stepped up onto the sidewalk and turned to face me. "Is 'partners' better?"

"I like partners," I said, and then joked, "Should we spit and shake on it?"

"That's how I bind my agreements." To my astonished delight, Emery then spit in his palm and offered his hand to me.

I laughed and spit in my hand, taking his. We shook. The gesture was absolutely disgusting, yet endearing. Silly thing is, it did feel like we had sealed the deal.

Dad's Volvo pulled up to the sidewalk. We quickly released hands. I swiped my palm across my jeans, turning to Dad with a smile.

He rolled down the car window. "Good timing. We were just about to head down and find you two."

From the passenger seat, Ben grinned largely at us.

"Detective Conlin needs the four of us at the lab," said Dad.

"What have they found?" Emery asked, quickly opening the back door and gesturing for me to go first.

Surprised, I thanked him, sliding into the backseat. Following me, he didn't respond. He stared at Dad, waiting for an answer.

"I'm sorry, Emery, but they haven't uncovered any solid leads yet. The police have completed their initial investigation and would like us to see if we notice anything different or missing in the lab."

Emery nodded acknowledgment.

After giving him an encouraging look, Dad turned back to the steering wheel.

As Dad pulled from the curb, Ben looked back at us.

With a friendly smile, he asked, "Hey, I noticed a soccer game going on down there. Were you playing?"

"Me?" I pointed to myself, grateful for Ben's diversion tactic. "You're asking *me* if I was playing soccer?"

"*You*? I wasn't asking you," he teased, reaching back and tugging my hair. "I know you're allergic to soccer balls, basketballs…" He listed all the sports balls I was apparently allergic to, which were all of them. After wrapping up the exhaustive list, he added. "So, Emery, did you play?"

"No. I've never played before."

Ben looked shocked. "You're kidding me. Never? That won't do. The game is awesome. Hey, I'll tell you what, I'll come over tomorrow and teach you. I can tell by your build you'd be a natural."

"Thank you. I'd like that," Emery said absently.

After a moment of appreciating Ben's heart of gold, I wondered why he was still here. "I thought you'd be surfing by now."

Ben turned his infectious grin to Dad. "Well, you know, your old man, he's a total slave driver, but try as he may, he's not stopping me from going to the coast today."

I could see Dad smile in the rearview mirror.

Ben's grin returned to me. "I'm taking off after the lab."

"But it's a two-and-a-half-hour drive. Don't you think it's getting too late to go?"

He motioned out the windshield. "Cassy Girl, the sky is clear, and there's a full moon tonight."

"So?"

"The best surfing is at night."

"You surf in the dark?" I asked in disbelief.

"I just told you there's a full moon tonight. It won't be dark."

"The water will be. Don't you want to see what's coming up to eat you?"

"No," Ben laughed. "It adds to the excitement."

Taking a moment from his thoughts, Emery smiled at this.

I was flabbergasted.

~~~

There was a different security guard at the lobby's front desk. This guard belonged more in a flowing gown than a bulky, khaki uniform, though she did compensate for its unattractiveness by keeping the shirt unbuttoned low, showing off impressive cleavage. With milky skin, big blue eyes, jet-black hair, and a button nose, she reminded me of Snow White. I didn't like her, right off the bat.

As the four of us approached the desk, her thick red lips stretched over her very white teeth. Her smile was radiant.

Dad greeted her. "Hello, my name is Drake Jones. We have an appointment with Detective Conlin in Professor Phillips's lab."

Her voice was smooth and satiny. "Yes, Mr. Jones. He's given you clearance. You'll need to sign in." She tapped the visitor's log with a long, creamy index finger. Her fingernails were painted siren red.

Dad peeked at her badge, avoiding the cleavage. "Thank you, Selma."

"Mr. Jones, I need your driver's licenses," she informed with a too-friendly smile.

While Dad dug around in his wallet, Selma leaned on the desk, showing more cleavage. This was obviously a calculated move.

"Mr. Jones, I must confess I took a little peek at the visitors list when I arrived today," she said, her voice turned sultry. "I was thrilled to see your name written down." Looking up at him through her long lashes, she smiled provocatively. "I'm sure I'm your biggest fan. There isn't a night that goes by that I don't watch you. Oh, on TV, I mean," she clarified with a steamy laugh.

My eyes burned with rage.

If Dad were taken aback, he certainly didn't show it. With his professional face plastered on, he replied courteously, "Well, thank you, young lady. I'm glad you enjoy the segment." He handed her his license.

Selma, also a professional, took the license from him, running her long fingers over his wedding ring.

If I had been required to speak at the moment, I would have been speechless. It took every bit of restraint I had not to leap over the desk and scratch her pretty blue eyes out.

To my horror, the expression on Ben's face was bewitched. Apparently, he'd fallen under the twisted Snow

White's enchantment. As he leaned on the desk, his grin stretched wide. "I'm Ben Johnson. Am I on your list, Selma?" He offered his license to her.

A mocking smile played on her lips. "Not mine, but you are on Detective Conlin's." She plucked the license from his fingers.

The daze cleared from his eyes as the enchantment broke. Straightening up, Ben glanced at Dad and mouthed, *Ouch*. Then he grinned.

"Gentlemen, please sign in while I copy down your information," Selma requested. However, she didn't do that. As Ben signed in and Dad waited his turn, Selma stared at Emery, that smile continuing to play. As she leaned toward him, I fought the temptation to cover his eyes.

"Aren't you Professor Phillips's son?"

His eyes locked on hers. "Yes. Are you new here?"

"Not very. You must have missed my shifts." As she leaned even closer, his eyes didn't waver from her face. "I'm very sorry about your mother." Her voice dropped low, taking on a velvety tone. "I was on duty the night of the fire."

Dad's head snapped to her. "You were on duty that night? Were you the security guard who discovered the fire?"

"Oh, no, not me. The other guard, Charlie Donaldson, was the first one on the scene," she answered, smiling up at him.

"You went up, though, didn't you, Selma? You must have noticed something unusual."

"Oh, I did, very unusual, Drake. May I call you Drake?"

"What did you notice, Miss Heart?"

Selma laughed. "Oh my, Drake, you've hurt my feelings." She feigned a pout.

With a slight smile, Dad didn't respond.

Her pouting red lips turned up. "I'd really like to tell you, Drake, but the police have asked me not to talk about it."

"Miss Heart, how do you think the kidnappers got past you and Mr. Donaldson?"

Slowly, she pushed herself back in the chair, keeping eye contact with Dad.

"*Was* Professor Phillips kidnapped?"

Dad rephrased. "Theoretically speaking, then, if she had been kidnapped, how would they have gotten her past you and Mr. Donaldson?"

"Charlie and I have discussed the possibility of her being kidnapped, and, honestly, Drake, neither of us see that as likely. No one came through here without proper authorization. I know, because I was right here." She tapped her nails on the desk. "Charlie and I both were. He only left when the fire alarm went off." She paused. "But let's say someone did sneak her out right under our noses. Charlie would be the one to talk to about theories of how that would be done. He's worked here for twenty years and knows this building inside and out." Her eyes moved to Emery. "Now, you probably know Charlie, don't you? Isn't he a good man?"

"Yes, *Charlie* is a good man," Emery agreed.

Catching the emphasis, her smile grew. "Charlie is heartsick about your mother's disappearance." Pausing, she waited for him to respond. When he didn't, her eyes shifted to Dad. "I wish I could have been more helpful, Drake. I'll keep my fingers crossed that the police find her soon." Holding up a hand, she crossed her middle finger over her index finger, smiling.

"Ours are, too, Miss Heart," Dad reassured, in a purposeful tone.

Without writing information down, she handed their licenses back to them. "Gentlemen, you should get moving. You don't want to keep Detective Conlin waiting."

As we ascended the stairs, Ben whispered to Dad, "I've met some trippy women in my time, but that one is a creep show."

Dad laughed low. "She did set off all the alarms. I can't imagine Bob didn't check into her carefully."

~~~

Standing in the lab's doorway, my mouth dropped. Almost a third of the room was charred. A huge, blackened heap near what had been the professor's desk looked to be the source of the blaze. Scattered around the heap were notebooks and files that had survived the bonfire, or at least, had partially survived.

The burnt smell hung heavy in the air. In the scorch, I picked out an unusual scent. It was strong, sweet, very distinct, and familiar. Unfortunately, I couldn't put my finger on where I had smelled it before.

Detective Conlin waved at us to come in. Detective Reed and a police officer also stood in the room.

Quickly, Dad and Ben ducked under the yellow crime scene tape, entering the lab.

I glanced up at Emery's face. He stared into the room.

"Are you okay?" I asked him.

He smiled, composed. "Ladies first," he said, gesturing at the yellow tape.

Somehow, that answered my question. Being the only "lady," I ducked under the tape.

After ducking under the tape himself, his eyes fixed on the torched heap to the left. Without saying a word, Emery briskly headed left, as I headed toward my crime scene on the right.

The stool lay on the floor, one leg collapsed, but the beakers had been removed from the counter. After a quick survey, I noticed them in the sink, filled with water. On the counter's top, there were no rings to indicate something wet had pooled. Running my fingers across the laminate surface, it was smooth. Formula 10X had left no evidence behind. Lastly, I observed my blood staining the counter's edge. There were also stains splattered on the floor.

Before entering the room, I had expected to experience a range of emotions. I thought, at the very least, I'd burst into tears. However, my eyes were dry and my emotions unstirred. Even breathing in the scent of my blood didn't produce much of anything.

A throat cleared behind me. "We tested it and know it's yours," Detective Conlin said.

I looked up at him.

He smiled. "That's a lot of blood. Like I said, you are a lucky girl."

Yeah, real lucky.

Dad approached us. "Bob, I wanted to ask you about the security guard downstairs."

Detective Conlin laughed. "I'm assuming you're referring to the bashful one. When she flashed those baby blues at me, all my red flags flapped, too. We raked them both over. Nothing came up on either, and they both have airtight alibis."

Detective Reed caught my attention. Standing near the door, he watched Detective Conlin nervously.

"No," Emery suddenly said, so low that only I could hear him. "Not this." Turning to him, I saw he sat next to the bonfire remnants. In his hands he held a severely seared notebook.

"I'll be right back," I mumbled to Dad and Detective Conlin, who continued their conversation. Moving quickly across the room, I knelt beside Emery. Glancing at the notebook he held, I observed only about a quarter of each page had been untouched by the fire. What survived was barely legible.

"Emery, what is it?" I whispered.

Staring at the notebook remnants, he shook his head slowly. "I told her to keep backups. She wouldn't. She's too old-fashioned. Now this is all that's left. It's gone. *Completely* gone," he said in disbelief.

The hollow tone of his voice frightened me. "What, Emery?" I asked in a dry whisper. "What's gone?"

Turning to me, his eyes were troubled, apologetic. "Cassidy, I'm so sorry, but this is all that's left of Formula 10X." He lifted the seared pages in his hands.

My thoughts were a confused swirl. "I don't understand. Please, tell me what this means," I pleaded, too loudly.

Suddenly, Ben stood over me. "What's wrong?" he asked me.

Raising my chin to look at his anxious face, I shook my head. I couldn't answer. I didn't know how to answer.

Bending over me, his eyes narrowed on the notebook, trying to decipher the undecipherable.

"What did you find?" Detective Conlin asked, leaning over Emery's shoulder. "What is that?"

Staring in my eyes, Emery answered him in an even voice, "This was my mom's gene therapy notebook."

The detective's expression was blank, not comprehending the significance.

Squatting on Emery's other side, Dad stared down at the singed page. His expression was apprehensive. "Is this her recent research?" he asked.

Studying Dad's face, Emery said, "You understand, don't you, Mr. Jones? You understand this is the only reason someone would abduct her."

"Why do you think that?" Detective Conlin demanded.

Turning his face up to the detective, Emery stated coolly, "This is the only thing that made her valuable. Don't you see? They didn't want her gene therapy. They only want her, and I don't know why."

Though I heard his words, processing them proved difficult with the words, *Cassidy, I'm so sorry,* screaming in the background.

Eleven

Crooked Cops

During the drive home, my mind began functioning, unfortunately. I understood that the scorched notebook Emery held had been my hope against hope. Formula 10X would most likely have to be recreated to help me. Now that it had been destroyed, I was all that remained of the secret formula.

Quietly nibbling on a tasteless chicken nugget, I realized hope wasn't completely dead. There was still a glimmer. We just needed to find her.

I glanced at Emery next to me. Munching on an onion ring, he stared down at his Droid, reading another text message. He had been texting with Riley since we had gotten into the car.

Let's see what she has to report, I said to myself, pressing my back into the seat and tucking my chin so I could glimpse the Droid screen. My eyes followed along as Emery typed out a response: *Will hang tight for now*.

He's leaving, I realized, my throat tightening up. *He can't leave! Not now. Not me.* My eyes filled with tears, and I could feel sobs build up in my throat. *I don't want to be alone. What am I going to do?* Before I could stifle it, a small sob slipped out.

Emery turned his head to me. Seeing my expression, his became concerned. His eyes jumped to Dad and Ben, who were chatting in the front seat. Confirming the men were preoccupied, he dipped his head to my ear. "I won't leave you," he whispered, understanding the cause of my panic.

My head jerked in an uncertain nod.

His hand moved to my jaw. Surprised, I allowed him to turn my face to his. "I won't leave you," he repeated, looking steadily at me.

Staring into those sincere onyx orbs, I felt fear and uncertainty melt away. Suddenly, I knew beyond a shadow of a doubt that I could trust Emery. He took his promises very seriously. "Thank you," I whispered, quickly brushing a tear from my cheek. "I know you won't."

A smile touched Emery's lips as his hand dropped from my face. Then he moved away and settled back in the seat.

Crisis diverted, I thought, watching him return to the text I had interrupted, as though nothing had just passed between us. The intensity of those seconds still had my heart thumping like a rabbit.

"You going to eat those fries?" Ben asked, interrupting my thoughts.

I looked at his grinning face and then down at the half-full container I clutched in my hand. I had completely forgotten about it. "Have at it." I handed him the container. "And don't forget the ketchup—you need your vegetables."

~~~

As we walked through the front door, Batman greeted us. This costume was obvious because his black T-shirt had *BATMAN* plastered across the front.

"Hi there, Batman," I said.

Not realizing he was labeled, Chazz grinned. "That's right, Cassidy." Pushing the black cape behind his shoulders, his face became solemn. "I'm glad you're here. Joker and his henchmen have been giving me some trouble. Will you help me get them?"

I wanted to give his cute round cheeks a million kisses. "Taking out henchmen is what I do best." I needed a diversion, even if that meant karate-chopping invisible bad guys.

"What about you, Emery?" Chazz asked in a deep voice.

"Yes, I'll help. I need to see what the Joker looks like first. Do you have a comic book with him in it?"

Thrilled to have willing participants, Chazz replied enthusiastically, "Yep, I'll get it. You and Cassidy go to the living room and wait." With that, he dashed up the stairs with the black cape flapping behind him.

Emery motioned toward the living room. "We need to talk."

"Yes, we do," I agreed, walking into the living room. I flopped down in one wingback chair, and Emery sat in the other.

"Your parents are in your dad's office," he said, looking at me. "Keep an ear out for them."

"Ears are out," I assured, leaning toward him. "Now, why were you going to leave?"

He smiled. "This wasn't the discussion I had in mind. For time's sake, we'll have to get back to your question. It will take Chazz only minutes to find the Batman comic books on Nate's dresser. They didn't get put back with the rest."

"You know where they are? Then why—" I began, and then thought, *Duh.* "Scary clever of you, Emery. So, tell me what's going on."

"Riley had a friend in law enforcement run a check on Selma Heart's social security number and driver's license. Both are fakes. In fact, according to the federal government, Selma Heart doesn't exist. It's a pseudonym. The home address she has listed with Wallingford is a real residence, though. Whether she actually lives there or not is another story."

I could feel the confusion on my face. Somehow, I had missed something major. "Okay…Selma Heart, the security guard. She was definitely suspicious and horrible, but

Detective Conlin said the police checked her out and that she was okay."

"Which makes one wonder."

Oh, geez! "Are you saying Detective Conlin is crooked?"

He shrugged. "I'm open to all possibilities."

This is too much! "Maybe Riley's friend is wrong."

"He isn't wrong. He ran the numbers I memorized from Heart's employment records. Detective Conlin would have had the same results."

"Well, maybe you memorized them wrong. Wait a second…When did you see her employment records?"

"When I left you in the lab."

"When you went to the restroom?"

He gave me a patient look.

"Okay, I get it. You didn't go to the restroom. But you were gone like, what, five minutes tops?"

"It doesn't take long when you're familiar with a computer system."

"You mean you're a *hacker*?" I asked, astonished.

"I know my way around computer networks."

"That's just a nice way of saying hacker."

He shrugged.

I pressed my fingers to my temples, willing my brain to think. I couldn't keep up with Emery. "All right," I said after a moment, staring at the floor. "Let me summarize: When you left the lab, you somehow got access to a university computer and retrieved Selma Heart's employment records. At which time, you *memorized* the information." I looked up at him. "All of it?"

He nodded. His expression said, *Of course.*

I gaped. "Do you have a photographic memory?"

His face became impatient. "Time is limited," he reminded me, not answering my question.

I refocused on the matter at hand. The intricate workings of Emery's mind would have to be a subject for another time, another day. "So, what now?"

"My friend Mickey has offered to follow Heart when she leaves the university tonight. Hopefully, she'll go directly home, or better yet, lead Mickey to my mom. He'll swing by and pick me up late this evening if it appears she's settled in a location. I'm planting a GPS tracking device on her car."

"You can do that?" I asked, stunned, and thought of a slew of reasons why he shouldn't. "But she could catch you, and hurt you, or call the police. You could be *arrested*."

"I won't get caught," Emery said, as if the certainty of this were etched in stone. "This brings us to your original question. I made arrangements to leave today because being here makes the things I need to do that much more difficult. I'm not usually under a watchful parental eye and so restricted. Because of you, my plans have changed, though my mission hasn't." He regarded me with an expression beyond his years. "As your dad said he would do everything in his power to find my mom, I will do everything in mine. I'll find creative ways to get around your parents when I need to. I don't want to burn bridges, not knowing my future role in your life." He stopped talking to scrutinize me. What he said next confirmed I looked as bewildered as I felt. "I'm sorry. I can see that last part is more than you presently want to think about. All I ask, for now, is that you help and support my efforts."

"Of course I'll help you. We're partners, right?"

He smiled. "Right."

"Okay, then," I said, collecting my thoughts. "Though this secret-agent stuff has me a little freaked, I can see we need to do it, and we'll just keep our fingers crossed that my parents don't catch us."

"Cassidy, I'm afraid you've misunderstood," Emery interrupted ruefully. "You can't come tonight."

"But you just agreed—"

"I know, and we are."

"Here I am, guys," Chazz called, running down the stairs.

"Then why don't you want me to come?"

"That isn't it," he whispered, glancing at Chazz speeding across the foyer. "We'll discuss this later."

"Yeah, we will," I said, redirecting my gaze to my brother.

Beaming, Chazz bounded into the room, holding *The Marvel Encyclopedia* in both hands. Apparently this had evolved into more than looking at Joker's mug shot.

"I looked all over, but couldn't find Batman," he explained, jumping up on the sofa. "But this book is way cooler. Okay, Emery, you sit here." He patted the cushion to his right. "Cassidy, you sit on the other side."

Emery stood up and followed orders, plopping down beside my ecstatic brother.

Sighing, I moved to the sofa. It was hard to resist Chazz's enthusiasm. For my cutie-pie brother, I pushed the pending conversation with Emery to the back of my mind.

"We're going to look at the A's," he announced, opening the book filling his lap.

"Joker starts with 'J,'" I pointed out.

Chazz gave me a stunned look. "Batman isn't in here. He's DC Comics."

"Silly me," I said, consigned to my fate. I figured I might as well learn about comic book characters, since I now closely resembled one.

Emery and I took the better part of two hours reading Chazz's favorite characters' bios out loud, with Emery taking text message breaks here and there. I enjoyed myself more than I thought I would. It was nice reading about lives more tragic than my own, though theirs were only fiction. We ended with *X-Men*. I related to Wolverine, not because of the animal thing but because of his power to heal. His bio said that his healing ability stretched out his natural life span, and that he appeared much younger than he actually was. This disturbed me, to say the least.

Finishing up with *Xavier*, Chazz dropped the huge book in Emery's lap and darted upstairs for comic books.

"Uncanny, isn't it?" Emery asked, thumbing through the book.

Leaning back in the cushions, I disagreed. "No, I would say *not plausible*."

After laughing at my indirect eavesdropping confession, he asked, "Who do you relate to?"

I rolled my eyes. "The mutants. Definitely the mutants. And you?"

"Doctor Octopus."

"The villain?" I asked in surprise.

"No. The scientist with lofty ideas who creates a weapon and releases it on the world." He smiled wryly. "Oh, wait. That is a villain, isn't it?"

"Enough about mutants and villains," I said, and then burst into a fit of giggles at my unintended joke. "Thank you, *Marvel*, for your knowledge and insightfulness." I flattened my hand against my chest and bowed to the book, playfully giving homage.

Emery looked a little uncomfortable, regretful even.

"Okay, give it to me straight," I teased, patting his shoulder. "I can take it. Am I or am I not a mutant?"

"I'm not sure how your genes have been affected," he answered stoically.

The smile fell off my face. "Well, okay," I said, putting on a brave front. "We'll just have to wait and see what your mom has to say about all that." I managed to drum up a half-grin. "So, partner, why are you excluding me from tonight's activities?"

"It's not exclusion," Emery assured me. "I simply have no way of explaining why you would come along." He shifted so he faced me. "Mickey knows I wouldn't involve someone who wasn't somehow beneficial to the mission. A fourteen-year-old girl isn't normally beneficial."

"I agree," I said, maneuvering. "A normal fourteen- year-old girl wouldn't be beneficial, but I'm presently not normal. Don't you see how much I could help?"

"You would provide tremendous advantage," he admitted. "But you're missing the point. You couldn't use your abilities with Mickey present, and again, in his eyes there would be no reason for you to be included. If I brought you, his suspicion would be roused, and under that type of scrutiny, you could slip up. My goal is to protect you, not expose you."

"Thank you," I said with a small, grateful smile. "That means a lot to me. But I want to help. I want to find your mom, too." *My life depends on it.* "Figure out some way to utilize me, okay? Or better yet, give me an assignment."

A sly grin came on Emery's face. "Your first assignment, comrade," he said in a low, confidential voice, "is to get me a front door key."

The front door opened, and Nate stepped into the foyer. He stopped dead in his tracks when he noticed Emery and me sitting on the sofa. His face became annoyingly suspicious.

"What's up?" he asked carefully, eyeing Emery.

"Bunch of gossips," I mumbled. Nate would have needed some assistance coming to *that* conclusion.

Glancing at me, Emery smiled and clarified for Nate, "Chazz has been enlightening us." He held up the encyclopedia as proof.

That was proof enough for my brother. "Poor you," he commiserated, walking into the living room.

To add to the proof that all was innocent, Chazz ran into the living room with more comics. Mom followed him in.

"Good, you're all here," she said with a smile. "Remember what night it is."

Sunday's dinner was what we called "Kid's Choice." That meant we kids chose the menu, but we also made it. Dinner usually became breakfast, since that was our favorite meal. We called this "Breakfast for Dinner."

"Yay, pancakes," Chazz cheered.

Mom groaned. "We had pancakes this morning." Chazz thought for a moment. "Okay, French toast."

"French toast isn't anything like pancakes," Mom joked. "But the menu is up to all of you. Dad and I will be upstairs. Call us down when you're ready."

~~~

We had just sat down to a French toast feast when the doorbell rang.

"Huh. I wonder who that could be," Dad said, getting up from the table.

As Dad left the room, Emery caught my eye, nodding slightly. I understood that he wanted me to listen. Nodding back, I looked down at my plate, tuning in to the foyer, while Emery distracted Mom and Nate with conversation.

Detective Reed was at the door. Inviting him in, Dad asked him to have a seat in the living room. I could hear the surprise and curiosity in Dad's voice. I don't think Dad knew the detective beyond casual chatting at police headquarters.

At first, Detective Reed tried to make small talk, but his voice gave away his nervousness.

Dad cut to the chase. "Paul, I can see you're bothered by something. Please, you can talk to me."

"Off the record, Drake?"

"You have my word."

The detective sighed. "This is extremely difficult for me. It involves the Phillips case. There are things going on in the investigation that are questionable, unethical. Protocol hasn't been properly followed. Evidence has been misplaced. Leads that would normally be followed up on aren't. When I pointed out these discrepancies, I was told I'd be smart to look the other way."

"Who told you to look the other way?"

"Conlin, Drammeh, Captain Woodrow... I don't know how far up the ladder this goes. I think it goes high, real high... Drake, I want to stop them, but I don't know how."

Dad let out a long breath.

"With the cover-up, soon every lead we have in finding Serena Phillips will be gone. I don't know who to go to. No one can be trusted on the force...Will you help me?"

"Yes, Paul, I will."

"Cassy, are you under a spell?" Chazz anxiously asked, breaking the connection to the living room.

I smiled at him. "No, buddy. Just thinking."

As Chazz turned back to his plate, I looked at Emery. He had been watching me. Frowning, I nodded to let him know it was not good, not good at all.

~~~

I'm calling this "the day that doesn't want to end," I thought while listening to Emery creep down the hall. It was eleven-thirty p.m. He was sneaking out to do surveillance with Mickey and I was stationed in my room, monitoring the household. What a joke.

An hour and a half earlier, while we were all supposedly preparing for bed, I had slipped Emery the spare front door key. "You don't need it, though," I told him. "I'm going to wait up for you in the living room. I'll let you in."

"No, I want you to stay in your room," he said, all authoritative-like. "If your parents should catch me, I don't want it to appear you were involved. From your room, you can monitor the household for me. If someone should hear me leave or return, you can create a distraction and cover me that way."

I started to argue, and then he threw my words back in my face. "Cassidy, you said you wanted to help. This is how you can help me."

So, here I was. Helping.

The front door creaked open, and I heard an engine idling out front. Then the door quietly closed.

"Forget this," I said to myself, springing out of bed. Within a second, I was at the front living room window, peeking through the drapes.

Emery climbed into the passenger seat of a Jeep Cherokee. Streetlight spilled over the car, but didn't reveal the driver in the dark cab. I could only make out Mickey's brawny silhouette.

"I can do better than this," I mumbled, playing with my vision. I felt my pupils expand, absorbing available light, and I made an ability discovery: I had awesome night vision. As Emery began to pull the car door shut, Mickey's shadowy outline became clear as day. My heart skipped a beat as I took him in.

Mickey's name was deceiving. A street name such as Snake or Sledge would have been more fitting. He wore a brown leather biker's vest and had a fierce dragon tattoo slithering down his thick, freckled arm.

It spewed yellow fire at an aqua circle made up of inter-locking knots. His shock of red hair was spiked in a short Mohawk, and a devilish grin split his whiskery face. A thin scar slashed across his right cheek. *A souvenir from a knife fight*, I assumed.

"Where'd you meet this guy, Emery? Prison?" I whispered to myself. My stomach felt as though it had dropped several inches.

The Jeep drove off, and Emery's straight-laced image went with it, or maybe that had flown out the window when he hacked into Wallingford's computer. I recalled my initial gut feeling of Emery, and now knew without a doubt that there was much more to him than met the eye.

The difference between then and now, of course, was that this enigma was now my friend.

Emery, Emery. What have you gotten yourself into? I agonized, pacing the living room floor. Between hand-wringing and the strange energy swirling in my chest, I felt ready to implode or swim across Elliot Bay. Either way, I had to ease the pressure — immediately. Clearing a space in the living room by pushing the wingback chairs and coffee table next to the sofa, I started with jumping jacks.

My arms and legs moved in rapid synchronization, my feet barely touching the floor. The swish of my pajama bottoms and sweatshirt were the only sounds I made. I was sure if anyone witnessed me, I would look like an exercise video playing in fast-forward. I kept this up until I felt calmer, until the frenzy in my chest was tempered. Even then, I still had energy to burn.

Having always been envious of gymnasts and the amazing physical feats they could perform, I decided to try a handstand. Simple enough. *Okay, here it goes*, I thought, bending forward and kicking up. My palms planted into the area rug and my legs pulled up with ease, creating a straight, solid line. Delighted, I held the position for minutes without even a hint of weakening or imbalance. Then I got creative. Keeping my spine straight and arms solid, my legs slowly separated into side splits. My legs dropped until my pointed toes touched the floor. *I'm like Gumby*, I thought in amazement, dropping my backside so my straddled legs lifted up. Holding the position, I waited for my muscles to cramp and give out. They never did. Eventually, I steadily lowered my legs and rear to the floor and then sprung to my

118

feet, inspired. From that point on, I found there wasn't a challenging move or weird body contortion I could think up that I couldn't perform agilely. *Pretty sweet for a girl who could only do a noodle-leg cart- wheel three days ago*, I thought, springing front flips across the floor, enjoying the moment.

Soon I became so engrossed in my discovery that I completely forgot why I was performing gymnastic routines in the dark, until the Jeep pulled up to the curb. *That didn't take long*, I thought, flipping lightly onto my feet from a back handspring. Landing in front of the fireplace, I glanced at the mantel clock in surprise. It was one-thirty in the morning. I'd been flipping, jumping, springing, and twisting for two hours.

I peeked out the window. Relief flooded me when I saw Emery climb out of the car unscathed, slinging a black backpack over his shoulder. I raced to the front door and unlocked it. When I heard the Jeep drive away, I began to slowly pull the door open. Emery's feet paused on the porch until he saw my face, smiling big to greet him. He greeted me with a frown, equally as big.

"If we were in the military, I'd make you drop down and give me twenty," he whispered humorlessly, stepping through the doorway.

"Twenty pushups?" I whispered back eagerly. "I'll do it right now."

He gave me a funny look. "Are you feeling a little…energetic?"

"A little," I admitted, closing the door. "I worked most of it off while you were gone."

The funny look held. "Worked it off?"

I bobbed my head. "Here, I'll show you." As I excitedly moved toward the living room, my thoughts swung back on track. I spun around to Emery and demanded in a whisper, "Where'd you meet that guy?"

The house creaked.

Emery's eyes shot to the stairs.

"Everyone's asleep," I assured him, pointing to my ears. "I'm paying attention. Now how do you know Mickey?"

"I met him through Riley," Emery said, grabbing my arm. "I don't want to talk in the open." He ushered me into the living room, maneuvering me to the wall. "From here we can't be seen, but can get up the stairs quickly if someone should come down," he explained, releasing me.

"Don't you ever stop thinking?" I teased.

"That wouldn't be wise when I'm sneaking in and out of houses in the middle of the night," he stated matter-of-factly. Coming from anyone else, a statement like this would have sounded sarcastic.

I fingered the backpack strap. "What's this?"

"My bag of tricks," he answered, a sparkle in his eyes. "Mickey put it together for me."

"Bag of tricks" was certainly intriguing. However, Emery's questionable taste in friends was foremost on my mind. "And Mickey? Is he all right? He looks kinda rough."

"Rough, but a very good man," he assured, staring at me strangely. I could almost hear thoughts clicking off in his head. "Cassidy, you do everything backwards," he told me. "Aren't you curious about what happened tonight?"

My cheeks heated up. He hadn't meant to embarrass me, but he did. Trying to save face, I replied, inserting sharpness into my voice, "Of course I am. I'm assuming since my parents aren't picking you up from jail that you didn't get caught."

He smiled apologetically. "No, Heart was unaware of the stakeout," he confirmed, savvy enough not to mention the humiliation he had caused. Then he dutifully began his report. "She does live at the address listed in her records. Her residence is a little over a mile from your house. As far as we could tell, she lives alone, and she had no visitors during the evening."

"And you got the tracking device on her car?"

"Yes, and I've loaded the software into my phone. When her car moves, my phone will alert me, as though I'm receiving an incoming call. I'll be able to track where she goes."

"Well, good," I said lamely. Emery's dauntless self-reliance had me thunderstruck once again. "I can't believe you're my age."

He smiled. "What did you want to show me?"

My face burst into a beaming smile. "Oh, yeah!" I quietly exclaimed. "While I was waiting for you, I decided to figure out what I can do." I stepped away from the wall and moved into the entrance to the living room, facing the foyer. "This is what I can do."

Swinging my arms down and then forward, I sprung backwards. My palms pressed to the floor and I pushed off, doing a somersault with a twist high in the air, landing on my feet. Smiling proudly, I pivoted around to Emery. His mouth hung open.

"That was…fast," he said, adjusting his glasses. He didn't look impressed, though. He looked worried. "Cassidy, do you remember our discussion about your returning to school tomorrow, or later this morning, rather?"

"The discussion where you told me to resist using my abilities because it would be too easy to cross the line?" I replied, sidling up to him, smiling. "The one where I told you resisting wouldn't be a problem because I have no intention of revealing my 'mutant-ness' to my friends?"

He smiled, too. "Yes, that one."

"Well, you have nothing to worry about," I assured him. "I can control this. With the exception of smell, it's all voluntary."

Emery didn't look convinced, which sparked my temper.

"You're harnessing a lot of power," he pointed out.

"I can handle it!" I snapped loudly.

My parents' bedroom door opened. Emery's hand flew over my mouth.

"Go to the stairs," he commanded in my ear as the upstairs hall light flipped on, washing down the stairwell. Feet padded down the hall. My sense of smell and the heaviness of the footfall told me it was Dad. Emery's next instructions showed he, too, knew my dad was checking out the disturbance. "Tell him you came down for a glass of water."

I nodded, feeling like a total idiot. Whatever confidence Emery had in my "harnessing" ability, I had just dashed away. He released my mouth, and I darted for the stairs. Taking a deep breath, I began to unhurriedly climb the steps. Dad appeared at the top.

"Hi," I whispered to him. "I just came down for a glass of water."

"I thought I heard yelling," he said, with that look someone has when they've been startled out of sleep.

"Sorry. I stubbed my toe," I fibbed, knowing this was one lie of many more to come.

He kissed my head. "Go back to bed, sweetheart."

"Night, Dad," I whispered, opening my bedroom door.

He hadn't noticed my door had been closed.

Twelve

Back to School

A t 7:10 a.m., I walked groggily into the kitchen. Three lunch bags lined up on the island knocked the wooziness right out of me.

"Good morning," Emery greeted.

I turned my head to him. Leaning against the counter, he smiled at me, his hands wrapped around a steaming coffee mug. *He would drink coffee*, I thought, surveying him, *and he probably takes it black.* Emery wore his typical attire: a button-down shirt neatly tucked into khaki pants and a brown leather belt that matched his loafers. However, there was an additional element to today's presentation that truly made me want to shake my head. Embroidered in navy thread on the pocket of his gray shirt was his monogram, EMP.

"Why are you up so early?" I asked in denial. The extra lunch bag said it all.

Smoothing his neatly combed hair, he answered casually, "I'm your guest at school today."

He doesn't think I can control myself, I thought, staring at him indignantly. *He thinks I need his protection, but I'll end up protecting him if he steps foot on school campus dressed like that.* "No, you're not," I informed him.

"Yes, I am," he countered, sipping his coffee.

"No. You. Are. Not."

Mom whipped around from the sink. "Cassidy Claire! What has gotten into you lately?"

Seated at the table, Nate chimed in, "Brain damage. From the whack on the head."

"Nate," Mom warned, giving him "the eye."

Ignoring them both, I continued to stare hard at Emery, who was quite unflustered and very determined. *He isn't going to budge*, I realized, feeling my temper climb, and then suddenly it occurred to me why. *I am so dense! This is his creative way of getting around my parents. He has no intention of going to school with me. Mickey must be picking him up.* This thought caused a little unease. But don't judge a book by its cover, right? Emery had said as much last night, and Mickey was helping him. *And I'm messing up his escape plan.*

"Have you had breakfast, Emery?" I asked quickly, swiping up the Cheerios box from the island.

His mouth curved in amusement. "The coffee is enough."

"Are you sure?" I dumped the cereal in a bowl. "Lunch period isn't until twelve-thirty." I smiled at him, resisting the urge to wink.

Mom sent me an approving look and Nate laughed, shaking his head. "You're a trip, Cass."

~~~

At 7:20, we three headed for the front door, lunch bags in hand. Luckily, Nate went upstairs to grab a hoodie while Emery and I collected our things from the hall tree in the foyer. This provided me the opportunity to talk with Emery privately. I wanted to assure him that Nate would be cool about his ditching us on the way to school.

"Nate won't say anything," I whispered, pulling on my zip hoodie.

Emery gave me a quizzical look.

"You know. About taking off with Mickey."

124

He looked down at his "bag of tricks" and unzipped it. "Cassidy, I hate to break this to you," he said, placing his lunch in the backpack, "but that is not my plan." He zipped the backpack and unhooked his black jacket from the hall tree. My dad owned a similar one.

It took me a second to figure out what his plans were. "Oh, geez, Emery. No," I gasped.

His face lit up in amusement.

"You really are coming to school."

"I really am." He shrugged on his jacket. "I told you I wouldn't leave you."

Nate jogged down the stairs.

"Well, I didn't think you meant *ever*," I whispered in frustration.

Emery just smiled and slipped on the backpack.

Nate patted Emery's shoulder. "Ready to roll, dude?"

Not dressed like that, I thought, glancing at the loafers anxiously. *My gosh! Principal Snider wears those shoes. This will be like a matador waving a red cape at a herd of bulls.*

"Emery, you have to change your clothes."

That stinkin' amused expression came back on his face. "I'm sorry, Cassidy. I'm not going to do that," he told me, hefting his laptop bag on his shoulder. Even that displayed his monogram.

"Borrow something from Nate," I urged, interpreting his refusal to mean he had no other options.

"Cass, he's like a foot taller than me," Nate pointed out impatiently. To Emery, he said, "You're fine. Let's go." Nate opened the door and walked out. Emery followed him.

Watching the boys cross the porch, I gnawed on my lip, thinking, *No way he's sliding under Dixon's radar.* Then I grabbed my backpack and bolted after them. I wasn't giving up this easily.

"Wait," I called, pulling the door closed behind me. The boys were on the front walk. They stopped and turned to me. "I'm really not trying to be mean, Emery," I assured him, scampering down the steps. "But look at Nate."

My brother's hair, a tumbled mess, had a cowlick sticking straight up on the side of his head that he'd slept on. The old jeans he wore had holes in the knees, and the navy hoodie was smeared with grease stains. From the smell of him, I don't think either article had made it to the laundry recently. "This," I gestured to my brother, "is what the general male population at school will look and smell like today."

Nate sniffed his armpits. *"Hey!* I smell better than them."

Emery laughed and said to me, "What would you suggest I do to fit in better?"

I'm not a miracle worker, I thought, but whole- heartedly took on the challenge.

"Bend your head," I commanded, poising my fingers.

Smiling, Emery offered me his head, and I aggressively messed up his hair. "Okay, let me take a look," I said, pulling my hands back.

Holding back laughter, Emery stood upright, his hair in complete disarray.

"Cass, you think Julia Parr would do that for me if I combed my hair?" Nate teased.

"Maybe if you washed it," I returned, strategically arranging Emery's hair to look naturally messy. After several seconds of fussing, I smiled, satisfied with the results. "There," I announced, stepping back. With hair nicely tousled, Emery looked quite adorable. However, it wasn't enough. Frowning, I considered further. "Untuck your shirt."

Nate grinned at Emery. "Sorry, dude. Gotta agree. Untuck."

Smiling ear to ear, Emery pulled his shirt loose. It had the perfect amount of wrinkliness. "Am I presentable now?" he asked.

"Dude, we're going to stick you on the cover of *Teen Vogue*."

I lifted an eyebrow to Nate. "Like *Teen Vogue*, huh?"

"I get all my fashion tips from *Teen Vogue*," he joked, primping his cowlick. Then he added, "Time to go. I don't want to tell Mrs. Courtney in the office I'm tardy because I was helping another guy get glam for school."

When we hit the sidewalk, Nate asked Emery, "How do you want to do classes? Half mine, half Cassy's?"

"He is going to *all* of my classes," I stated, sounding a wee bit possessive.

Both boys looked at me in surprise.

Nate smiled devilishly. "Oh, is that right? *All* of your classes, huh? Emery, does that work for you?"

The unflappable Emery said, "If you don't mind, Nate. Cassidy had already asked me."

"I have better electives," I lamely defended myself.

"She's right," Nate conceded, nodding. "Her electives are way better than my lame-o ones. Good you thought of that, Cass." He snuck me an exaggerated wink.

"Cassidy! Nate! Tall boy! Wait up!" Miriam's voice called from behind us.

Nate groaned. "Trust me, Emery, don't look back, don't stop. Just keep walking."

Glaring at Nate, I stopped and spun around. "Hi, Miriam."

With a curious expression, Emery stopped, too, turning to see who would provoke such a warning.

Nate being Nate, he took his own advice and kept walking.

Miriam knew how to make a first impression. Bounding toward us, her pretty curls bounced and her cheeks flushed a lovely pink in the cool air. Her face was completely animated, displaying the most charming smile. Emery stared at her like she was some kind of exotic creature, and I had to admit, though I didn't want to think about it, she smelled rather exotic. This was going to be a challenging day.

With sparkling eyes, Miriam stopped in front of us, catching her breath. "That is one steep hill," she exclaimed, glancing at Nate's back. "I love you, Nate," she called after him.

Nate's shoulders shook in laughter.

Miriam laughed, too. "Gosh, your brother is cute. He cracks me up." She looked at me. "What happened to your forehead?"

This morning I had exchanged the gauze for a bandage, hoping not to be as obvious. "I fell. It's only a cut."

"Oh." Her eyes darted to Emery's face.

"Miriam, Emery. Emery, Miriam," I introduced them.

"Nice to meet you, Emery."

"It's nice to meet you...too." Emery watched Miriam blatantly look him over.

Finishing her examination, her eyes popped up to his face. Though she smiled, I knew Miriam was disappointed. Emery had the tall-dark-and-handsome thing going, but he didn't appear to have fallen off a Harlequin Romance cover, which was what Miriam kept an eye out for. Generally, her eye has been disappointed.

As we resumed walking, Miriam asked polite questions, though her mind had already wandered elsewhere. "So, Emery, where did you move from?"

"I don't live in the Queen Anne neighborhood. I'm staying with the Joneses."

She looked up at him curiously. "Oh, you're a family friend." Her eyes narrowed. "Why haven't I met you before?"

Time to divert.

"Miriam, sweet boots," I exclaimed, admiring her feet.

Briefly stopping, she admired her feet, too. "You like them? My grandma bought them for me Saturday."

"Oh, yeah? What did you do in Portland?"

Miriam's energetic mind was easily distracted, especially if the new subject was herself. Not that she was self-centered; she just enjoyed everything she did and was always eager to share, and she shared right up to the school's office door, without hardly taking a breath. As I reached for the doorknob, she abruptly asked Emery, "Why are you here?"

It took a second for him to register that he was the subject. "I'm Cassidy's guest at school today."

Her eyes widened with excitement. "You can do that?"

"According to my mom, you can," I said, turning the doorknob. "He has to sign in. We'll see you in biology." I opened the office door, and almost a dozen heads turned our way, their eyes looking over me to Emery's face. *Thanks, Mom*, I thought, walking to the front desk, feeling ogling eyes follow us.

~~~

In first period, the intense gawking ceased once I introduced Emery to the teacher and we took a seat. Not that eyes didn't continually wander towards him, taking in his attire, the glasses, and the bright red visitor's badge he wore. Amazingly, Emery was quite unruffled. Cool-headed, he would meet the gawker's gaze and slightly smile, causing the gawker to quickly look away.

I wasn't quite as cool-headed.

A couple of Nate's friends, obviously privy to the sports field gossip, continually eyed Emery and me. To hide my nonstop blushing, I placed my elbows on the desk and leaned forward, cupping my face between my palms. Worse than the embarrassment was the anger seeping through my body, like a slow, deadly poison. I felt an aggression toward both boys that truly frightened me, as if there was a feral beast in me waiting for an opportunity to tear loose.

When the bell rang, I uncupped my cheeks and breathed a sigh of relief. The relief didn't last long. Next period would be the real challenge for Emery and me. Though a junior, Dixon was in that class. Not only was he in my biology class, our seats were also assigned at the same table, which I suspected wasn't a fluke, because Miriam and Rodrigo were our other tablemates. I was convinced Mr. Levy, our teacher, was evil.

However, I must admit that Mr. Levy's discipline techniques, which consisted of massive detentions and humiliation, had worked wonders with Dixon. Every day now, Dixon walked scowling into the room, sat in his chair, crossed his arms over his chest, and kept his mouth shut until the period's dismissal bell rang. He wasn't usually so pleasant.

After introducing Emery to Mr. Levy, I led him to our table. So far, Miriam was the only occupant.

"Hi, Emery," she greeted as we sat down. "How are things going so far?"

"Fine, so far," Emery answered pleasantly, sitting next to me.

Turning to me, her bright eyes danced. "I'm going to bring my cousin, Lexy, to school when she visits," she announced.

I laughed, louder than I normally would. "Miriam, this is only happening because my mom made it happen. You can't normally just bring someone to school."

She smiled confidently. "I bet you ten bucks she'll be sitting riiiiight—" she reached around me, patting Emery's shoulder "—there in about three weeks."

"No bets." I felt Emery's gaze on my face. "I have no doubt you'll—" I stopped short, getting a whiff of someone I knew had to be Dixon. Only Dixon would smell that foul, like something gone sour. My eyes shot up to the door, catching Dixon's hostile gaze.

"What are you looking at, Jones?"

My insides and fingers curled. "Hey, Dixon."

Ignoring me, he plopped heavily in his chair. "Take a picture, butthead," he snarled at Emery. "It'll last longer."

Emery calmly regarded him.

Dropping in the chair next to Dixon, Rodrigo smiled mockingly.

"Be nice," Miriam warned, dragging out the *s* sound.

Dixon's menacing eyes shifted to her.

Watching Dixon, Emery's eyes sharpened in his composed face.

My muscles tightened.

Leaning back in the chair, Dixon crossed his arms over his broad chest. Glaring across the table at Emery, he demanded, "What's your name?"

"Emery. What's yours?"

This threw Dixon for a moment. Scrambling for a new tactic, his eyes settled on the monogram.

"What does the P stand for?"

"Phillips."

"What about the M?"

"Mendel."

Dixon smirked. "What did you say? Mental?"

Rodrigo snickered.

I took a deep breath, trying to calm myself.

Emery's expression was unperturbed. "No. Mendel. As in Gregor Mendel."

"Who's that?" Dixon spat.

"He was the first geneticist."

I was shocked that Emery answered the question honestly. *Give me some help here*, I sent him, anger warming my gut. *Don't stir the pot.*

Dixon stared at Emery in disgust. "You *look* like you'd be named after some geek." Then his lips turned up in a caustic, challenging smile. "'Mental' fits you better."

Under the table, I dug my fingernails into my palms. *Deep breaths, deep breaths.*

"You're mental," Miriam jumped in, smiling at Dixon. *Oh, crud.*

His eyes shot over to her. "Shut up, Big Mouth." *Keep it together. Breathe.*

"Brilliant, Dixon, *as usual*," Miriam taunted.

Uncrossing his arms, he leaned toward her. "Someone needs to shut you up," he said slowly, between his teeth.

My spine stiffened. My hands clenched. I *so* wanted to hurt him. *Breathe! Breathe! Breathe!*

Miriam's smile recklessly broadened. "Brilliant *and* a charmer. You're the full package, Dixon."

Hatred filled Dixon's eyes.

Next to me, Emery tensed, preparing to intervene.

Breathe! I sucked in a long breath. My lungs expanded like balloons.

The bell rang for class to start.

On cue, Dixon sank back into his chair. Crossing his arms over his chest, he pressed his lips into a tight line while he glared at Miriam.

I slowly released the breath, feeling fury blow out with the hot air. *I did it*, I thought triumphantly. *I reined in the beast, and no one is the wiser.* My internal battle had gone unnoticed.

Relaxing in my chair, I watched Dixon's hands clench and unclench, his eyes latched on Miriam. Dixon had no intention of reining in his beast.

Thirteen

Partners in Crime

As soon as the dismissal bell rang, Dixon rose from his chair and headed out. Rodrigo was at his heels. At the door, Dixon shot Miriam a chilling look that said, *Later.* Collecting her things, Miriam took no notice.

Leaving the classroom, Miriam streamed one way down the hall while Emery and I streamed the other, heading to my third period class.

"Sorry about that," I said to him. "Dixon is a total jerk."

"Dixon is a classic bully, and your friend, Miriam, is rash. She's a train wreck waiting to happen."

Stopping dead in my tracks, I felt as if Emery had delivered a kick to my stomach. I knew my reaction was extreme, but his words had triggered a heart-clenching trepidation in me. Perhaps because I knew they were true.

"Did I offend you?" he asked, studying my face.

Feeling a deep sorrow, I shook my head and began walking.

Emery grabbed my arm. "Not so fast," he said, pulling me to the side.

Standing next to a bank of lockers, I looked at passing faces, avoiding his.

"Cassidy, please look at me."

Reluctantly, my eyes shifted up, meeting his steady gaze.

"I'm not here for the educational experience," he reminded me. "I'm here to support you in any way I possibly can. In order to do that, you have to tell me when you're struggling."

"Well, isn't it obvious?"

He smiled. "Aside from the occasional blush and tears, you're a difficult person for me to read."

I was shocked. "I'm like an open book."

"You may feel that you are, but you keep your expressions very controlled, which I find astounding with all the emotions I know you must be experiencing. Don't get me wrong, though. I'm relieved you have this skill. You need to create a veneer for all of *them*." His eyes gestured to passersby. "However, with me, you must be completely honest."

"So, you're saying I have a poker face," I interpreted in disbelief.

"A very good one. Please, tell me anything I've missed."

I shared my battle with "the beast." He listened attentively, his own facial expressions difficult to decipher. I wondered if Emery knew he had a good poker face, too. Something told me he did, having carefully crafted it.

After I finished talking, he frowned slightly. "I'll learn to read you better," he promised himself more than me. "I'll need to."

Before I could ask him what he meant, his cell phone vibrated in his pants pocket. Quickly retrieving it, he looked down at the screen and pressed a button on the keypad. A slow, satisfied smile spread across his face. "Heart has left her apartment. I have to go," he said, looking up at me. "I need to get my backpack and jacket. Your locker combination is 9-32-11?"

"Yeah. I think," I answered, confused. "I don't understand. What are you going to do?"

He watched the GPS. "Search her apartment."

"Wha—how? Alone?"

"Yes, alone." He glanced down the nearly empty hall. "The final bell will ring soon." He consulted his wristwatch.

"Fifty-eight seconds, to be exact. You had better go to class."

"What about Mickey?" I proposed anxiously. "Couldn't he do it instead?"

Emery's eyes were back on the GPS. "It's *my* mom. The dirty work is up to me." His gaze flicked to his wristwatch. "Forty-seven seconds."

"Oh, how do you even know when the bell rings?" I asked in exasperation, overwhelmed with the idea of Emery playing Lone Ranger.

"I pay attention," he replied, eyes on his watch. "Forty-two seconds."

"I don't care!" I put my hand over the watch face, resolved. "I'm going with you."

He regarded me quietly.

I went on, as though we were in a heated argument. "Nuh-uh. I'm not being left behind again. I'm not! We're in this together. A team. Partners. Remember? Comrades."

Emery put his hand up. "All right, *compañera*. What are the repercussions if you don't show up for class?"

"Oh," I said, thrown off. I'd expected him to put up more of a fight. I pondered his question briefly. It wasn't like I knew. I had never skipped class before. "Okay, I'm pretty sure worst case is the office calls my mom. If they do, I'll tell her you were having a hard time, you know, about your mom, so we decided not to go to class."

"It isn't a complete fabrication. I am having a difficult time," he admitted, glancing at the Droid. He frowned. "Her car just stopped. She's about half a mile from her apartment. There isn't time to weigh out pros and cons. If you're decided, let's go."

The bell rang.

At my locker, Emery exchanged his laptop bag for his backpack and snapped up his jacket and my hoodie. "Keep

135

the hood on and your hair tucked in," he instructed, handing me the hoodie. "The color is too distinct."

"Got it," I said, swinging the locker door shut.

His phone vibrated again. He looked at it and said, "She's on the move again. So are we."

We rushed out of the building. While we walked, I slipped on my hoodie and pulled the hood over my "distinct" head. Emery zipped up his jacket, concealing the monogram, and produced a baseball cap from his "bag of tricks." It made me wonder what else he had in there.

We walked briskly and silently as Emery watched Selma's movements on the cell phone. I was thankful for the silence. I couldn't wrap my mind around what we were about to do or how we would do it. It took all my concentration just to keep one foot stepping in front of the other.

Before I knew it, we stood in the parking lot of a contemporary apartment building. I had passed this taupe and smoky gray stucco building a million times, never paying attention to its sleek, clean lines, or the patios with stainless steel rails jutting across each of the four floors.

"I bet the front doors are locked," I said, biting a fingernail. "How are we getting in?" I looked at Emery. He was looking at the Droid.

"She's stopped again," he reported calmly, not answering my question. "With all these frequent stops, she's likely running errands. Let's move. We may not have much time."

"I guess I'll find out," I mumbled to myself, scrambling after his long strides.

An apartment resident was coming out of the building as we approached. Emery grabbed hold of the closing glass door, motioning with his head for me to go inside. I scooted through the doorway and he followed me in.

Okay, we're in. Now what? I wondered, nervously staring down the wide corridor, decorated in the same color scheme as the building's exterior. A powerful citrus scent hung heavily in the air, masking other scents. I assumed the fragrance was some kind of air freshener. It was nauseating.

"Heart's apartment is on the second floor, 2E," Emery said, scanning the hall. "We're going to take the stairs. Keep your head down. The hall is monitored with security cameras."

Oh, my gosh! My chin dropped. Keeping my eyes on the slate tiled floor, I trailed Emery's feet.

On the other side of the elevator, he pulled a door open, stepping aside so I could go through. "Keep your head down," he reminded me as I entered the stairwell.

I nodded, tasting Cheerios in my mouth. *Please don't let me hurl*, I prayed as we jetted up the stairs. *Please don't let us get caught.* Emery opened the second-floor door for me. I walked through, my eyes meeting slate. *Please help us get into Selma's apartment.* I followed after Emery's feet. *Oh, geez! How are we getting in?*

"Here, Cassidy," Emery said, his feet stopping. "Move close to the door and angle your body right." I did what he asked. He unzipped the backpack and pulled out a soft leather case. "You're shielding me from the camera behind you," he explained, flipping the case open. Inside were seven steel lock picks and two tools that looked like mini wrenches.

My eyes widened. "You know how to use those?"

"I do." He examined the keyhole and then selected a pick and a wrench. "Will you hold this?" he asked, handing me the case.

My anxiety dissolved briefly as I watched Emery insert the wrench into the keyhole, easing it clockwise. "Who taught you how to do this?" I asked, fascinated.

"No one. I'm self-instructed." He slipped the pick into the keyhole, too. "I thought it would be a useful skill to have." He jiggled the pick, and there was an audible *click*.

137

He smiled at me and grasped the doorknob. "Apparently, I was right. Should we see if she's set the alarm?"

"No," I gasped, but Emery proceeded to turn the knob. I squeezed my eyes shut and held my breath. There was silence and then the sound of creaking hinges.

"You can breathe now," Emery teased. I opened my eyes to his amused grin.

My breath came out in a gust. "I haven't been this stressed since playing Ding-Dong-Ditch," I claimed, putting my hand over my pounding heart.

"Ding-Dong-Ditch," he echoed, poking his head in the apartment. "So you are an adventurer. All clear. Ladies first." He pushed the door wider so I could go in. I scampered in, and Emery followed me, closing the door.

"Take these," he said, handing me the pick and wrench. I slipped the tools into the case as he locked the door and set the security chain. My eyes ran over the combination living/dining room furnished in chrome and black with punches of red. Everything looked expensive—very expensive.

"How can a security guard afford all this?"

"It depends on who you're a security guard for," Emery replied, his eyes roaming the room. "Her computer must be in the bedroom."

The temperature seemed to drop twenty degrees in the bedroom. Silvery walls encompassed white and mirrored furniture sitting on plush white carpet. An extravagant chandelier hung over the frosted four-poster bed, dripping with crystals that looked like icicles. "Sleeping quarters fit for the White Witch," I remarked with a shiver.

"Appropriate comparison," Emery commented, closing the bedroom door. "Can you pick up her scent?"

Mortified, I felt my cheeks flush. *What does he think I am? A hunting dog?*

Emery glanced at me, taking note of the blush. "You're not allowed to feel embarrassed with me," he said as his eyes wandered from me, settling on a laptop computer camouflaged on the white desk. "We're accomplices now. Lawbreakers," he continued teasingly, sitting down in the transparent desk chair that looked like a block of ice. He set the backpack in front of him and unzipped it. While rummaging through the backpack, he listed our crimes. "Trespassing. Breaking and entering." He pulled a portable hard drive from the backpack. Turning his head to me, he smiled and shook the hard drive. "Theft."

"Ha, ha," I said sarcastically, and then answered his question. "I smell her."

"Could you recognize her scent elsewhere?" He plugged the hard drive into the laptop.

"I don't know."

"Then it would be good to find an article of clothing to take with us," he said, striking keyboard keys. "In case you need to track her."

I let out an amazed laugh. "That is the weirdest thing anyone has ever said to me."

Absorbed in what he was doing, Emery didn't answer.

I blew out a consigned breath. If tracking Selma Heart like a bloodhound was what it took to find Emery's mom, then I would just have to do it. "I'll check her closet."

"Good idea," Emery said, and then announced, "I'm through the screen lock."

"Hacking, picking locks. You do make one wonder," I joked, setting the lock pick kit next to his backpack and moving to the walk-in closet. The closet light automatically came on when I opened the door. Black clothing lined the bars. "What a shock—the twisted Snow White is partial to black."

"You're good with these analogies," Emery remarked. His Droid vibrated.

"Selmazzz on the move," I said to myself, stepping into the closet. A tall black boot with a wicked spiked heel lay across the floor like the arm of a tollbooth preventing entrance. I nudged it with my toe, as if it could spring to life and attack. Then I began to gingerly finger through her ebony wardrobe, consisting of skin-tight clothing and leather. Her style was hip in a vampirish sort of way.

"Speaking of the twisted Snow White," Emery spoke up a minute later, "it appears she's on her way home."

The air wheezed out of my lungs. "Well, let's get out of here!" I screeched, jumping out of the closet and spinning to Emery. He sat at the desk, looking down at the Droid in his hand.

"Not until the data transfer is complete," he said calmly, narrowing his eyes on the cell phone's screen. "She's on Raye."

"Raye! She's almost here! We have to go!"

"Not until the data transfer is complete," he repeated, watching the GPS. "She'll be here before then. Cassidy, I need you to find some way to delay her."

Delay her! Who does he think I am? Jason Bourne?

"Heart is a block away. She's driving a red BMW M3."

Zipping to the bedroom's sliding door, I peeked through the thin gap where the curtains met. Selma pulled into the parking lot.

"She's here," said Emery.

"No duh!" I shouted, ready to hyperventilate.

"Keep your head, Cassidy. Find a way to delay her, but be discreet."

"That's a little contradictory, don't ya think?" I squeaked, watching Selma angle out of the sports sedan. She was dressed in the khaki uniform. *Okay, head, think, think, think. What would Jason Bourne do?* Selma opened the BMW's back door and dragged out a couple of dry cleaning bags. *What would he do? What would he do?* She closed the door and pointed her keychain at the car, setting the alarm. *That's what he would do!*

Watching her walk toward the building's entrance, I unlocked the slider and cracked it open. "One delay coming up," I whispered, listening to Selma's shoes click on the cement. She was no longer in my line of sight. The clicking paused as she unlocked the glass door. When I heard the door open, I flew into action, forgetting the "discreet" instructions Emery had given me. Yanking the curtain back on the rod, I threw the slider open and dove for the patio rail, grabbing onto it and flipping up. As my legs swung over, I released the rail, dropping the two stories. I landed on my feet in front of an old man pushing a walker.

Uh-oh, I thought, straightening up.

He squinted at me through his thick lenses. "Where'd you come from?"

"Over there." I pointed erratically and then dashed toward the BMW. I had to set off the car alarm before Selma got into the elevator. Wired with nerves and adrenaline, I pressed my palms to the smooth hood, giving the car a shake—literally.

The BMW let out a deafening wail.

Oh, geez! Slinking low, I scampered several cars over and crouched behind a Suburban's back wheel. Heart pounding, I listened for the building's door to open beneath the blare of the alarm. It didn't. *Oh, no! She must be in the elevator! What do I do? What do—* The door swung open, and I caught a whiff of Selma. Pressing my hand to my chest, I thought, *Thank you, thank you, thank you*, while listening to the rapid *click- click* of heeled shoes coming my way. Inhaling a ragged breath, I drew in her scent anew. It occurred to me then that I wouldn't need her clothing for scent. Her scent appeared fixed to memory. Lucky me.

Suddenly remembering I had forgotten to close the slider, I cut my eyes to Selma's patio. The glass door was closed, the curtain back in place, and when I adjusted my vision, I could see Emery watching through the curtains' gap. Impulsively, I gave him a nervous little wave.

The car alarm turned off. Selma's shoes shuffled on the concrete. I assumed she was looking around. *What if she walks this way?* I wondered in a panic. My nerves were stretched like a rubber band, ready to snap. *What do I do? Jump her? Run?* To my utter relief, Selma reset the car alarm and I listened to her shoes clicking away. Of course, we weren't home-free. Emery might still be waiting for the data transfer. Something told me, Selma or no Selma, he wouldn't leave without it.

The slider opened. Emery slipped out onto the patio and closed the door. Rocking back onto my rear from the low crouch, I sat on the concrete, watching him calmly vault over patio rails until he reached the end of the building. Then he climbed over the side of the last patio and lowered himself to the patio rail below it. I couldn't see where he went from there, and it only occurred to me after he casually sauntered my way that maybe I should have gotten off my duff and helped him.

He pulled me to my feet. "We need to move."

I nodded, dazed. "Sorry I didn't help you down."

"I didn't need help." He put his arm around my shoulders and steered me toward the sidewalk.

"Thanks for fixing the curtain," I said, and then slapped my hand to my forehead. "Oh, no! I left the closet door open."

"I closed it," Emery said, wheeling me left onto the sidewalk.

I mentally went through the house. "The front door. The chain."

"Taken care of."

"Your lock picks."

"In my backpack."

"The chair. It was pushed under the desk."

"Check." He paused. "A piece of advice, Cassidy."

I glanced up at him. His face sported a grin. "What?"

The grin grew. "Look before you leap next time."

I smiled and jabbed his side. "Oh. That's funny." The smile swept off my face as though the wind had blown it away. A heaviness weighed on my chest like a lump of lead. I was suddenly so sad. "Did you get what you needed?" I asked bleakly.

"Yes." His voice sounded far away. I wanted to cry. "I'll take a look at her computer files during your lunch period." I could feel Emery's eyes on my face. "I'm sure they're encrypted, though."

"Lunch," I echoed hollowly, tears collecting on my eyelids. I sniffed and dabbed at my eyes. "I can't go back to school…I can't go back there—ever." I had no idea where that came from or why. I had no idea where any of this was coming from.

Emery patted my shoulder. "This feeling will pass soon. It's a crashing effect from the adrenaline drop."

"How do you know?" I demanded, tears rolling down my cheeks. "You can't know everything, can you?"

"You'll feel back to normal when it balances," he assured me confidently.

"Normal," I snorted, and then fell into an oppressive silence.

By the time we reached school, the tears had dried up, and I felt almost "normal." We entered the building, and Emery took off the baseball cap and stuffed it into his backpack. After combing his fingers through his flattened hair, he pushed my hood back.

"Feel better?" he asked and began pulling my hair loose.

I looked up at him numbly. He smiled, resembling any other boy my age. But he wasn't, nor was he like any other adult male. In the last fifty minutes, he had broken into an apartment, stolen data from a laptop, and made a narrow escape with James Bond finesse. Now here he was, as comfortable as can be, straightening my hair.

"Who *are* you?" I asked.

My question didn't take him aback in the least. The tone of his quick response sounded prophetic, as though he'd seen our futures in a crystal ball. "The most loyal friend you'll ever have," he told me, freeing the last of my locks. "The bell is about to ring. Are you ready to go to fourth period?"

Before I could answer, the bell rang.

Fourteen

Dodgeball Out of Control

On the way to the cafeteria after fourth period, Emery's Droid alerted us that Heart was on the move again. "She's on her way to the university for her shift," Emery informed me, analyzing her route on the screen. "Which means she found nothing amiss."

"Did we really break into her apartment?" I asked, glancing up at his face. Now that we were immersed in the humdrum predictability of school again, our off- campus adventure seemed like a dream.

"No," he teased.

I laughed. "That's a relief."

The cafeteria door flew open in front of us. A combination of body odor and warm food slammed into me, causing me to suck in my breath. "That is so disgusting," I gasped, covering my nose.

"I can only imagine," Emery said, catching the door. "Find a way to dampen the smell."

"Easy for you to say." Lowering my hand, I entered the open room that was a swirl of moving bodies, noise, and odors. Who would have guessed smells could be so chaotic?

Sitting sideways with her feet on the bench, Miriam saved a place for us to sit at our usual table. Carli and Bren sat across from her, looking very yin and yang. All arms and legs, Carli was a ray of optimistic sunshine with long blond hair and a peaches-and-cream complexion, where tiny Bren had skin a shade lighter than espresso, straightened black hair bobbed at her jawline, and dark, feisty eyes. They were opposing, yet complimentary forces of life.

The three girls were debating whether actor Zac Efron's eyes were blue-green or blue-hazel.

"They're blue-green-hazel," I announced as Miriam flipped her legs under the table. Emery and I quickly stepped through the bench and sat down before bodies could expand into the unoccupied space.

"Blue-green-hazel," Bren repeated, grinning. "That is totally lame."

I shrugged. "I read it somewhere."

"Cass is right," Carli piped up. "I read that, too."

To Emery, Miriam mouthed, *They're blue-green.*

"Whatever," said Bren, popping a grape in her mouth.

"Where are my manners?" I joked, and made quick intros. I explained to Carli and Bren, "Emery is staying with us while his mom is gone." I didn't mention, of course, that his mother was the missing professor head- lining news.

Miriam nibbled on her sandwich, looking bored. She already had this information.

"So, where do you live, Emery?" Carli asked brightly.

"Near Wallingford University."

"I use to live near Wallingford," Carli exclaimed, all cheer and braces. "Which elementary school did you go to?"

"Emery was homeschooled," I answered hastily for him.

The three girls looked at him like he had two heads.

"Does your mom teach you?" Bren wanted to know. She hadn't picked up the past-tense usage.

Emery smiled at her. "No, I had tutors."

Again, the girls missed the past-tense reference. It made me wonder how many small yet significant details went over my head, too.

"Tutors," Bren echoed, unwrapping her sandwich. "I guess that would be better than your mom. Can't imagine my mom homeschooling me."

146

We girls grunted agreement.

"Hey, did you guys hear about Chad Dunham?" Carli whispered, switching the subject to the most popular, stuck-up boy in school. Her eager tone promised a juicy Chad tidbit, and Emery inquiries were thankfully dropped. As Carli filled us in, I caught one of Nate's friends, Ahmid Mazur, staring at me two tables away. He sat next to Bobby. Jared sat across from them, his back facing me.

When my eyes met Ahmid's, he gave me a grin that said, *Caught me.* Turning his head to Bobby, he shielded his mouth, saying something. Bobby laughed, glancing at me. Jared's back visibly stiffened.

Now, this was a predicament. I couldn't read lips, like Ahmid feared I could, but I did have a more effective means of eavesdropping. *Sorry, Emery,* I thought. *This is a temptation I can't resist.* Staring at Ahmid, I weeded out the surrounding clamor, tuning in to his voice.

"Man, I can't believe she's so into the dude," Ahmid said to Bobby, wickedly smiling.

"Nate said the guy's cool, but I've got my doubts."

"Nate's delusional. The guy's a total geek."

I gave Ahmid a dirty look.

He laughed. "Dudes, she's giving me the evil eye."

"Stop looking at her," Jared demanded.

My heart sped hearing his voice.

"You're just jealous because she's into that loser," Ahmid needled. Looking at Jared's face, his expression became concerned. "Just kidding, Jared," he backpedaled. "Why would you be jealous over *her*, anyway?"

The way he emphasized "her" made me want to crawl under the table.

Bobby came to Ahmid's aid. "Yeah, Jared, we're the jealous ones. You've got Robin Newton all over you. Man, we all want your problems."

Ouch! Emery jabbed me in the ribs with his elbow. Losing concentration, I lost the boys' voices among the other gossip, slander, and idle chatter in the room. Glaring up at Emery, I rubbed my side.

Calmly, he smiled at me, sticking a pretzel in his mouth.

My glare turned to Ahmid and Bobby. *I'll show you who the losers are*, I thought, feeling hot, angry blood pump into my veins. *I'll show you.*

~~~

Slouching in my desk in literature class, I pretended to review the pages in *Jane Eyre* that Miss Lake had told us we'd discuss in class today. My outrage had dissolved into deep depression, wrapping around me like a lead blanket. *Fitting*, I thought dismally, staring down at the book page that might as well have been blank. *Plain Jane and I share too much in common.*

From this thought, my mind slipped into schizophrenic dialogue. *Why are you letting those idiots get to you?* I scolded myself. *Rise above it.* From there, I screamed internally, *Of all people, why her? Why Robin?* My mind pointed out, *She's a plastic Barbie doll. Why should you care if a couple of morons view her as a goddess?* The crueler side of me, or perhaps the most honest, answered, *You care because that plastic Barbie doll is going to sweep Jared away and out of your reach forever. Like Ahmid said, why would anyone be jealous of you? You're a sardine.*

I glanced at Emery, who was looking over Selma's disk content on his laptop. He had confirmed in the cafeteria that the computer files were indeed encrypted. Now he would have to break the encryption. *Emery has real problems*, I thought, watching his fingers rapidly strike keys. *My gosh, I have real problems. I'm a mutant, for crying out loud.*

Giving my head a little shake, I commanded, *Pull yourself out of this. Stop being stupid and shallow. Get on task.*

Complying with my mental demand, I focused on the words in front of me, almost laughing out loud. Ironically, Miss Lake had us review the pages where Mr. Rochester brings the beautiful Blanche Ingram to his home.

"All right, class," Miss Lake spoke up. I glanced sideways at Emery as he closed the laptop and placidly looked up at Miss Lake. My eyes shifted forward to her. "Mr. Rochester returns to Thornfield with a group of elegant, high-society guests," she continued. "Among this aristocratic group is a young woman named Blanche Ingram. What does Charlotte Bronte tell us about Blanche, and what are your impressions of her?"

A dozen hands flew in the air. Pleased, Miss Lake pointed at fingers for responses.

"Miss Ingram is beautiful." *The knife plunges into my gut.*

"She's popular."

"People envy her."

It twists.

"Blanche is shallow." *It begins to pull out.*

"She's greedy."

"Stuck-up."

The knife dislodges.

"Doesn't matter," an off-response rang out. "Mr. Rochester will still go for her."

The knife plunges again, this time properly gutting me.

~~~

When the dismissal bell rang, I turned to Emery. "So, what did you think of the class?" I asked, forcing a smile. I had decided to test my poker face skills. Emery had enough

149

to worry about without getting pulled into my internal torment.

He scrutinized my face. "Interesting, though I've never read *Jane Eyre*. The novel seems like a good character study."

"Yeah, it's pretty true to life," I agreed, adding a laugh.

Emery continued to study my face. Apparently, Jane Eyre wasn't the only good character study. "One more class, and you can get back to more important things," I said, infusing cheer into my voice. "Unless you'd like to blow out now."

"No, I'll see this through," he replied, staring at me.

"Well, okay then. Time for P.E."

We slipped in with the bodies streaming down the hall. Moving among them, I felt detached, like a phantom. The hollowness and insignificance was so profound that it wouldn't have surprised me if one of the dashing bodies had run right through me. One thing I knew, walking down that corridor, was that I didn't want to be a sardine anymore.

~~~

"Hi, Mr. Saunders," I greeted my P.E. teacher with a pasted-on smile. "This is my friend, Emery. He's visiting the school today."

"Glad to meet you, Emery," Mr. Saunders bellowed, his generous belly vibrating. He eyed the loafers. "Too bad you don't have gym clothes. You're missing dodgeball."

Inwardly, I groaned.

Ben hadn't been kidding about my "allergies." Anything that was round and bouncy, I ducked when it came my way. This made me absolutely useless in most sports, especially dodgeball.

As I walked Emery to the gym's bleachers, he asked, "What is dodgeball?"

150

"Oh, it's a game of terror and humiliation, but a lot less complicated than soccer. You have two teams and numerous red bouncy balls. When you're hit, you're out. The last man, or woman, standing wins the game for their team."

"You make it sound so exciting," he teased.

"Yeah, it's real exciting, especially when an innocent bystander gets pegged in the head." With that, I bopped his head lightly and ran toward the locker room. The smile dropped off my face.

My dire mood deepened in the locker room, becoming full-blown when I heard Robin laugh with her remoras. Glimpsing her perfection, I joined my friends. Their conversation was but a hum as I removed my gym clothes from my backpack. Depression swaddled me as if I were a papoose, and try as I may, I couldn't shake it. Lost in gloom, I realized that I hadn't been properly gutted in literature. P.E. would prove that there was more to dig out. Jared and Robin were in this class. Athletic, revered, blond, and beautiful, this was where they shined, and I'd have to watch from the insignificant sidelines.

Slipping into my maroon gym shirt, our school mascot caught my eye. Looking down at the grizzly bear outlined in orange, an idea popped into my head, one that I wouldn't even attempt to resist.

As if a forbidden door stood before me, I reached out, grasping the doorknob firmly.

Pulling up my black shorts, I thought, *Never again will I be compared to Robin and come up short.*

I turned the doorknob.

Forcing my feet into untied tennis shoes, I promised myself, *Today, I step away from the wall. I will end the game and be the last "woman" standing.*

Kicking the forbidden door open, I barreled through, and ran into the gym.

151

As I rushed out to the floor, Mr. Saunders stared hard at me. "You're tardy, Cassidy."

Smiling, I nodded at him and glanced at Emery. Sitting midway up the bleachers, he smiled back, and then looked down at the laptop resting on his thighs. *Good. He's working on breaking the encryption*, I thought, feeling lighter than air. *He wouldn't be happy if he knew what I'm about to do.* A small voice at the back of my mind whispered a warning, pleading with me to question the source of my sudden high and to pay attention to that strange stir of energy in my chest. I told that voice to shut up. I was going to win. Win big.

"Robin and Bobby, you're captains," Mr. Saunders bellowed, his belly shaking.

Robin. What a shock, I thought as she and Bobby trotted up to the front. Standing with the other picks, I looked down at my sloppy shoelaces. Locking in on the shoelaces, I had an abrupt compulsion to fix them. Dropping to the floor, I began to work out the knot in the first lace while Robin chose her first player.

"Jared," I barely heard her call, the shoelaces my primary focus.

Getting out the knot, I carefully retied the shoe, making sure the loops were even.

Back and forth, Robin and Bobby chose, quickly at first, slowing down when the picks became more difficult. The crowd thinned around me as I sat, fussing with my laces. Satisfied at last, I looked up from my shoes, almost jumping out of my skin. Standing next to "Barbie," Jared watched me with a fascinated expression.

Realizing I had looked like a complete moron tying my shoes for the last couple of minutes, I stood up, resentfully blushing. *What the heck was that?* I asked myself, glancing down at my shoes. *Am I OCD or something?* The small voice whispered again, *Pay attention. This is too big for—*I shook my head, silencing the whisper.

Looking up, I startled. Robin had pulled herself close to Jared's ear, whispering as she surveyed her options. Moving her face to his, she gazed into his eyes, waiting for a response. Beautifully grinning, he shook his head. Robin turned from him, scrutinizing us more closely.

Jealousy whipped up in me like a tornado. *Don't pick me. Don't pick me*, I willed. I had a winning strategy worked out, and that strategy would be null if I were on Robin's team. She was the one I planned to beat.

"Kayla," Robin called, and anger shot through me like fire as I assumed Jared had advised her not to choose me.

You didn't want her to choose you, I reminded myself. *You can't beat her if you're on her team. I've got to get Bobby to pick me.* Grabbing his gaze in mine, I encouraged Bobby with a smile. Surprised, he smiled back. "Okay, Cassidy."

Yes! Walking briskly past him to join his team, I had to resist kissing his cheek.

Once they had hemmed and hawed through the remaining undesirables, the teams were chosen. Mr. Saunders directed our teams to different sides of the gym, placing the red balls along the line dividing the center of the gym.

When I stood next to Bobby, preparing to run for a ball, he looked at me, mouth hanging open. "Are you going for a ball?"

I smiled. "Yep."

"Are you suicidal?"

Broadly smiling, I shrugged.

He shrugged back, laughing.

From the corner of my eye, I noticed Emery look up from the laptop. I turned my head to him, grinning. His usually composed face showed an anxious expression. Staring intensely at me, he shook his head in a demanding way. *Clever boy. He's figured out that I usually play this game plastered against the back wall*, I realized, mouthing to him,

153

Relax. When he didn't do that, I rolled my eyes. When they rolled all the way around, I looked at him. The demanding had turned to anger. I wondered if he would try to pull me off the floor. Glaring, I thought, *Just try to stop me, Emery. Now that would be interesting.* Feeling invincible, I turned away.

Waiting for the whistle, I sought Robin, making eye contact. She looked at me dully, uninterested. *I can't wait to get you out, Barbie*, I thought as her bored eyes wandered from mine.

The whistle blew.

Before anyone moved, I had a ball and sought my first target. In that split second, I felt adrenaline pour into my veins. *Throw lightly*, I reminded myself, launching the ball. It sped through the air, hitting my target square in the chest. I heard the air rush from his lungs. *Oh, no! That was too hard,* I thought anxiously, staring into Jared's shocked eyes. For a moment, I regretted my choice, though it was good strategy.

"No freakin' way," Bobby shouted next to me. "Cassidy got you out, Jared?"

It was a question, not a statement. Jared had been the assumed "Last Man Standing." He usually was.

The game paused momentarily. Looking away from me, Jared nobly walked to the bleachers. Eyes followed him as he took an unprecedented seat.

Robin let out a war cry. The ball flew from her hand, but her aim was off. It headed straight for Bobby, who was still staring at Jared. Everything had happened so quickly, fractions of seconds apart, that Bobby didn't have time to react.

Oddly, for me those fractions slowed down. Suddenly, I was aware of every movement, sound, and scent at once, yet could distinguish each element. The sensation was so clear, precise, and absolute that I felt I had entered another dimension of time. Watching the ball move toward us was like watching a movie, frame by frame, and I could hear the *whooshing* sound it made, cutting through the air. Stepping in front of Bobby, I caught it easily to my stomach. The ball lifted in my right hand before Bobby registered what had happened, fractions of a second later.

I took aim, keenly aware of my strength. With the rush of adrenaline and emotions, the intense strength fought to escape. I knew that if I threw too hard, Robin could be decapitated, so I took pains to be aware and careful. Pulling back the reins on the frightening, wild strength, I threw the ball. Still, it was too hard.

The ball truly did cut through the air. Upon impact, Robin's nose appeared to explode, red splattering her pretty face. She landed hard on her rear end, blood streaming over her mouth and chin. Her face contorted in pain while her eyes blazed.

Time froze for everyone as we stared in disbelief. Like an injured animal, Robin curled up in a crouching position, hiding her nose protectively in her hands. Her eyes became wild as her remoras gathered around her. While they circled, she slapped their hands away, ducking her nose toward her shoulder. The scene was surreal.

Running to Robin, Mr. Saunders held a towel to her face. With fists pounding the floor, she howled cuss words.

What have I done?

Snapping out of my daze, I rushed to Robin's side and dropped to my knees next to her. "R-robin, I'm s-so sorry. Please, f-forgive me," I sobbed, guilty tears streaming down my cheeks.

Pushing Mr. Saunders' hand away, she lurched at me. I let her. Grabbing my shirt collar, she yanked me to her, my face inches from the streaming blood. With hate-filled eyes, she bared her blood-stained teeth, screaming, "I WILL NEVER FORGIVE YOU, CASSIDY JONES."

Stunned, I blinked at her, knowing she meant it. However—and I hate to admit this—the most self- centered, pathetic thought popped into my head: *She does know my name.*

~~~

Soon after Robin's vow, I slipped alone into the locker room. No one took notice with all the hysteria. Keeping tuned in to the commotion, I numbly changed back into my clothes. On the bench in front of my locker, I lay on my back, staring up at the ceiling. My thoughts were harsh and condemning. If horrible me had been thinking clearly, Robin would be sitting in the bleachers right now undamaged. I had caught her ball; she was already out when I pegged her. *What an idiot*, I thought, shaking my head in disgust. *What an idiot.*

As girls flooded the locker room, I continued to stare at the ceiling, condemning myself. Approaching me, friends attempted to comfort, but I refused to receive it. I didn't deserve comfort. When the dismissal bell rang, I didn't move. Alone in the locker room, I waited another couple of minutes before getting up to face the music. I had to face it, even if I didn't like the tune.

Walking into the gym, my feelings were conflicted when I saw Emery waiting on the bleacher bench. When he looked up at me, my eyes dropped to the floor. Guilty, ashamed, dejected, afraid, I walked toward him, ready to hear the tune.

"Do you know why Mr. Rochester shows interest in Blanche Ingram?"

My eyes sprung up. "*Jane Eyre*? Why are you talking about *Jane Eyre*?" *What is wrong with him?*

"You said it was 'true to life.' I thought that I should consider how." He actually looked guilty. "I've been distracted today. I'm sorry for that."

156

"Why are you sorry?" I snapped. "You didn't bust Robin's nose? You weren't being a jealous idiot." Shocked the words had come out of my mouth, I dropped wearily on the bench next to him, burying my face in my hands. "I didn't do it on purpose," I wept into my palms. "I didn't want to hurt her. I just wanted to win...My God, I could have killed her."

Emery placed his hand on my back, as he had at the sports field. After a long silence, he said in a soothing tone, "Cassidy, you don't see yourself very clearly. Between what occurred yesterday at the sports field and today, I've gotten a glimpse into your muddled view of yourself." He paused. "This will be awkward for both of us. Nevertheless, I believe you need to hear what I'm about to say. It may not be new to you. It's the sort of way your parents have most likely described you numerous times; however, the impact will be different coming from me...Would you look at me for a moment?"

Turning my face in my palms, I slid my eyes toward him. His expression was so sincere.

With a smile, he stated, unhesitant, "You are a beautiful, intelligent, brave girl, and inferior to no one."

My eyes slipped to the floor as I soaked in his words. Emery was right. My parents had described me this very way, but they were my parents; they loved me and *had* to view me like that, or so I believed. Having a relative stranger—a boy my age, no less—echo their words validated them to a degree. Not that I agreed in the least, but still, it was nice to be perceived in this way.

"Wow," I said, straightening up. Emery's hand moved from my back. "That isn't at all what I expected you to say. I figured...oh...forget it." I turned my face to him and met his gaze. "Thank you. I did need to hear that, and maybe someday I'll even believe it." I smiled. "Are you sure you're only fifteen?"

"Chronologically I am," he said, returning the smile. "I've always known I wasn't typical for my age. I had just never realized the extent of my difference until today." He glanced around the gym. "This has been eye-opening."

"I'm sorry."

"Why? I am who I am," he stated simply and beautifully.

"And I like who you are," I admitted, grinning. "In fact, I want to be more like you. Here, I'll be like you right now and get my head back in the game. Did you have any luck breaking the encryption?"

"I'm close."

"Good. And that's with distraction," I said, standing up. "Let's get going so you can put some serious time into it." As Emery rose to his feet, I added sheepishly, "I'm really sorry about this stupid diversion."

"It wasn't stupid. It was necessary," he corrected generously, hefting his laptop bag over his shoulder.

"You're right," I agreed. "It taught us both something important."

He gave me a curious look. "What's that?"

I looked him in the eye. "I'm dangerous."

Fifteen

Bullies

"Cassidy Jones!"
Great.

Turning from my locker, I looked into Miriam's face. Her eyes widened in delight when she observed I'd been crying. Sucking in a thrilled breath, she blurted, "It's true. You broke Robin Newton's nose."

"Not intentionally."

"Who said it was intentional?" She grinned mischievously. "Was it?" Her voice dropped low. "Come on, you can tell me. I won't say anything."

Observing, Emery smiled slightly.

I slammed my locker door. "Of course it wasn't intentional. It was an accident."

Unmoved, she shrugged. "Either way, it couldn't have happened to a more deserving person."

I gave her a stern, disapproving look.

In response, Miriam became more unruly. "Oh, come on, Cassidy. You know it's true. Robin Newton is terrible. She has caused countless amounts of misery. I look at this as 'What goes around, comes around.' She's paying her dues."

I shook my finger in her face. "Remember that, Miriam. It's like you said, what goes around, comes around."

The most ridiculous, naughty look came over her face.

My caution continued. "You can't kick a dog and not expect to get bit."

Miriam doubled over in laughter. Watching her, Emery smiled at her absurd display while my lips straightened into a reprimanding line.

Bent over, arms wrapped around her gut, she peeked up at me and then broke into new rounds of laughter. After a minute of this, she got control enough to say, "Really, Cass, you are *so* funny. You do that better than my mom." After brushing a tear of merriment from her cheek, she grabbed Emery's arm. "You were there. Tell me exactly what happened."

Grinning, he said, innocently, "It happened so fast, I didn't see a thing."

I rolled my eyes. *Ha. Ha.*

Miriam shoved him in mock frustration. "Fine. Don't tell me. I'll ask around. There are plenty of witnesses to choose from." With mischief sparkling in her eyes, she smiled up at him. "I can always ask Robin."

He smiled, I think, because he was at a loss for words.

Apparently, Miriam thought this, too. Laughing, she patted his chest once. "You have the cutest facial express—"

"Miriam, we need to head home," I interrupted her. Emery was eager to get back to decrypting, and I was eager not to waste any more of his time.

She smiled at me. "Well, I'm ready."

~~~

Treading down the hill from the school campus, I was flooded with relief, until the three of us turned down a quiet residential street. Midway down the street, Dixon leaned against a parked car, arms crossed over his chest. Toby and Rodrigo stood on either side of him, glancing at us in anticipation. Though Dixon smirked, his eyes burned, fixing on Miriam.

"Crud," I mumbled, slowing my pace.

Adjusting her pace to mine, Miriam glared back at him. "Who does he think he's looking at?"

"You," I whispered in frustration. "Now, just keep your mouth shut." *Will this day end already?*

Of course, reckless Miriam wouldn't take the advice. "Who do you think you're looking at?" she called loudly.

Dixon sneered back.

"Crud." My feet paused.

Next to me, Emery whispered in my ear, keeping a steady eye on Dixon. "Don't you do anything. Let me handle this. I promise you, he won't touch her. Now, keep walking."

Shaking my head, I stood firmly in place.

Dixon and his toadies laughed, low and rough.

Several feet ahead, Miriam paused, looking back at us, unconcerned.

"You don't know this guy," I whispered to Emery.

"No, I do know this guy. Trust me, everything will be fine."

I moved close to his ear. "Okay, I'll trust you, but if things get out of hand, all three of them are going over a fence."

His lips turned up. "I'll have to be sure it doesn't get out of hand then. Walk."

With a lump in my throat, I walked, knowing within minutes they all would know that something not right had happened to Cassidy Jones.

As we silently moved forward, Emery repositioned himself between Miriam and me, his eyes locked on Dixon.

Briefly, Dixon's eyes moved to Emery, narrowing. Sizing him up, his expression became apathetic. His glare shifted back to Miriam.

Fifteen feet from him, Miriam stopped walking. Emery and I stopped with her. "Dixon, *what* is your issue?" she demanded in an annoyed voice.

"You're my issue." He smiled maliciously. "I want to finish our conversation, Big Mouth. Remember the one about how brilliant and charming I am?"

Her eyes rolled up like she was trying to remember. "Huh? Brilliant and charming? No, that's not how I would have described you. You must have confused me with someone else. Now, if you want my description, I'd have to say…"

I held my breath.

"…that you, Dixon, are mean, spineless, and totally lame."

His smile broadened. "Now, why did you have to go get all nasty like that?" He pushed himself away from the car. Dixon had never looked so huge and intimidating.

"I don't have time for this," Emery muttered, walking purposefully toward Dixon.

A mixture of annoyance, malice, and amusement played over Dixon's face as Emery rapidly approached him. "Tobe, Rod, *Mental* isn't afraid to take a punch," he mocked, jabbing an open hand at Emery's shoulder.

In one fluid motion, Emery trapped Dixon's wrist with his left hand and cupped his elbow with his right. Rolling the elbow toward him and twisting it up, he pushed Dixon's arm up and back like a lever, locking his shoulder.

Simultaneously, I saw this move in two ways, fluid and frame-by-frame. The strange, indescribable experience took me more by surprise than Dixon being in an elbow lock.

Dixon cried out in shock and pain.

Toby, Rodrigo, and Miriam stared in disbelief at the "nerdy" boy humbling Dixon. I experienced a separate disbelief.

"Didn't see that coming," Toby mumbled, gaping.

Seconds into his predicament, Dixon attempted to escape the hold, howling in pain with the attempt.

"Don't struggle, or your arm will rip out of the ball socket," Emery warned coolly.

Rodrigo took a step forward.

Without looking at him, Emery cautioned, "That would not be wise."

To encourage Rodrigo to take heed, Emery slightly lifted Dixon's elbow, causing him to scream out, "Chill, dude!"

Rodrigo stepped back.

"We're leaving now," Emery stated. "Do you have a problem with that?"

"S-sure, sure, no pro-blem," Dixon agreed in pain.

Emery released him.

Without looking at Emery, Dixon carefully stretched out his arm. Glaring at his toadies, he commanded, "Tobe, Rod, let's go." Stepping past Emery, he stalked down the sidewalk, rubbing his shoulder. Glancing at Emery in awe, the toadies quickly caught up with Dixon's angry stride.

"Cassidy and Miriam, let's go," Emery said calmly, beginning to walk. Under his composure, I recognized the stir of adrenaline he was controlling.

Glancing at one another, Miriam and I caught up with him.

"Thank you," Miriam said guiltily, glancing up at Emery. "...and I'm sorry."

"Why?" Emery asked with an easy grin. "He is mean, spineless, and totally lame."

Though my nerves were a jumble, I laughed to hear something so adolescent come out of Emery's mouth.

"Well, I couldn't have *lived* with myself if you'd been hurt," Miriam stated dramatically. "Where did you learn to do that, anyway?"

"My dad."

His dad?

~~~

On the rest of the walk home, Miriam relentlessly attempted to elicit personal information from Emery. For the most part, his answers were vague and cryptic, except for silly questions like what was his favorite color or flavor of ice cream. I think Miriam tossed in those questions to be playful or to craftily throw him off enough so he might accidentally reply to a more serious question. Basically, the interaction became a game for both.

Letting them play, I mulled over what had happened when Emery humbled Dixon. He had made his fancy martial arts move quickly, faster than the eye could register, except for the mutant's eye. From the moment Emery's right hand lifted to the moment Dixon's elbow was hiked up, I saw each movement like individual snapshots. In my mind's eye, I could pull up any one of those snapshots, seeing it clearly. Strangely, I believed I could now perform the same move.

As we reached the front gate to Miriam's Victorian home, she stopped, gazing up at Emery with gooey admiration. "Thank you for being my hero today."

I choked down laughter.

Briefly stupefied, Emery came up with a witty response. "Today? Do you need daily heroes?"

Miriam laughed. "No, I don't usually get into this much trouble, but now I know who to call when I do." Giving him a captivating smile, she added, "Why don't you leave me your phone number just in case?"

Not having a clue how to respond, Emery laughed, shaking his head.

Miriam looked at him like he was the first Harlequin Romance escapee. "I'll see you tomorrow, Emery."

"He won't be at school tomorrow," I said quickly.

Miriam's eyes sparkled. "I'll *still* see him tomorrow. Bye, Emery." With that, she traipsed up her front walk.

Watching her ascend the porch steps, Emery called, "It was nice meeting you, Miriam."

Her shoulders shook in laughter. On her porch, she turned to us, brilliantly smiling at Emery. "You are adorable. I'll see you tomorrow. See ya, Cass."

"See ya," I called.

After one last smile, she closed her front door behind her.

As we resumed walking, I teased, "Now, she's an interesting character study for you, isn't she?"

Grinning, he shook his head. "I don't believe I'm up to it."

I laughed. "Not many are." Pausing, my mood became thoughtful. "Emery, I'd like to try something." I set my backpack on the sidewalk. "I want you to grab my shoulder."

Looking at me curiously, he reached for my shoulder. Before his hand made contact, I had him in an elbow lock.

"Ow. Easy." He stared into my face, stunned.

"Oh." I released him, feeling sheepish. "Sorry."

Still staring at me, he rolled his shoulder.

"Uh, is your arm all right?"

Not answering, he narrowed his eyes on my face. "Tell me how you processed that move."

"Do you mean, how did I learn it?"

"Yes. I want every detail."

After I described the experience, he asked me, "You're able to recall the event frame-by-frame, as you put it?"

Nodding, I explained, "It's like a video has been stuck in my head, and I have a fast forward, rewind, and pause option. Does that make sense? I just don't know how else to describe it."

"Yes, it does," he replied thoughtfully. "Your example is a good visual."

"What do you think happened? How did I do that?" I asked in a quick breath.

"Let me think about it for a while," he requested, picking up my backpack and handing it to me.

Falling into silence and deep thought, we continued home.

Sixteen

Karate and Me

While Emery was upstairs attempting to break into Selma's computer files, I did homework at the kitchen island. Mom milled around the kitchen, scrubbing and baking chocolate chip cookies. The school hadn't called her about my absence from third period, not yet, anyway.

As I finished up homework, Chazz tromped into the kitchen, climbing up on the stool next to me. "Cassy, *Clone Wars* is over. Now I'm getting a cookie." He took a cookie off the cooling rack in front of us. Chazz had a funny way of informing about the obvious.

Flipping my binder shut, I asked, "Want me to get you a glass of milk?"

"Yes, please." Melted chocolate already lined his lips like lipstick.

As I placed a glass of milk in front of Chazz, Emery came into the kitchen. His expression was inscrutable.

"Finish up your emails?" I asked, watching him closely.

He looked into my eyes. "Yes."

He broke into the files, I understood, staring back at him, *and he isn't happy about what he found*.

Nate burst through the front door then, shouting, "Cassidy, you brute, where are you?"

Still staring at Emery, my eyes widened with dread.

Bounding into the kitchen, Nate exclaimed, beaming at me, "I can't believe you did it."

I stuffed a whole cookie in my mouth.

He glanced at Emery. "That you *both* did it."

Alarmed, Mom's head bobbed between Emery and me. "What is going on?" she demanded to know. I had conveniently forgotten to mention Robin and Dixon when she had asked earlier how the day went.

Grinning ear-to-ear, Nate answered, "First, my sister broke Robin Newton's nose—"

Mom gasped.

"Second, Emery kicked Pilchowski's—"

"I only put him in an elbow lock," Emery corrected quickly.

Nate considered this. "Still cool. I should have figured Miriam exaggerated. Man, she is totally hyper. When I walked by her house, she practically tackled me, all eager to tell someone about her 'hero.'" Nate grinned, rolling his eyes. "It was insane how she went on about you, dude. 'Emery is so brave, so strong, so handsome.'" He imitated Miriam. "And blah, blah, blah, blah, blah…Man, you are in so much troub—"

Cutting him off, Mom, who hadn't heard a thing beyond "broken nose," blurted at me, "Cassidy Claire, how did you break that girl's nose?"

"It was an *accident*," I clarified. "We were playing dodgeball in P.E. I threw a ball, and it hit Robin in the face. Her nose bled, but I don't think it was broken."

"Oh, yeah, it's broken," Nate butted in. "And that's not how *I* heard it, even though I have my doubts about the accuracy, but Jared is a reliable—"

"Jared? What did he say?" I asked in a quick breath.

Surprised, Nate observed my face for a moment. Then his lips turned up into a knowing smile. "Oh, you're wondering what *Jared* said about *you*? *Jared* told me he had never seen anyone move like you did today. He said you took him out before he even realized you had a ball, and then you caught a ball that Robin pitched at Bobby, and with that same ball, you busted her nose." Pausing to watch my reaction, he added, "Jared said you were awesome. A total animal."

"Animal?" I repeated, nauseated.

Nate grinned like I'd received a wonderful compliment.

Dropping my head to the island top, I moaned, "I'm going to be sick."

With my head down, Mom wrapped her arm around me, speaking encouraging words I couldn't comprehend. All I heard were my own thoughts. *Jared called me an animal? I thought I was a little more subtle, like I had suddenly just become really, really athletic.* "Animal" implied inhuman, mutant—not athletic.

Sticky fingers massaged my cheek. "Don't be sad, Cassy," Chazz said. "You didn't mean to hurt her."

Lifting my head, I looked at him. With milk dripping from his chin and cookie smeared around his mouth, he flashed me a smile. His teeth were coated in chocolate.

"Feel better?" Mom asked, squeezing my shoulders.

I cocked my head to her. "Yeah, thanks, Mom. What you said helped."

Smiling, she squeezed me one more time before walking over to the sink, probably to get a sponge. Chazz's cookie wasn't smeared only on his face.

"So, Emery, how much karate do you know?" Nate asked.

Twisting around, I looked at Nate and Emery.

"A lot. I'll teach you some moves if you like." He glanced at me. "Is there an open place I can demonstrate?"

I stared at him in surprise. *He wants to do karate at a time like this? Why?* I wondered. It struck me then that his martial arts offer had to do with what he had found on Selma's files. What, though, I hadn't a clue.

"Our attic," Nate said eagerly.

"*Wa-hoo*," Chazz cheered, leaping off the stool.

Emery looked at me. "Come on, Cassidy."

169

Flow with him, I said to myself, following the boys out of the kitchen. *Emery has his reasons.* If I had learned anything about the guy thus far, it was that Emery didn't do anything without a reason.

~~~

Nestled under our home's pitched roof, our attic had been transformed during the remodel. The wall studs had been covered in drywall, textured, and painted wheat, and two large skylights had been added on the slanting roof to bring in more light. During bad weather, the attic replaced the outdoors for us. Berber carpet covered the floors to help with the acoustics because we tended to become rambunctious. Stairs coming up from the second floor cut the room in two. One side, intended for more restful activities, featured a sleeper sofa surrounded by floor pillows, and shelves filled with board games, books, and DVDs for the television against the wall. The other side simply had a treadmill, several large yoga balls, and an extra-large tumbling mat, perfect for karate demonstrations.

Heading up the narrow attic stairs, Chazz announced, "I'll be right there. I got to put something on." With that, he darted away, slamming the attic's door behind him.

When we reached the top of stairs, Emery looked around approvingly. "This is perfect," he commented.

Flow with him, I reminded myself.

As we unfolded the tumbling mat, Chazz reappeared, wearing Nate's Halloween ninja costume from two years ago. The black robe hung to his knees, and the legs bunched up around his ankles. I have no idea how he kept the pants up. So he could see out of the long, horizontal eyehole, he had bunched the top of the hood with a black hair band. It looked like a large egg on his head. We all smiled when he told us to call him "Ninja."

Nate and I were in awe during Emery's demonstration. He definitely knew the practice of martial arts, and he knew it well. His "classified," "accountant," unreachable father must have been a good teacher. Emery used Nate to illustrate different moves while Chazz and I watched. Though observing for me was interesting, especially the way my mutant eyes saw the action, Chazz soon lost interest. With sudden inspiration, he darted down the stairs, yelling, "I've got to change. Someone else is coming to see you." That "someone else" never came back.

An hour into the instruction, Mom called up the attic stairs, "Nate, come down and do your homework."

"Okay." Nate called back. "Darn. Emery, this is so cool. Will you show me more later?"

"Sure," Emery replied. Glancing at me, he wore a pleased expression. "I'll bring up my laptop and show you some great fight videos I have stored." He added to Nate, "Come up when you're finished. The participants are ranked among the best. The matches are intense."

"Real brutal?" Nate asked with a grin.

"Extremely." Emery smiled back at him. At the top of the stairs, he looked at me. "I'll be right back."

As they tromped down the stairs, I lay on the tumbling mat, frowning. *Why would he think I'd want to see a couple of extremely brutal guys knocking the living daylights out of each other? What in the heck was in those computer files?*

When I heard Emery coming up the stairs, I flipped up into a sitting position. My mouth dropped open as his head appeared. A single element missing from him created such a dramatic transformation, that if I had to come up with one word to describe him, it would have been *Wow!* Without glasses, Emery went from tall, dark, and handsome to tall, dark, and dashing. Those Clark Kent glasses really were an effective disguise.

Staring at his familiar, yet totally unfamiliar face, I asked awkwardly, "How can you see without your glasses?"

Setting the laptop on the sofa, he answered casually, "I'm wearing contacts. I just prefer the glasses."

As he walked toward me, I shamelessly gaped.

He smiled. "Cassidy, you're looking at me like I'm from another planet."

"Well, you kind of are. I mean, I've never seen anyone look so different when they take their glasses off." My eyes squinted. "You look really, really different."

"You're going to give me a complex," he teased. "Now, get up. I want to try something."

My eyes narrowed on him. "What did you find in Selma's computer files?"

"This first."

Flow with him.

As I jumped to my feet, he asked, "When you observed the demonstration, did the moves register and process in the same way as they did earlier?"

"Yes, they seemed to stick."

Smiling, his black eyes sparkled. "Good. Let's go out to the center of the mat."

Fight videos. No glasses. Center of the mat. I saw where this was going. "I don't know if this is such a good idea."

Emery rolled up a sleeve. "Of course it is." He rolled the other sleeve. "Just don't hurt me."

I shook my head.

"Cassidy, if this proves out, then I can explain to you why you were able to observe the move I made on Dixon and learn it. Now, come on." He walked past me, stopping dead center.

Reluctantly, I joined him.

"Now, all I want you to do is block me...Remember, be careful."

I gulped.

He threw a punch.

My hand flew up and blocked it.

"Good." He smiled. "Now, I'm going to do a series of punches."

Easily, automatically, I blocked those and the kicks that followed, and the combination of kicks and punches after that. With each series, Emery became more aggressive and fast, but cautious. He really didn't want to get hurt. Though my adrenaline spiked, I seemed to have better control over the strength than I had in P.E., maybe because I knew what to expect this time, or maybe because this wasn't laced with emotions. This was only two friends, casually sparring.

Like the kids playing dodgeball, Emery appeared to move in slow motion. Maybe that was why I considered this casual. Seeing punches and kicks slowed down wasn't terrifying. Because the motions appeared so slow, I must admit, I became bored blocking. It got to the point that I could anticipate his moves and defeat them before he really had a chance to make them.

"Okay," Emery panted, bending over, resting his hands on his thighs. Sweat dripped from his forehead, splashing on the mat. "I can't do anymore."

"You're tired?" I asked lamely. I wasn't even close to breaking a sweat.

His face lifted to me; his expression was incredulous. "You're not even out of breath. Incredible. Absolutely incredible."

Now Emery looked at me like I was from another planet or like I was a new toy he'd just been given. Standing up, he wiped his brow with his forearm. "Let's sit down and talk."

"You're really good," I said, following him to the sofa.

He laughed. "That's a compliment, coming from you."

"Why would it be? You're natural. I'm not."

Picking up the laptop, his only response was a slight smile. "Go ahead and sit." He motioned to the sofa.

I sat next to him. "Okay, I give up. What did you find in those files?"

"This first," he said again.

"All right, 'this first,'" I agreed in frustration.

"For lack of a better word, I'm going to call what you are doing 'imprinting.' Basically, you observe a physical event, and like a stamp adhered to an envelope, your mind fixes that event to memory. Instantaneously, it is imprinted, and you can perform it. Add your other abilities, and you're not only able to perform what you observe, but you're able to perform exceedingly well."

This explained the strange occurrence "exceedingly well." It made sense. "Okay, I get it. Now what?"

He opened his laptop screen. "Now we train you. First, I'll have you watch fight matches involving a variety of martial arts forms. Later, we'll move on to something more combative." He smiled at this.

"You're boggling my mind. Why do you want to train me?"

"Because it may be useful."

"Useful for *what*?"

He looked me steadily in the eyes. "I've broken the encryption on two files. One file had surveillance photos of my mom and me. Apparently, whoever Heart is working for has been watching us for a while. The other file contained copies of email correspondence between two undisclosed individuals. The communications were in code. However, I did decipher that an assassin was the subject of the correspondence and King Pharmaceutical was mentioned."

"Is that like a drug company?"

Emery nodded. "Company headquarters are here in Seattle. You and I will go there tonight."

"And you want me to learn to fight in case we run into trouble," I concluded.

"Exactly."

I turned my wide-eyed gaze to the laptop. "Show me what you have so I can start imprinting."

He played the first video.

Concentrating on the screen, I slowed the images with my mind, imprinting the moves between the fighters. Eager to cram as much as possible into my head, I encouraged Emery to speed them up on the laptop until the video was moving in fast-forward. My eyes caught everything, stamping the moves into my memory.

About half an hour into this, Nate joined us, forcing Emery to play the videos at normal speed. Irritated, I focused on the images that appeared to be moving through Jell-O. It was excruciating.

Musing, I likened myself to the laptop, thinking it ironic that the computer had downloaded *me* with its "software." Musing further, I viewed my body as a machine able to physically perform the downloads, as Emery said, exceedingly well, and I had to be able to fight exceedingly well. Anything involving an assassin couldn't be good.

In the midst of musing, a mental radar went off in my head, warning me that something was wrong. I had no idea what alerted me to danger, but all at once, my senses instinctively sharpened. My ears picked up the disturbance first.

Two car doors slammed. Four sets of feet tromped up our front walk, two sets of them heavier, either because of body weight or footwear. Dispatch transmitted over their portable radios.

I gasped.

Emery grabbed my forearm. "Careful," he whispered, studying my anxious face.

A fist pounded on the door.

"We need to go," I said, jumping up. Heeding his intuitive warning, I descended the stairs at human speed. Emery and Nate followed.

The front door opened as I sprinted down the hall. "May I help you?" Mom asked with fear in her voice.

"Mrs. Jones, I'm Detective Bob Conlin. I'm a friend of Drake's."

Dashing down the stairs, I saw Detective Conlin's solemn face over Mom's shoulder.

"I'm sorry, Mrs. Jones…I have bad news."

Seventeen

Where is My Dad?

W ith Chazz on her lap, Mom sat centered on the living room sofa. Pressing close to her, Nate and I sat on either side. Detective Conlin and his partner, Detective Drammeh, sat across from us in the wingback chairs, solemn-faced, yet matter-of-fact. Emery stood off to the side, leaning his back against the room's entryway molding. His expression was unreadable as he looked on the dire scene. Beyond him, a police officer stood in the foyer, standing guard. Another officer was posted at the back door.

Determined to keep a cool head, I battled inexplicable rage as Detective Conlin began the bleak account. "At approximately three-thirty this afternoon, two men pulled Drake into a white van near Pike Place Market. According to Ben, the vehicle pulled up to the curb where Drake was standing, and before he and other witnesses could intervene, the van sped away. The two men and driver wore nylon masks. A witness took down the vehicle plate numbers. We ran them. The van was reported stolen three days ago."

"What's happening?" Chazz asked quietly.

Her eyes wide with terror, Mom pulled his head to her shoulder and whispered, "Somebody has taken Daddy. But don't be afraid, sweetheart, he'll be okay."

Detective Conlin watched Chazz somberly. "I understand this is a shock for all of you. But we are doing everything we can to find Drake."

Liar! I screamed internally, and then caught myself. *Focus.* Closing my eyes, I visualized Dad. *Losing control could mean his life. Be smart, Cassidy, be smart.* Drawing air in through my nose, I opened my eyes and trained them on the Detective Conlin's face, slowly exhaling.

"In order to move quickly, we need to gather any information you have that could aid us in the investigation."

"Since Drake has been abducted, shouldn't the FBI be in charge of the investigation?" Mom asked in a strained voice.

The detectives exchanged a look.

Detective Drammeh answered, "The FBI will take over the investigation tomorrow morning. Until then, we're leading it."

Not knowing if this was unusual or not, I glanced at Emery for interpreting help. His gaze was fixed on Detective Drammeh.

"Mrs. Jones, can you think of any reason someone would abduct Drake?" Detective Conlin asked.

She shook her head. "I can't think of any."

"Was he working on a provocative story?"

"No. The last three days he has been focusing on leads in Serena Phillips's disappearance."

Mom! No!

Anxious, I quickly looked at her. Her eyes were narrowed on the detective's face. *She's trying to figure him out*, I realized. *Dad must have told her about his conversation with Detective Reed.* Inwardly, I sighed with relief. She would be very careful what she revealed to these men.

Detective Conlin became gruff. "What leads?" he demanded.

My jaw clenched at his tone. *Control. Keep control.*

Mom's arms tightened around Chazz. "I'm not sure," she lied.

The detectives eyed her suspiciously.

"You understand, Mrs. Jones, we need to know everything," said Detective Drammeh, watching her face. "It could mean your husband's life."

I listened to Mom's heart speed. She was conflicted. Breathing deeply, she looked Detective Drammeh in the eye. "I have told you everything I know."

The room fell silent while the detectives stared at Mom.

Abruptly, Detective Conlin broke the silence, informing us, "We're going to trace calls to your house and cell phone. We'll set up here, in the living room. Until we have a clear picture of what we're dealing with, the officers will remain posted at the front and the back of the house. No one is to leave the premises, and no one will enter without proper authorization. This is for your protection." He surveyed us three kids. "Understand, kids? You stay inside."

Yeah, I understand. Anger expanded in my chest. *This is just a more subtle way of kidnapping. We're your prisoners.*

Detective Conlin waited for our compliance. With my brothers, I jerked a nod. I *so* wanted to hurt this man, my dad's "friend."

"Is Ben all right?" Mom asked.

"He's fine," Detective Conlin answered, his voice edged in irritation. "He's at the station giving a statement. When he's finished, he'll come here. He asked me to pass that along to you."

Mom nodded.

Detective Drammeh spoke up. "Mrs. Jones, I'd like to take a look around. Does your husband have a home office?"

Mom stiffened. "Yes, he does."

"Could you show me?"

With an uncertain expression, her eyes rested on Chazz's face.

Detective Conlin forced a smile. "Please, Mrs. Jones, go with Detective Drammeh. Your children will be fine. We'll take care of them."

"We'll be fine, Mom," I agreed tersely. "Go help the detective." I didn't want him alone in Dad's office.

As she looked in my eyes, a tear slid down her cheek. Quickly she brushed the tear away as I slapped down rage. I understood she wanted to fall apart but couldn't. Neither of us could do what our emotions dictated.

Kissing my forehead, she said softly, "I want you all to go to the family room and stay there until I come to get you." Without clearly knowing our present danger, she apparently thought there was safety in numbers, as if these crooked cops would pick us off one by one. After kissing Nate, she moved Chazz to my lap, kissing him, too. Standing up, she crossed the room. Detective Drammeh followed. Passing Emery, she quickly touched his cheek as she stepped into the foyer.

Following her instructions, we stood to leave. Before we left, Detective Conlin peppered us with questions, such as "Have you overheard any conversations that made you feel uncomfortable?" and "Have your parents seemed nervous or scared lately?" When we answered "no" to everything, he let us leave. Escaping his presence was a relief. His very smell infuriated me.

On the sectional, Chazz curled up on my lap and wept. Resting his head against the back cushion, Nate rubbed Chazz's back, his expression lost and afraid. Emery, who sat facing us, fixed his inscrutable gaze on my hand balled next to my thigh, a visual of the internal tempest I was fighting to subdue.

"I need to go to the bathroom," Chazz sniffed.

"I'll take you, buddy," Nate offered gently, taking Chazz's hand. "Let's go."

When we were alone, Emery moved next to me. "You're struggling," he whispered, covering my fist with his hand.

I nodded, unable to form words. For a long moment, we stared at one another, our expressions closed and controlled. Then Emery allowed himself to relax. Sadness replaced his calm, causing me to choke up. My fist unfurled under his hand. His fingers slipped into my palm, grasping it.

"I'm sorry about everything," he said in a low, thick voice, looking at our hands.

"I know. But none of it is your fault."

Not acknowledging this, his eyes narrowed. "I really believed at this point we wouldn't be dealing with this on our own...There is something I haven't told you, that I haven't told anyone." He paused. "I do know how to contact my dad. It's a secret way, sort of like sending out a distress call. When my mom disappeared, I sent out that call. Normally, he would have been here by now, which tells me something has gone wrong. If he had simply been delayed, he would have contacted me somehow. The fact that he's silent, means...well, it isn't good."

"I am so sorry."

His face turned to mine. "I'm telling you this for a reason. We're not sure if law enforcement can be trusted. There will be no one coming to help us."

"What about Riley? Or Mickey?"

"No, I can't involve them any further. It's too dangerous. From this point on, we're on our own. It will be up to us to find your dad and my mom."

"So, what do we do? Beat the truth out of these detectives?"

Emery smiled faintly. "No, that wouldn't be prudent. If they're on the kidnapper's payroll—"

"If?" I questioned, squeezing his hand. Shock and pain crossed his face. "Oh," I gasped, releasing the hold.

"That was intense," he said in amazement, carefully opening his hand. "With a little more force, you would have fractured bones."

"I'm really sorry."

Staring at his hand, he ignored the apology. "I understand how extremely challenging it is for you to keep your

181

emotions in check, but you must. For both our parents' sake." He looked at me and frowned. "There's no room for guilt, Cassidy. My hand is fine." He opened and closed it as proof, and then picked up where he had left off. "We don't know for certain Detectives Conlin and Drammeh are on the kidnapper's payroll. We'll err on the side of caution, though, and assume they are. Fortunately, we have an advantage they're unaware of—Heart's computer files and a location where our parents may be held captive."

"King Pharmaceutical. We should go now!"

Emery put a finger to his lips, reminding me to keep my voice down. "Not yet," he said in a hushed tone. "We can't afford to run into anything haphazardly. We'll be patient and see how things unfold. I also need time to access the remaining files. They may contain information crucial—" He stopped talking, hearing Mom speaking low in the hall.

She entered the room, her hands resting on my brother's shoulders. "Are you both all right?" she asked us, glancing around warily.

Emery and I nodded.

My ears alerted me to someone at the front door. Tuning in, I heard Ben's voice and inhaled his scent.

Briskly walking into the family room, Ben surveyed us, his forehead creased with worry. In long strides, he walked over to Mom, wrapping his arms around her. "Elizabeth, I'm so sorry. I was too far away to stop them."

"I know you did everything you could, Ben." Her voice cracked. "Please don't feel responsible."

Pulling away, he nodded miserably with downcast eyes.

After making a round of hugs, whispering to each of us he was sorry, Ben collapsed on the sectional diagonally from me. Mom sat next to him, pulling Chazz into her lap. Nate returned to his place next to me.

Turning his head to Mom, Ben whispered, "I can't tell what's up or down. I mean, I always thought Bob was a good guy. He helped Drake and me out on a few stories. I seriously didn't see this one coming."

She nodded, glancing at Nate and me. "Did you and Drake go earlier?"

Ben's brow knitted in frustration. "Yeah, we did, and the guy's whacko." With his eyes, he quickly motioned to the living room. "Those jokers told me the guy checked out. Even after I told them what happened, they said they were aware of his 'eccentricity.'" He imitated quotation marks with his index and middle fingers. "But they found no link between him in either case." Ben's response had started as a soft whisper to Mom, but in his vexation, his voice rose so we could all hear.

"Who are you talking about?" Nate asked.

Ben looked at him, startled. Forcing a smile, he answered, attempting to sound casual. "Oh, this head case your dad and I met with earlier. The guy is a trip. Want to hear about the crazy meeting?"

Glancing at Ben, Mom slightly widened her eyes, warning him caution.

Understanding, Ben smiled at her. "Really, Elizabeth, it's all right for everyone to hear. You'll want to hear this, too, before the detectives need you."

After she nodded consent, Ben began. "Your dad got a lead on this guy who met up with your mom, Emery, last Wednesday at her lab. His name is Arthur King."

My heart skipped a beat. *King Pharmaceutical. Arthur King has my dad!*

"He's the CEO of this swanky company. Your dad contacted King, and the guy was willing to talk, so we went to meet him at his office."

Sensing my anger climb, Emery moved his hand next to mine, which pressed tensely into the cushion. His pinky began to slowly brush the side of my hand. The calming gesture said, *Control your emotions, Cassidy.*

"Now, I thought I knew this city inside and out but, somehow, I missed this crazy place. The building is random, shaped like a pyramid, and the weirdness continues on the inside. Okay, you have to picture the set of some futuristic sci-fi movie. The lobby is posh, everything is expensive, but it's also white. *Everything* is white—the walls, floors, furniture—everything. The only thing that isn't is this huge black monitor mounted to the wall behind the lobby's front desk, and the sad little receptionist who is also dressed completely in black. Black and white. That's it. No color. At least, there was no color until King popped up on that screen behind the desk."

Anger shifted into fascination. *This is completely bizarre,* I thought, relaxing my hands. Emery's pinky relaxed, too.

"Talk about random. King is this little bald guy with this honkin' hook nose. Even on the screen, the guy looked real short. I think he tries to compensate for the shortness by dressing loud. Get this, King had on this crazy purple and green pinstriped suit, a hot pink shirt, and a purple tie. He was ludicrous! The scene was so Twilight Zone that I secretly flipped on my camera. I couldn't pass up such rare footage.

"Anyway, King looked down at us from the monitor all serious and Napoleon-like. When he spoke, I expected him to say, 'Greeting, Earthlings.' Instead, he said, 'Welcome, Mr. Jones and Mr. Johnson. Allow my security officer, Mr. Spade, to escort you to my office.' Then, right on cue, these doors slid open in what looked like a solid wall.

"Okay, now, if you've seen the movie *Matrix*, you'll be able to picture the dude that stepped through the doors. Mr. Spade is huge and totally cut, in this tight black shirt, black leather pants, black boots, and long, black leather trench coat. The only thing missing from the look was the Uzi. To go with his slick gear, the guy was totally deadpan, no facial expression whatsoever. Only his eyes moved. It was creepy, like he was a robot or something, very Terminator-ish.

"Staring all stony-like at us, he then moved his eyes towards the open doors. We took this to mean he wanted us to go inside. As we walked toward Mr. Spade, I saw that behind the doors was an elevator. Before stepping in, I looked at the wall for a button, and there wasn't one. Strange, huh? Anyway, the entire back side of this elevator was glass, looking down this long white corridor lined with monitors. There were all these mopey employees, dressed in black, shuffling down the hall. They reminded me of morticians. It was depressing. Couldn't pay me enough to work in a place like that.

"Mr. Spade stepped into the elevator after us. The doors closed without him even pushing a floor button. In the corner of the elevator was another monitor, and guess who popped up, making me almost jump out of my skin? King, of course, and, man, was he full of himself. He had Drake start his questions right there and then, and your dad, being the pro he is, flowed with it, not letting the whacko throw him off. While Drake asked his questions, I discreetly positioned my camera to the screen. Funny thing is, Mr. Spade noticed. I was sure when I saw his eyes shift to the camera, he was going to tell me to turn it off, but he just looked back up.

"Each floor we passed was the same, white halls, black monitors, gloomy morticians. The elevator stopped on the top floor. The doors opened up to another long, white corridor with monitors lining the walls. At the end of the hall were these tall doors, like fifteen feet high, with two more Matrix dudes standing like statues in front of them. Without even doing the eye thing, Mr. Spade stepped out of the elevator, and we followed him. King popped up on every monitor. It seriously gave me the heebie-jeebies. But Drake, cool as a cucumber, kept asking his questions while we walked.

"Standing in front of those doors was like going to see the wizard. The two Matrix dudes grabbed these long glass handles on the door, pushing them open. Behind them, kind of posing for us, was King. If I wasn't so creeped out, I think I would have busted up looking at the little egomaniac in his loud suit. He was a total circus—the tent, ringmaster, and clowns all rolled into one.

"Drake went to shake the guy's hand, but King ignored him, saying, 'Mr. Jones, we're finished here. Mr. Spade will show you out.' Then he turned to the Matrix dudes, holding the doors open, and said, 'Mr. Club, Mr. Diamond.' Though I was trippin', I almost lost it when I heard their names—Spade, Club, Diamond, just like playing card suits."

Spade, club, diamond, and...heart. For some reason, the realization shocked me. Selma Heart had to be the missing card suit.

"Insane, huh? Anyway, King stepped back in his office all regal-like, and Mr. Club and Mr. Diamond closed the doors, moving back in front.

"Before Mr. Spade could 'show us out,' your dad's cell rang. While he was taking the call, I noticed we were standing in front of this wall with hundreds of small, black-framed pictures. Each frame had a black-and-white photo of his morticians. Man, I get goose bumps just thinking about it. It's like his trophy wall or something. I mean, why would he do that? And can you imagine being desperate enough working for such a head case? His crazy face probably follows them around all day on those monitors."

Making a *Brrr* sound, Ben shook his body from head to toe at the thought. I had the same reaction. My dad had walked right into the lion's den.

Flipping his thumb toward the living room, Ben said to Mom, "And *they* didn't think King's behavior was suspicious, or they didn't believe me. Heck, I'm glad I taped it, otherwise I'd doubt it myself, thinking the tacos I had for breakfast were bad or something."

"What did King see my mom about?" Emery asked tonelessly.

"According to King, he wanted to hire her to develop a genetic tonic to stop hair loss. He said your mom turned the offer down and he hasn't seen or talked to her since. But the guy is sketchy—"

"Who's sketchy?"

The sudden addition of Detective Conlin's voice in the room made us all jump. *Should have been monitoring for lurking detectives*, I thought, tensing up. Emery's pinky went back to soothing. *Control the anger, Cassidy. Control the anger.*

"King," Ben answered with uncharacteristic irritation.

Detective Conlin in turn looked irritated. "I told you, Ben, I agree the guy is off his rocker, but you're barking up the wrong tree. There are lots of crazies out there—I've arrested my share—but *crazy* doesn't make you a kidnapper. There is no connection between King and Serena Phillips's disappearance, and he would have no motive to kidnap Drake."

The edge in the detective's voice softened. "Now, Ben, we have the same goal, and that is to find both missing persons and bring them home. Work with me to do that."

"Okay, Bob, I'll work with you...This morning, Drake and I went to see this nut—"

Detective Conlin cut him off, glancing at Mom. "Mrs. Jones, we're set up in the living room. We'll need you with us now, in case a call comes in."

Anxiously, Mom looked at Ben.

Patting her hand, Ben smiled. "Don't worry, Elizabeth. I'm staying with the kids." He threw Detective Conlin a dirty look. "I'm not going anywhere."

~~~

When Mom left the room, Nate let out a long sigh. "Dudes, I need to turn my brain off. Can we play Xbox for a while?"

Wish I could turn all of me off, I thought wearily, sitting as if my vertebrae were fused together.

"Xbox is an excellent idea," Ben said in a tight voice, snatching up a controller from the ottoman. When he sat back down, Chazz climbed onto his lap, cuddling up. Ben kissed his head and asked, "Want to help me annihilate your brother?"

Already positioned on the floor to play, Nate smiled up at him gratefully.

Emery stood up and stepped toward the hall.

"Where are you going, dude?" Ben asked him.

Surprise flickered on Emery's face. "Upstairs for my laptop."

"Okay, but come right back."

Emery looked incredulous as he left the room. *Clearly, he isn't "accustomed" to answering to an adult*, I noted, staring unseeingly at the combat game the boys played. *Was it only yesterday he said that? Seems like eons ago.*

A few minutes later, Emery returned. Sitting next to me, he took out the Droid from his pocket. "Cassidy, I have some games downloaded. You can play them if you like."

"Thanks," I said in a hollow tone, taking the Droid from him. Emery's "games" were fight videos. He flipped open his laptop, going to work, as did I, thankful for the training opportunity and the distraction.

While the boys artificially fought, I trained for a real one. Muted images flashed on the tiny screen, each imprinting on my brain. Emery had upped the intensity of the training to Japanese jujitsu and Krav Maga, both brutal. Strangely, the hand-to-hand combat didn't make me cringe like I thought it would. Instead, the fighting sequences stirred up a sort of eagerness in me. I decided this must be "the beast" reacting, because normally seeing blood intermixed with sweat wouldn't do a thing for me. As the brutality heightened and the forms became more like street fighting, I wondered where Emery found these videos. These matches didn't seem exactly legal.

The tune "Walking on Sunshine" sang from Ben's jeans pocket. Pausing the video, I looked over at him.

Pulling out his cell phone, his eyes widened as he looked at the caller ID. Nearly dropping the phone, he flipped it open. "Hello," he answered anxiously. His face clouded over. "Give me a second," he said into the receiver.

Abruptly, he stood up. "Be back. I gotta take this," he mumbled with a frown, stepping over Nate and Chazz, who were absorbed in the game. In big strides, he left the room. Tuning in to him, I followed his strides down the hall. "Gotta take a call," he explained to the police officer posted in the foyer. Then the door to Dad's office closed. Leaning forward, I dropped my face in my hands, concentrating.

"Yeah," Ben said.

I strained to hear the caller.

"Are you alone now, Mr. Johnson?" the caller spoke in a throaty tone with a foreign accent.

"Yeah, who is this?"

"I have your friend, and if you want to see him again, you'll do exactly what I tell you."

"What do you want?"

"The video from your camera. The one from today."

"No problem. Where?"

"Understand, Mr. Johnson, you are being watched. If you try anything stupid like making copies, we'll know."

"I won't, but I want Drake for the video."

The caller laughed, low and cruel. "Yes, that is how these things work, and how they also work is that you come alone, or you won't like the way you get your friend back."

"Yeah, yeah, got it, alone. Where?"

"Pizza!" A voice boomed in the room, startling me and causing connection loss. The "foyer" police officer stood in the doorway, beaming, holding four large pizza boxes. "Detective Conlin ordered these," he informed. "You can serve it up in the kitchen."

As Nate and Chazz jumped up, I desperately sought Ben's voice. Locating it, I listened anxiously.

"Eight o'clock, Mr. Johnson."

"Yeah, eight o'clock." Ben hung up.

"No, no, no," I moaned in my palms. "Awful, awful timing."

"What is, Cassidy?" Emery asked quickly. "What's happened?"

"That was the kidnapper. Ben is meeting him," I explained in frustration. "The problem is, I know the when, just not the where."

Eighteen

Saving Ben

I quickly summarized Ben's conversation with the kidnapper, adding in anguish, "Ben can't do it, Emery. He'll be walking right into a trap. We need to stop him."

"Ben knows that. He also knows this might be the only opportunity to save your dad."

"I know, but Ben isn't going to be some sacrificial lamb. We *need* to stop him."

"We're not going to stop him."

"What?" My eyes narrowed on his composed face. "Why not?" I almost shouted.

"Keep your voice down," he warned, glancing at the hall entrance.

"Why don't you want to stop Ben?" I asked between my teeth.

"Calm down and listen...We're not stopping him, because we're going to help him. You are going with him. Ben will have to drive to this meeting. Before he leaves, you'll sneak into his car. When he meets with the kidnappers, you'll overtake and detain them. They won't have your dad with them, but we'll get them to talk."

"So, I'm going alone," I verified with uncertainty.

"We can't both leave this early in the evening. Our absence would be discovered quickly and we would lose any advantage we had. You're the obvious person to go with Ben, and I'm the obvious person to stay here where I can cover for you and work on accessing those files, and I *must* access those files." He gave me a level, discerning look. "Don't lose the fire when you need it most."

In other words: Don't be a *bawk, bawk, bawk*.

Emery sure knows how to deliver a punch, I thought, feeling this one between the eyes. I understood his challenge, which was: When push comes to shove, will you choose to rise up or crawl away, Cassidy? *Rise up, of course*, I almost said out loud. This was Ben we were talking about, and I would be willing to fight anyone to save him. I just didn't know if I could. "Are you sure I can do this? I only imprinted a handful of matches."

Emery's expression was unwaveringly confident. "Fighting for you will be mostly instinctive. The matches were only to teach you different forms. I've witnessed your capabilities. You're a powerful force, maybe an unstoppable one. This man will literally not know what hit him—or them."

Them?

A really good question came to mind. "What if he—or *they*—have guns?"

"They will. That's why you need to take them by surprise. I have no doubt that with your speed, you can unarm them quickly. You'll have to incapacitate them, too," Emery said casually. "Of course, our complication will be the lack of communication between the two of us, since you don't have a cell phone. Ben does, though. You could take his...but then, my number could be traced. You'll need to find a pay phone. When you call with your location, I'll figure out a way to meet up with you."

"Too much to think about," I said, close to hyper-ventilating. "I'll cross that bridge when I get to it." Taking a deep breath to calm my racing heart, I added, "I hope there will be a bridge to cross."

"Cassidy, you are *not* to think like that." Emery's black eyes bored into mine. The intensity made breathing even more difficult. "Apprehension is normal, but you can't let it get the best of you. You're right, there is no way to anticipate what will happen, but you will cross bridges when you get to them. This will be successful. We will find our parents. Know that you are exceptional, and stay focused on the mission."

The way he held himself, and the commanding way he spoke, made me think of a war general rallying his troops. The pep talk worked. Air entered my lungs again. "All right, the mission," I agreed with a nod. "I'll cross bridges and call you after I knock the kidnappers out cold." Placing my index finger on my lips, I pondered a moment. "Huh, I better bring a rope."

Emery smiled. "I have a better way for you to bind hands, if that's what the rope is for...Now, do you have black clothing?"

"No, nothing black."

"I didn't think so, but I have it covered, anyway."

How would he know if I had black clothing or not? I wondered, eyeing his face, which told me nothing. "What do you have covered?"

Ignoring my question, Emery said with a new urgency in his voice, "We don't have much time. It's eight minutes after seven. We don't know where Ben has to meet the kidnappers, so we don't know when he'll leave here. What I need you to do now is to go to the living room and tell your mom you're exhausted and want to turn in early. Don't overplay it. We don't want her to worry and check up on you—"

"Ben," I warned, listening to him clomp down the hall. Until now, he had been in Dad's office, probably devising a plan of his own.

Forehead creased, Ben walked into the family room. "Where are the boys?" he asked, attempting a smile.

Feeling worry roll off him in waves made my heart ache. *You'll be all right, Ben. I'll have your back*, I reassured him silently. Aloud, I replied, "In the kitchen. Detective Conlin ordered pizza. You should go get some before those big police officers devour it all."

Inhaling deeply, he glanced at the wall clock. "Yeah, pizza sounds good." He looked at us. "You two coming?"

"When I finish my emails," Emery replied, tapping away at his laptop.

I stood up. "Maybe later. Right now, I need to talk to Mom."

"She's in the living room with the detectives," Ben said distractedly, walking to the kitchen entrance through the family room.

See you soon, Ben, I sent him as he disappeared into the kitchen.

Closing the laptop, Emery pointed up. Giving him a thumbs-up, I scooted off to the living room.

~~~

Mom was encouraging about my decision to turn in early. I presented it as a way for me to escape the stress. She certainly understood this. Before I tromped upstairs, she said, her sad eyes brightening, "Hopefully when you wake up, your dad will be here."

"I have a good feeling he will," I replied, resisting the urge to stick my tongue out at the detectives.

When Emery had pointed up, I assumed he was telling me to meet him in my bedroom. My assumption was correct.

As I cracked open the door, he impatiently pulled me in, closing the door behind me.

He handed me Nate's black pullover sweatshirt. "Put this on. It'll be cold tonight."

The smell almost gagged me. "No way. I'll wear mine."

"You said you didn't own black. Now, put it on. There isn't much time."

Okay, the mission, I reminded myself, holding my breath. After I tugged the sweatshirt over my head, Emery handed me a wad of black polyester.

I laughed. "You've *got* to be joking."

His face was serious and determined. "We don't have time to joke. If Ben leaves without you, he probably won't survive the meeting."

With my heart in my throat, I quickly pulled on the ninja robe and tugged the pants over my jeans. The costume was tight but doable.

"I guess it was lucky Chazz dug this out today," I commented, tying the black belt.

Emery ripped the bandage off my forehead.

"Ow! What's the big—" Jerking my head up, I saw his middle and index fingers covered in purple goo, moving toward my face. "Purple? Why?"

The paint was cool against my cheek. "It's the darkest color Chazz has left in his face paints," Emery explained, scooping out more.

"Of course it is. What superhero would humiliate himself by wearing purple?"

Emery grinned, smearing my forehead. "I guess you'll be the first."

"Funny."

His eyes narrowed on my face. "Now, hold still. I have to get around your eyes well. This is the part they'll see around the hood's eye opening."

"Purple," I muttered, looking up. "Good thing I'll have a hood on. With the hood, why bother with the paint, anyway?"

His fingers moved above my eyes. "In case the hood comes off. We don't want anyone to be able to identify you. I'll safety-pin it to the robe, as well."

I sighed. "You think of everything."

"There." He smiled at me. "Do you want to take a look?"

"Definitely not. Where's the hood?"

"First." He pulled the black hair band from his monogrammed shirt pocket. "Do that, you know, twisting thing with your hair."

"Braid?" I asked, grinning as I gathered my hair. "You graduated from college and you don't know that this is called a braid?" I clucked my tongue as my fingers quickly braided.

He handed me the hair band. "Well, I know now."

Looping the band around the end of the braid, I tossed the braid behind my back. "Is this supposed to be my queue?"

"No." He grabbed the braid and pulled the robe's collar from my neck. "I don't want anyone to see your hair or use it against you," he explained, dropping the braid down the robe.

I cringed at the thought. "Yeah, I don't either."

Emery smiled, bending to the floor behind me. Straightening back up, he handed me my old sneakers. "And you said you didn't own black."

Grimacing, I picked them up by the laces. "I tried to forget about these. The last time I wore them I stepped in horse manure. Sorry." I glanced at his hands.

"So you threw them to the back of your closet," he commented, unfastening the safety pins.

Tugging the shoes on, I asked, "Under normal circumstances, you wouldn't snoop in my closet, would you?"

"No, I value my health too much," he teased, handing me the hood.

After I pulled it on, he quickly pinned it to the robe.

From his shirt pocket, he produced a folded piece of paper and a few quarters. "My cell phone number and change for a phone. Put these in the front pocket of your jeans."

After I tucked away the paper and change, Emery pulled out four plastic disposable handcuffs. "Hand restraints."

"Bag of tricks?" I asked, taking the handcuffs.

"Mickey's very thorough."

"He isn't the only one." I regarded him, stuffing the cuffs into my back pockets. "How'd you get this together so fast?"

196

Walking to the window, Emery explained, "I had already collected the costume and face paint when I came up earlier for my laptop."

"You were gone, like, two minutes." My eyes narrowed on his face questioningly. "Are you sure I'm the only mutant here?"

"If you weren't, I'd be tempted to leap out there with you." He smiled and opened the window.

Nineteen

I am Not an Animal

True to form, trusting Ben had left his Explorer's doors unlocked. He'd even left the windows partially rolled down. Crouching, I climbed into the passenger seat and curled up to wait until the vehicle's cab light went out. This was when things got dicey.

The cab light was still on when I heard the front door open. Ben and the police officer were talking. Luckily, Ben's head was apparently turned away from the street, because he didn't give any indication of noticing the light. Though sweating bullets, I couldn't help but laugh when Ben told the officer he'd be back after he "fed his cats."

As the light went out, I peeked up. Ben was closing the front door. In a panic, I dove over the backseat, landing in a pile of fast food wrappers and paper cups. In the gaggy odor, I recognized Deluxe remnants. Holding my breath, I rolled into the back of the Explorer and landed hard on Ben's surfboard. I quickly pulled damp towels that smelled like salt over me. At least the salt smothered the stench from the backseat.

My heart pounded as the cab door opened. It was so loud that I was nervous Ben would hear it. When the engine turned, Foo Fighters blasted in my ears. Thankfully, he had good taste in music.

~~~

As the Explorer rolled to a stop, I cautiously glanced out the back left window. We were at some kind of construction site. I could see the outline of a light- colored van. I would guess that the color was white. Three shadowy figures leaned against it. One figure held a lit cigarette to his mouth. I recognized the smell—the sweet odor from the lab.

I adjusted my vision, cutting through the night so I could see the men clearly. They were all burly and rough-looking, with dark eyes, black hair, and bronze skin. I felt my jaw slacken, recognizing one of the men. The smoker was the custodian with the silver tooth. I had forgotten about him until this moment. Exhaling the sweet-smelling smoke, Silver Tooth sneered a smile.

The engine turned off. Letting out a long, agonized breath, Ben said to himself, "Well, here goes nothing." Hearing the door handle pulling up, I ducked down before the cab light caught me in the window. Ben stepped out, slamming the door behind him.

I heard the same low, cruel laugh I had heard on the phone. "I told my friends you were stupid enough to come." As the caller spoke, one of the men flipped on the van's headlights, illuminating the surrounding dark.

"Where's Drake?" Ben demanded loudly.

"Careful, Mr. Johnson. You'll wake the dead," the caller warned.

His friends snickered.

"Where *is* Drake?"

"Where *is* the video?"

"First, Drake."

"There is no Drake, you idiot."

"Well, no Drake, no video," Ben said defiantly.

The cab light switched off. Cautiously, I peeked. Silver Tooth held a gun on Ben.

Fury ignited in my chest, sweeping through me like wildfire. Feeling heat in every taut muscle, I took in the scene through the red haze burning in my eyes, wanting blood—the blood of the man pointing a gun at my friend. My body tensed, preparing to spring into action, and my hand shot to the tailgate's latch. Then, somehow, reason broke through the feral impulse, clearing the red haze.

Control the anger. Be smart. Think.

Pulling my hand back, I evaluated the situation. The gun was aimed at Ben's chest, and the other two thugs, standing only feet from him, had holstered guns strapped to their sides. The holsters were exposed, making the guns easily accessible. Any sudden moves on my part, and all three thugs would have guns in their hands in a split second. At this distance, I wouldn't be able to take them out quickly enough, not before Ben got hurt.

I had to wait.

"How do you think this is going down?" Silver Tooth asked in a throaty voice. "I've got a gun, and you are unarmed. Get the video, or I put a bullet in your useless brain."

"My useless brain decided it was better not to have the video with me. Give me Drake, and I'll give you the video."

"You're a fool," Silver Tooth hissed in contempt. "Tie him up and check his car."

While Silver Tooth kept the gun trained on Ben, the other men roughly grabbed him, pulling his arms behind his back, tightening a nylon zip tie around his wrists. Ben glared boldly at Silver Tooth as one thug taped his mouth with duct tape. The other dropped a burlap bag over his head, loosely wrapping twine around the bottom to secure it in place.

"For your sake, Mr. Johnson, the video better be in your vehicle. Check it out," he said to his thugs. "Then toss him in the van. We'll deal with him later."

I ducked, my heart speeding with a mixture of excitement and fear. The two men shuffled toward the Explorer. *Time to be the element of surprise.* My hand grasped the tailgate's latch. *Showtime.*

I wrenched open the tailgate and dove out head- first. My hands made contact with the rocky dirt and I flipped up, landing squarely on my feet. Silver Tooth already had the gun on me.

My eyes zeroed in on a jagged-edged rock at my feet. In one fluid movement, I reached down, grabbed the rock, and hurled it toward the gun. My movements were so quick that Silver Tooth didn't realize what had happened until the rock tore through the top of his hand, embedding in the thin flesh.

Letting out a piercing scream, Silver Tooth dropped the gun. Diving forward, I had it in mine before it hit the ground. When he looked up, he was looking down the barrel of his own weapon.

Though in pain, he kept his voice even, menacing. "Who sent you?"

I couldn't very well answer in my young female voice, so I kept silent, clasping the gun that I had no idea how to shoot.

Peripherally, I saw one man's hand move toward his holster. Before his hand moved a fraction of an inch more, I turned the gun on him. His hands flew up in the air in surrender. I moved the gun to the other man, who mimicked his friend, raising his hands in the air. Silver Tooth flinched. The gun moved back to him.

Silver Tooth laughed low. Holding up his limp hand, he asked me, "Do you mind?" Taking my silence as consent, he savagely ripped the rock from his flesh.

Perspiration beaded on his forehead. "Why don't you tell me what you want," he said steadily.

I kept quiet.

He lifted his chin toward Ben. "Do you want him?" Still, I didn't respond, at a loss of how to cross this bridge.

"The silent type, eh? How about I do the talking. You want what we all want: the assassin."

Who is the assassin?

His lips lifted, revealing the silver tooth. "No reason we can't share, eh? Be partners. Together, we take these Kings out of the equation." Smiling, he waited.

After seconds of silence, his face contorted in frustration. "Do we have a deal or not? Talk!"

Well, I certainly couldn't do that, and I wasn't using the gun in my hands. Simultaneously, I tossed the gun behind me and kicked Silver Tooth square in the chest. I could hear the wind leave his body. He flew backwards and landed on his back, gasping.

Adrenaline rushed through my veins. The night sky brightened, revealing everything around me in a new light. I perceived every physical detail of my adversaries, breathing in the smell of their skin and hair, tasting their fear on my tongue. Time and space slowed. Everything slowed but me.

The other men went for their guns. I leapt toward the nearest thug, grabbing his hands just as he drew his gun. Squeezing his hand hard, I felt bones crack and give way. Crying out, he released the weapon, letting it drop to the ground. Still clenching his hand, my other arm swung around, punching him in the gut. His body folded around my fist, and he flew backwards ten feet, bouncing off the van. Before he hit the ground, my left leg swept the other thug's legs as he trained his gun on me. His feet flew up, and he landed on the back of his head with a thud. As he lay dazed on the ground, the gun rested in his fingertips. Darting forward, I retrieved the gun, twisting back to grab the one at my feet. With slack jaws, each man looked blurry-eyed in my general direction, unable to visually track my fast movements.

Sensing movement from behind, I dropped the guns and spun around, catching Silver Tooth by his outstretched arm as he went to grab me. Twirling him in a circle, I let go, and he flew through the air, his airborne limbs resembling a rag doll's. Hitting the ground, he landed flat on his back with the wind knocked out of him for a second time.

One of the thugs made a feeble attempt to get up, but I was on him like a fly on stink. Grabbing him by the collar, I threw him against the van. As his body began to slink down, I eagerly grabbed him up again, throwing him at the Explorer. A scream tore from his throat as he flew sideways across the ten-foot gap. His body bounced off the Explorer, falling into a heap on the ground. Excited, I sprung at him, gathering him up by his collar and pulling him up so we were eye to eye.

Petrified, he didn't struggle, only stared at me with terrified eyes. As I looked into his dark, wide eyes, an image flashed before me: The black cat playfully tossing the mouse in the air, toying with its prey before the kill. This image punched a hole through the adrenaline- induced cloud in my head. Through this clarity, I recalled John Merrick in the movie *The Elephant Man* crying out in anguish, "I am not an *animal*!" Releasing the thug's collar, I watched him sink to the ground at my feet.

I am not an animal.

Slowly, I reached down to the terrified man, grabbing his collar again. His body was rigid as I dragged him across the dirt to the van, depositing him next to the other thug. Both men stared at me, frozen with fear. I put up a single finger, warning them to stay. They complied fully, reluctant to even take a breath. From the corner of my eye, I noticed Silver Tooth inching across the ground, afraid to make any sudden moves. Unarmed, he didn't pose much of a threat.

The guns.

In a heartbeat, I collected the scattered guns, placing them on the Explorer's floor. Closing the Explorer's door, I turned around and assessed the men: the two thugs hadn't moved an inch, and Silver Tooth had inched a few more feet. Then I stepped behind Ben, who had stood frozen during the entire altercation, and snapped the cord from his wrists. Still, he didn't move. I gave his back a reassuring pat. He flinched, but otherwise stayed silent and still. I assumed he was in shock, and then realized I, too, was in shock. Drawing in a ragged breath, I lowered my face into trembling hands. *It's the adrenaline*, I realized, my heart pounding like a jackhammer in my ears.

The van's engine started.

My head jerked up. The thugs were scrambling in through the side door. As I contemplated what to do, it peeled away, Silver Tooth driving with his good hand. In a running leap, I sailed through the air, grabbing the rack on the van's roof. Pulling myself up, I flattened my body out on top, hoping I didn't stick out like a sore thumb against the white.

~~~

As the van sped through the city streets, I fought a battle of my own. My body shook uncontrollably. Overwrought with aggression, I had to fight the urge to punch through the windshield and grab Silver Tooth by the throat. Deep breathing and the cool air rushing over my body eventually calmed me. The men's foreign tongue, which I decided was Spanish, soothed the beast in me. Like a lullaby, I listened to the cadence of the unfamiliar words pouring from their mouths, while tears trickled from my eyes.

Once able to form constructive thoughts, I came up with a plan. Deciding to avoid more confrontation, I planned to play "fly on the wall," to be an observer and collect information—unless, of course, these men were taking me directly to my dad. Then there would be trouble. My fingers crossed at this happy thought.

We drove down into the warehouse district. The narrow streets weaved together like a maze around old, dilapidated brick buildings with bars over windows of broken glass. The smell of rotting fish hung in the stale air, trapped between the brick walls. The streets were eerie and still, with not a living soul in sight except for the rats caught in the headlights as they scurried away behind dumpsters and piles of trash.

The van pulled up to a warped wood freight door. One of the thugs hopped out of the passenger side door, unlocked a huge deadbolt on the freight door, and slid it open. The door protested, moaning and groaning along the rusted metal tracks. The van slowly drove through the opening.

With the thug who had opened the freight door still outside and the other ones in the van, I knew this would be my best opportunity to find a place to hide. I scanned the cement floor, but the only likely candidates were the wood crates stacked about. Looking up at the open wood rafters, I noticed a small storage loft ahead. The only thing leading up to it was a tall ladder with peeling red paint. Deciding a bird's eye view was best, I stood up and leapt to the loft. As I landed, the structure shook, threatening to collapse. I counterbalanced the swaying with my weight, settling it as the van's engine cut below. Slowly, I lowered myself to the floor, lying flat on my stomach, praying the men hadn't noticed the structure swaying.

The van doors slammed. Their words still flowed in agitation but not urgency. I hadn't been noticed. A buzzing sound filled the room as long, rectangular fluorescent lights hanging slightly below me came on. Huge rat droppings covered the tops of the lights.

Surveying the dark street, the man at the freight door pulled it shut. He joined the others, who congregated around two stacked wooden freights serving as a table under the fluorescent lights. On top of the makeshift table sat three pink pastry boxes and eleven open cans of soda. Breathing in the musty air, I picked up a whiff of cinnamon rolls. My stomach growled, reminding me of my neglect. The grumbling ceased when I glanced back at the rat droppings. Who knew what floated around in those open soda cans or who had helped themselves to the boxes' contents?

Riled up and animated, the men spoke a million miles a minute, passionately slamming their fists on the table or kicking a crate periodically. Pausing from the rambling, Silver Tooth wrapped his injured hand in a dirty-looking rag. With his good hand, he flipped open one of the pink pastry tops, revealing several plump, generously frosted cinnamon rolls. Grabbing one of the rolls, he savagely sank his teeth into it, yanking a chunk off. Tossing the roll back into the box, he snapped up one of the open cans and took a swig. Visualizing what was scattered on the lights, I closed my eyes and covered my mouth to keep from hurling.

The freight door slid open. Silent and alert, the three men below pulled guns from their holsters. Apparently, they had extras. Two huge men with big guns of their own, dressed in tight black clothing, black boots, and black leather trench coats, stepped through the door. They were both maybe in their late twenties, with chiseled jaws, slicked-back hair, and blank expressions. Their void eyes mechanically moved through the room as they sidestepped from the door's opening.

Two more stepped through the door with guns drawn. It didn't surprise me to see her here—the missing card suit, Selma Heart. The man accompanying her appeared like the other two, expressionless and void, but Selma's face lit up in mocking delight, that sardonic smile playing upon her lips. The khaki suit had not done her justice. Tall, slender, yet solid and well endowed, she wore a tight black dress that clung to her curves, high-heeled black leather boots that hugged her calves, and a black leather trench coat with a stiff collar sticking up.

Between them stood "The Circus," or more like "The Freak Show." King would have been hysterically funny if one didn't look beyond the green and purple pinstriped suit and white dress shoes. His presentation appeared even more odd and surreal on his tiny frame. However, looking at the man himself and not his outfit, one would quickly realize there was nothing funny about him. Depravity oozed from his expression; insanity shone in his flinty eyes. I understood why Ben had downplayed King. He didn't want to give us nightmares.

Observing the scene and cast of characters left my emotions strangely unstirred, perhaps because the situation was so surreal. I looked on as if watching a play, morbidly curious to see what would happen next.

Flanked closely by Selma and her partner, King sauntered in, looking around. "Like what you've done with the place." His voice sounded nasal, as if his nostrils were clamped shut.

Though their guns remained drawn, Silver Tooth and his men were visibly shaken as their eyes followed the little man admiring their décor.

Approaching the table, King raised his hand in the air. "Please, *amigos*, lower your weapons. We're all friends here, right? Come on, be more hospitable. Show me around, pour me a cup of coffee, and we'll sit at your lovely table and have a nice chat."

The three men glanced at one another uncertainly.

"Oh, come on, boys. Take a look at your itty-bitty guns and our big ones. There's no contest here. Oh, this is all so silly. You know who's callin' the shots, amigos. Now put those ridiculous things away before I become impatient with you."

Reluctant, but thoroughly intimidated, the men lowered their guns. One of the men, deciding to be hospitable, slowly picked up the open pink box, cautiously offering it to King.

"Oh, for me?" King cried in mock gratitude. "Oh, how classy of you, and here I thought you were a bunch of low-life buffoons. But you know, I do have a sweet tooth. Can't seem to get enough goodies...Mr. Spade?"

The card suit standing next to him stepped forward, picked up a roll from the box, took a bite, and swallowed. King's eyes narrowed on Mr. Spade's vacant face. The room fell silent as we all waited for Mr. Spade to keel over. After a couple of tense moments, King shrugged, yanked the pastry from Mr. Spade's hand, and took a bite.

Slowly rolling his eyes, King exclaimed, "Oh, amigos. This is really yummy. You have to tell me where you got these. I'll have Mr. Spade pick me up a dozen. No." His finger shot up in the air. "I'll buy the whole stinkin' bakery."

The three men grunted in response.

King took a huge bite, smacking his lips and groaning. The room became still. All eyes watched his lunatic display. Anticipation grew, waiting for him to swallow.

King licked his sticky fingers. "Okay, amigos, enough wining and dining. Get me what I came for." He casually glanced around the room. "Hand over the video and the kid."

The men glanced at one another nervously.

King's trumped-up amiable expression twisted. "Come on, no more games. Is the kid in one of these boxes?" He motioned to the crates.

I cringed.

Silver Tooth cleared his throat. "Please, *Señor* King, we are sorry, but he is not here."

King's face continued to twist, but the tone in his voice remained pleasant. "Took care of him for me, huh? You know how I like to keep my fingers clean. Thoughtful of you

. . . *Now, hand over the video.*" He said this slowly, enunciating each word.

"There is a problem, Señor King," Silver Tooth said, his eyes watchful, moving between Miss Heart and Mr. Spade.

King took another bite of the roll. "Don't mind them," he said, his lips smacking as he waved lazily at his security officers. "They won't be a problem as long as *your* problem doesn't involve my video." He thoughtfully licked his fingers. "Amigos, I'm a very busy man, so why don't you run off and GET MY VIDEO SO I CAN GET OUT OF THIS PIT!"

My breath caught. The abrupt change in his voice was shocking. The way his face writhed reminded me of a rabid weasel.

"Señor King, please, listen," Silver Tooth pleaded. "Please, we had Ben Johnson and the video when we were attacked by a very powerful man."

"Oh, come now. Are you telling me three strappin' fellows such as yourselves—*with guns*—couldn't put down one man?" King's face twisted into amusement. Looking around, he asked, smiling, "Okay, amigos, where are they?"

Terrified, the men looked around and at one another, confused.

"Señor King, it is only us," Silver Tooth assured. "There is no one else here."

Like those of a gleeful child, King's eyes continued to bounce around.

"Please, Señor King, tell us who you are looking for."

King's face twisted with fury. "THE HIDDEN CAMERAS, STUPID! Do you think I'm such an idiot that I would believe the three of you couldn't put down one man?"

Wide-eyed, Silver Tooth shook his head. "Señor King, please listen. This was no ordinary man. It was a ninja with skills I've never witnessed. Yes, he defeated us, but he had the strength of twenty. He moved like the wind, like a ghost."

"WIND! GHOST! BLAH!" Sticking out his pointy tongue, King brought his fingers to his mouth like he was going to gag himself. Suddenly, his fingers paused and his body froze. His flinty eyes moved back and forth like he was watching a tennis match. "Would Takahashi dare?" he asked himself.

Selma looked doubtful. "Takahashi, sir?"

"Of course, Takahashi, *Heart*." He spat her name like it tasted bad. "Who else would have access to ninjas of this caliber?" He smiled crookedly. "He's not the only one with ninjas." He grinned like a madman pushed over the edge.

Selma tried again. "Excuse me, sir. This isn't Takahashi's style, and there is no possible way he would know about the assassin."

"Oh, Heart, don't be naïve," he ridiculed. "We rich and powerful men have ways of finding these things out. He's sending his assassin because he wants my assassin. Let him send all his ghost ninjas. I'm ready!" Then his voice took on a low, creepy tone. "And Takahashi will be the first honored with a visit from mine." He howled with deranged laughter.

My ears picked up a slight scratching noise ahead of me. Lifting my eyes to the rafter, I met two little beady eyes. A scraggly, disease-ridden rat waddled toward me. I yelped.

Suddenly, bullets flew around me. Survival instinct kicked in, along with a rush of adrenaline. The bullets slowed around me, leaving a visible trail behind them. I dove to the rafter in front of me, using it as a springboard to the next. Like a ping-pong ball, I flipped from rafter to rafter, skirting bullets. During a leap, something blazed across my left arm. It felt like a hot iron had been pressed across my bicep, burning the flesh. The pain kicked me up to a new level of survival. I moved so rapidly that the villains below couldn't track me to take proper aim.

The room became silent. They were out of ammunition.

Before they could reload, I dove toward the floor, flipping backwards and landing on my feet before King. Now that we were eye-to-eye, his mouth hung open. His forearms were awkwardly bent up like he'd been trying to cover his ears. His right hand still clutched the cinnamon roll.

Inspiration struck me. Snatching the roll from his tight fist, I leapt through the open freight door and disappeared into the night.

Twenty

The Dynamic Duo

Hopping down into my bedroom from the window ledge, it surprised me to see *9:54* glowing on the alarm clock on my nightstand. I had only leapt from my window two-and-a-half hours ago. It felt like a lifetime had passed.

My room was dark, empty, and lonely. This saddened me, until I caught a whiff of tomato sauce and yeast. Adjusting my eyes better, I saw on the dresser two slices of pepperoni pizza on a plate, with a napkin folded underneath and a glass of water next to it. The thoughtfulness of the gesture brought me to tears. *This crashing adrenaline really stinks.*

Yanking the hood off before it became saturated, I walked to the dresser and picked up a cold slice. In my mouth, I tasted spicy pepperoni and the salt from my tears. I was ridiculous. The crash would have been much worse without the nice five-mile run home. Besides discovering I could dodge bullets, I found I had developed a keen sense of direction. The warehouse district wasn't exactly in my neck of the woods, but my advanced senses had no problem guiding me out and back to more familiar ground. The tricky part had been finding darkened, quiet streets that didn't take me too far off-course. Overall, though, I had made good timing.

I had gnawed down to the pizza crust on my second slice when I heard footsteps coming down the hall, and they weren't Emery's. In a panic, I rushed to my bed and flung the covers back. Shoving aside the pillows Emery had formed under the covers to look like a sleeping body, I jumped into bed, shoes and all, and pulled the bedding over my head.

The door creaked open, and the hall light flooded my room. Forcing myself to breathe, I mimicked deep sleep, snoring a bit.

As Mom walked toward me, I prayed she wouldn't get the urge to kiss me goodnight or gaze at my sleeping face. I'd have a difficult time explaining why I was wearing Nate's ninja costume and purple face paint.

Her feet paused. "Oh, Cassidy," she whispered, irritation in her voice.

My mock snore caught.

Her feet moved quickly toward me, passing by the bed. I heard the window close. Then her feet moved toward my bed, pausing. She rested her hand on my back. With a moan, I wiggled like she was disturbing my sleep. Pulling her hand back, she left, closing the door quietly behind her.

Staying under the covers, I heard her go into Nate's room, leaving a minute later and descending the stairs. There was a soft tapping on my door. Throwing the covers back, I bounded lightly for the door, opening it slightly. Emery slid through, closing it behind him. I was so happy to see his face.

"Where have you been?" he whispered tensely. "Ben came back over an hour and a half ago."

"Would you believe, hanging out in a criminal lair and getting shot at?"

His eyes widened. "Shot at? Did you get hit?"

"Uh-huh. In the arm."

He flicked on the wall light switch. The reading lamp on my nightstand lit. "Which arm? Is the bullet lodged?"

His worry touched me. "No, it—" Before I could finish, he found the tear where the bullet had ripped through the costume and the sweatshirt.

He ran his fingers along the skin through the tear. "The bullet passed through." Examining the skin, he laughed softly. "Unbelievable. Your skin is healed. Aside from a bit of blood, there isn't any mark or indication that you've been shot…Now, tell me who shot you."

After summarizing the surreal experience, I munched on the pizza crust while Emery processed.

Anger passed over his face. "I can't believe this type of element has my mom. I don't understand what King would want with her."

"Maybe she knows the assassin they all keep talking about," I suggested.

He stared at me. "I know my mom is eccentric, but really, Cassidy, she's only an obsessive scientist. She doesn't keep company with criminals."

I regretted bringing it up, but I would have regretted more verbalizing my next thought: *Well, what about your "classified" dad?*

Emery continued, "We should get going. The bus is due at the bottom of the hill in half an hour. If we miss it, there won't be another routed to King Pharmaceutical until midnight."

"We?" I asked, looking Emery over for the first time. With his backpack slung over his shoulder, he wore a knit shirt under his jacket, cargo pants, and cool combat boots, all black. My first thought was, *Why didn't he wear these clothes to school today?* My second thought was, *Not a chance, Emery!*

"Didn't you hear a word I said? King is dangerous. A complete psycho. He knows I'm coming, and he'll be ready.

Who knows what he has planned? At the very least, it will involve bullets—"

Emery put his index finger to his lips.

With an eye roll, I lowered my voice. "Do I need to point out to you that I'm the only person here who can dodge bullets?"

Somehow, my reasonable argument entertained him. Smiling, he stated with finality, "You are not going alone."

Curling my fingers in frustration, I dropped down on the bed. "I shouldn't have come home," I griped at myself. "I should have called you and gone straight to King Pharmaceutical. Why did I come home?"

He sat next to me. "Because you know you need help. You'll be on King's turf, in his playing field. This will involve more than ripping doors off hinges. This will require planning."

"Yeah, yeah, I get it. You're the brains, and I'm the muscle."

A grin spread across Emery's face.

"But no matter how brilliant you or your plans are, it doesn't change the fact that you can't dodge bullets."

"You'd be surprised what I can dodge," he answered.

I opened my mouth to restate my bullet point, when his expression became suddenly impatient.

"We've wasted enough time discussing this," he announced, reaching into the backpack and pulling out a black ski mask. "We'll both have to go out your window. I thought you could go first, and then you can break my fall."

The guy is unbelievable. "What if *I* decide *I'm* not going to do that?" I challenged. "What if I decide I'm going without you?"

He shrugged. "I'll still go out the window, and I'll still go to King's." Standing, he added, "Put the pillows back under the covers and grab your hood." He picked up the backpack and walked to the window.

Doing his bidding, I roughly stuffed the pillows under the covers, muttering to myself as he opened the window. Stomping lightly to my dresser, I swiped up the hood.

"Get the lights, Cassidy."

"Yes, Your *Excellence*." I flipped the switch.

As I turned toward him, he smiled in the dark. "Ladies first," he whispered, gesturing to the window.

Yanking on the hood, I pushed past him, climbing up on the windowsill.

He pulled the mask on over his grin. "Remember, aim for the shadows. I'll drop the backpack first."

"Just don't scream on the way down." With that clever remark, I sprung, landing lightly on the soft grass. My eyes darted to the living room's side window. Inside, the detectives sat on the sofa, looking at a laptop screen together, while Mom curled up on a wingback chair with her eyes closed.

"Psst."

As I looked up, the backpack plummeted towards me. I caught it with one hand. Though it had been easy to catch, it was heavy, as if Emery had packed it full of rocks.

Emery's legs dangled from the window's ledge.

An idea popped into my head, causing a smile to stretch ear to ear. Emery expected me to break his fall— and I would break it, completely. I waved my hand to Emery to come down. I held out my arms to catch him as he fell fast. My left arm hooked his legs first, and my right wrapped around his back so I cradled him.

His eyes widened with shock.

I bounced him in my arms. "My, Emery, you're as light as a feather," I whispered, delighted.

He scrambled out of my arms. "And you're funny, Cassidy," he whispered back.

I giggled, picturing his cheeks bright red under the mask.

Slinging the backpack over his shoulders, he motioned to the street. We followed the shadowed fence line to the sidewalk. Stepping onto the sidewalk, we turned right, walking briskly.

Three houses down, Emery abruptly stopped, pulling the ski mask off. "Give me yours." He put his hand out to me.

"No way," I shook my head. "I'm not going on a city bus with a purple face. Won't that be suspicious?"

He plucked the hood off. "A purple face is a lot less disconcerting than a hidden one." Smiling to himself, he stuffed both in the backpack.

"You're enjoying this. You're making me go on the bus like this because I caught you in my arms," I accused.

"Don't be silly." His smile widened. "Thank you, by the way," he added, and resumed walking.

Glaring at his back and breathing furiously, I quickly caught up with him.

~~~

The bus stopped in front of King Pharmaceutical. When we stepped off the bus alone, Emery quickly pulled me under the sheltered depot.

"Someone as paranoid as King will have outside security cameras," he explained, sitting on the depot bench.

The bus pulled away. Now we were really alone. Peeking around the depot wall, I looked at the impressive "random" building. The fifteen floors created the building's unusual pyramid shape, each floor tapering going up. Cloaking the steel gem were floor- to-ceiling tinted windows, the kind that looked like dark mirrors during the day and reflected ominously at night.

From the roof, a green beacon shaped like a diamond hovered over the building, glowing in the night sky. The opulent symbol made a definite statement: wealth, power, and madness.

I noticed several windows on the top floor shone a little brighter than the rest. I assumed this meant someone was home and waiting.

"Come, sit down, Cassidy."

Turning away from King Pharmaceutical, I looked at Emery. On his lap, he held a large paper made up of six pieces of printer paper taped together. I sat next to him, taking a closer look. "What is this a blueprint of?"

He looked pleased. "You can see this in the dim light? I'm going to need the flashlight. Do you mind pulling it out of the backpack?"

"I never mind when someone *asks*," I hinted.

Squinting at the blueprint, Emery appeared not to have heard me.

Sighing, I unzipped the backpack. Emery had filled it with my dad's tools. "What are you going to do with these?" I asked.

"I'm using those to dismantle the emergency generator before I turn off the electricity. That reminds me." He turned his head to me. "I'm assuming you can also see well in the dark."

"Yep, as clear as day."

"Good. The plan hinges on you having night vision. *Please*, pass me the flashlight." He put his hand out.

"Oh, so you were listening," I said, pulling out the flashlight and placing it in his hand.

"Thank you." He turned the flashlight on. "I'm usually aware even when I don't appear to be." Pointing the light on the paper, he explained, "This is a blueprint of King Pharmaceutical."

"Compliments of Selma Heart?"

"A valuable stone turned over," he replied, confirming his decrypting success. "As I've pointed out, this is King's turf, which puts us at a disadvantage. However, we have your night vision in our favor. My job will be to turn off the electricity, and your job will be to get here." He pointed to the top floor. "To King's office."

His finger moved to the bottom of the blueprint. "Here we are at the main entrance. Through these doors is the lobby. Now, if you look to the left…" His finger moved left. "…you'll see the elevator that Ben told us about. This elevator appears to be a private one for King, because if you notice…" His finger ran up the shaft to the top floor. ". . . it goes to the top floor where King's office is located, and it's the only elevator in the building that does. The only other way to get to that floor is the stairwell.

"The security cameras in the elevator, the stairwell, and throughout the building pose a huge problem. If I'm able to turn the electricity off, you'll be all right. If not, there is only one area of the building that won't be monitored." His finger moved back to the shaft.

"You just said they'll see me in the elevator. Besides, the elevator won't run without electricity," I pointed out.

"I didn't say you would be *in* the elevator."

What he was saying dawned on me. "This is your plan? I'm climbing the elevator cables all the way up to here?" I pointed to the top floor.

"There are no security cameras in the shaft."

"But there is an elevator!"

"Don't panic. It really won't be that difficult."

"Easy for you to say! You're not going to be crushed by a two-ton elevator."

He actually paused to think about this. "I don't think it weighs that much. Now, please, just look at the shaft. See these open spaces on each floor? Those are the elevator doors, and your way out if the elevator should start running. There's a trip lever at the bottom of the door. Push that lever, and the door opens."

"What if the lever sticks?"

"One side of the shaft is safety glass. Kick it out and escape that way."

"Just like that," I muttered, having doubts about Emery's brilliance. The gym rope flashed to mind. "I can't climb. I'm totally pathetic at it. You should see me in P.E."

Unmoved, he said, "I have seen you in P.E., remember? Trust me, climbing will be no problem for you."

"Okay, I'll trust you. So, you cut the electricity. Where?"

"In the basement."

"Okay, you turn it off, dismantle the generator, and I climb to the top floor. Then what?"

He smiled. "We cross that bridge when we get to it."

Briefly contemplating the possible bridge, I asked, "How do we know King has your mom and my dad up there?"

"We don't, but it's likely that he does. This is his fortress, his design. From the top floor, he monitors everything in the building and has made it difficult for anyone to get up to him. If he needed to escape quickly… Look." He pointed to the building's roof on the blueprint. "He has a helicopter pad, and I'm assuming a helicopter. You probably noticed the lights on the top floor. Someone is there, and most likely it's King. If he doesn't have our parents at this location, we'll find out where he does."

Again with the confidence. "All right, what now?"

"You're going to take out the security cameras in the lobby. Then I'll come in, and we'll locate and open the elevator door. I'll go to the basement, and you'll go up the shaft. From there—"

"I know, I know, we'll cross that bridge. How do I get into the lobby?"

"You're going to rip the door off the hinges."

"I thought you said there would be no ripping doors off hinges."

He grinned. "I said this plan would involve more than just ripping doors off hinges. I didn't say it wouldn't be included." He pulled the hood from the backpack. "Put this on, and I'll pin it down."

After he safety-pinned the hood, I hugged him, which seemed appropriate before entering a criminal's lair. "Good-bye, Emery."

He hugged me back. "I'll only be a few minutes behind." Releasing me, he smiled. "Now, rip that door—"

Before he finished his last command, I stood before the tall, tinted glass doors of King Pharmaceutical.

Twenty-One

The Coliseum

My eyes pierced through the obscured glass. The lobby, illuminated in dim light, appeared pristine, spotless, sterile, and without a security guard in sight. There appeared to be an unpreparedness about the scene, an invitation. I knew it was a trap.

Tuning in, I listened for ambushers, thinking perhaps they hid behind the long, sleek desk. I detected no movement, no breathing, only silence. Straining my ears beyond the lobby, I found only silence. I was dumbfounded. Why would King leave the entrance to his fortress unprotected?

An episode from the campy 1960s *Batman* television series popped into my mind, where the Joker trapped Batman in a room, releasing a poisonous gas. I wouldn't have put poisonous gas past my Joker. Wondering if my lungs had super strength, I decided there was only one way to find out. I reached for the door handle. Grasping the polished steel handle reminded me of the forbidden door I had imagined when I made the fateful choice in P.E. Stepping through this door, I knew, would produce unfathomable consequences. My hand hesitated, until I realized Dad's rescue could be the consequence or outcome of this action. For my dad, I could face the unfathomable.

As I yanked the handle, the door pulled off the hinges, hitting the concrete and shattering into thousands of pieces. An alarm blared that sounded like an old police car siren, and colorful lights bounced erratically off the white walls, floors, and ceiling. Stepping through the doorway, I entered King's fortress.

As I walked across the stainless white floor, the alarm turned off. King's face appeared on the huge monitor behind the desk. The strange strobe effect of the bouncing lights made his face appear ghoulish. He was the thing nightmares were made of.

"Hi, there, ninja. What took you so long? It's not right to keep a guy waiting like this. So I see you've come alone. Arrogant little fella, aren't you? Think you can come in here and take me on yourself, huh? Not that I have a beef with arrogance. Usually, I'd respect a man for it, *if* he hadn't been sent to kill me. Don't get me wrong. I've got nothing against you personally. I mean, come on, you were amazing earlier. Poom! Poom! Back and forth like that, and *then...*" King burst into a giggling fit. "The cinnamon roll stunt, now that was creative. It really gave me a chuckle. You know, I could use a fella like you around here. A busy guy like me needs a good laugh now and then."

A voice in the back of my mind whispered, *Cassidy, don't listen. Take out the security cameras. You don't have much time*, but King's rambling drowned out the whisper's wisdom. Like a mouse locked in the mesmerizing stare of the cobra, I was locked in King's madness. As if in a trance, I stared at his ghoulish face on the monitor and continued listening.

"If only I had found you before your lousy boss did. Now understand, ninja, my problem isn't with you. My issue is with that no-good, two-timing Takahashi. Sending you after me... Who does he think he is? WHO DOES HE THINK HE'S DEALIN' WITH?" He paused to take a breath. "Okay, I admit, I'm a little rough around the edges, but I'll give a guy a fair shake. For instance, in a situation such as this, when an assassin shows up on my doorstep and stupidly gets caught, I might let him get down on his hands and knees and beg for mercy. Heck, I'd even hire the guy if he jumped fences and massacred the scumbag who sent him. That is, if I didn't already hate the scumbag's guts.

"Unfortunately for you, I hate your scumbag boss's guts, and the only way I'm okay with all this is if I send you back to him in pieces, packed up in a nice pine box, with a BIG, FAT BOW ON TOP... So, ninja, now you know how this is goin' down tonight. You die. But before the gore fest begins, I've got one question. It's been buggin' me, really gnawin' at the brain. What's with the purple face? Don't think I didn't notice. I'm not blind." He circled his fingers around his eye area. "All that purple. Now, that is just *weird*. Is it like some kind of tradition in your ninja order? Like a ranking thing? You know, instead of belts, you bozos get different- colored faces?

"Be a pal, ninja, tell me. What? Cat got your tongue? Well, if the cat doesn't have it, I will. Hey, I'll mount it to my office wall and salute it with a cinnamon roll now and then."

Entwining his finger, he placed his hands behind his head. His weasel face was smug. "Kind of amateurish of you, just standing there like that, or maybe it's the arrogance. Doesn't matter, anyway, 'cause either way, you're going to give me a good show. This will be fun. I get goose bumps just thinking about it.

"Now, you and bullets, I've already seen. Don't get me wrong. It was exciting and all, but I don't like reruns. We're going to spice things up. Do it like real men used to. Hand to hand. Steel to steel. Blood, guts, the whole shebang." Lifting his lips in a sneer, he growled. "Grrrr. Barbarians." His eyes looked thoughtfully skyward. "I've always been partial to the Roman Coliseum. What I would pay to see those gladiators shred each other."

As I overcame my numbness, my instinctive radar warned me of approaching danger. Senses alert again, I heard them coming down the hall and inhaled their scents. I counted seven. Their footsteps were heavy, and a clanging sound, like metal hitting metal, told me they were armed. Bending my knees, I crouched down in a defensive position. My heart galloped with anticipation.

I am not an animal, but I will defeat these men.

"That's more like it, ninja! You can taste the blood, too. Hope you like the taste of your own. Now, if you don't mind, I'm going to lean back in my big leather chair and be entertained by *my* coliseum. Don't let these animals take you apart too quickly. I want to get my money's worth." His insane laughter rang through the room.

The strobe lights turned off. Overhead, a spotlight shone down on me, creating a wide circle. I understood the stage had been lit. My attackers were near now. I could smell them.

Then they appeared. Entering the room single-file, they fanned out, unhurried. The sight of them would have made me laugh if they hadn't been there to kill me.

Done up King style, the huge men were ludicrously dressed as gladiators. They wore metal mesh tunics, tall gray boots, and scalloped metal breastplates slung over their broad shoulders. Their muscular chests were bare, shiny, and hairless. On their heads they wore steel helmets with nose guards and colorful plumes sticking out of the tops. Each man carried a medieval-looking weapon: a long-handled ax; a thick, studded club; or a spiked metal ball hanging from a chain.

One gladiator carrying an ax held it in the air. As he let it drop, the others let out a battle cry, rushing toward me with weapons raised. Though the advancing men were dream-like, my mutant side didn't allow me to get lost in it.

Without delay, survival kicked in, releasing adrenaline. With my blood rushing and lungs expanding, vision became my dominant sense, slowing the men's motion and blocking auditory and smell. In the quiet, a focused calm took over as my sharpened eyes followed every man's movement. My body prepared to engage. As the first weapon swung toward me, a dance began.

My body instinctively moved into a spontaneous choreography, following the rhythm of the swinging weapons and eluding them. Missing me, their weapons struck one another. During these moments when deadly metal bit into flesh, stimuli seeped in through my eclipsed senses, and I dimly heard screaming and clanging metal, and smelled fresh blood. But none of this interrupted the dance's flow.

Seconds into the dance, I decided to end the gory performance. Now choreographer, my body moved fluidly through step combinations influenced by earlier imprinting. The other performers couldn't keep up. When the performance ended, limp bodies, strewn weapons, and blood covered the white stage, and I stood in the center of it all. King had his gore fest.

Quickly evaluating the fallen men, I heard strong heartbeats and air flowing into their lungs. Though unconscious and bloodied by the weapons, no one was mortally wounded. Knowing this didn't lesson the horror at my feet.

With the attack ended, my mind released me from the intense focus. I could now hear King's prattle that had been an irritating background buzz during the attack. He hadn't shut his mouth once.

"HOW'D YOU DO THAT?" he howled like a dog gone mad. "YOU! YOU CHEATED! YOU'RE A STINKIN', LOUSY, CHEATIN' NINJA!"

Looking at his seething face, rage burned in my gut. *This evil, sick man took my dad from me, from my family*, I fumed, *and all of it is a game to him. This is a game you will lose entirely, Arthur King*, I vowed.

Scanning the walls, I spotted four security cameras, one in each corner. Running toward the first corner, I leapt like I was making a slam dunk, grabbing the camera and pulling it off the wall. As his digital eyes came down, King's rage matched mine.

"STOP! STOP! THIS IS VANDALISM! DESTRUCTION OF PROPERTY! I CAN'T SEEEEE!"

With the cameras down, I leapt up on the desk, making momentary eye contact with King on the monitor before ripping it off the wall and slinging it across the room. With his insane voice out of my head, I plopped down on the desk, sitting so my legs dangled from the edge. My eyes wandered over the unconscious, bloodied men, and then dropped to my black polyester pants, splattered with blood.

"Cassidy, are you all right?"

At the sound of his voice, my dry eyes filled with tears. Dropping my face into my hands, I wept.

Emery's hands gently touched my knees. "I know this is shocking for you, but we have to move before reinforcements come. Focus only on the mission, and don't let anything else crowd your mind. You can't afford to lose concentration."

Lifting my face, I looked into his determined eyes. "But look at what I did," I whispered.

"They will all survive. You showed them mercy, and that's more than they would have given you, and that's more than King will give your dad and my mom if we don't rescue them."

As I took a deep breath, the smell of blood stuck in the back of my throat. But I resolved to move forward. "Okay, I'm ready. What now?"

"Now, we find the elevator."

Hopping down from the desk, I kept my eyes up, following Emery to the wall that appeared solid. In the area indicated on the blueprint, we ran our fingers along the wall, searching tactilely for the hidden doors.

"Found it," Emery said, pulling a crowbar from the backpack and putting the end against the thin crevice. "Cassidy, you'll have to force this in and pry the doors apart."

Pushing and wiggling the bar simultaneously, I worked it between the metal doors until I had enough leverage to force them apart. The doors popped out and slid open, revealing the corridor on the other side through the glass elevator shaft. Gloomily lit, the long passageway appeared like a white tunnel, lined with doors and black monitors. There were no pictures, no potted plants, nothing but sterile white, and each floor would be the same.

Tears welled in my eyes. "It's so sad," I choked out, staring down the white, cheerless expanse.

"You're crashing," Emery stated, looking up the shaft. "Know that is all it is, and keep focused. The elevator is at the top. You'd better start climbing. I'm heading for the electrical room." Turning away, he began to jog across the lobby. That's when I realized his face was uncovered.

"Emery, your mask."

Stopping next to a sprawled body, Emery turned and looked at me, shocked. With a furrowed brow, he quickly unzipped the backpack. At his feet, a bloodied gladiator began to lift his head off the floor. Dropping his eyes to the man, Emery whacked him hard in the head with the backpack. The gladiator's head dropped to the floor, and he went limp. With an impassive expression, Emery lifted the backpack up in his arms, retrieving the mask from it. Slinging it over his shoulder, he pulled the mask over his calm face. "Go," he said to me as he turned, resuming his quest for the electrical room.

Turning to the shaft, I leaped toward the center and grabbed the thick cable. Legs dangling, I began quickly pulling myself up. I rapidly progressed, focusing on the elevator overhead. I pushed bloodied images from my mind and reviewed the plan. Around the ninth floor, a fatal flaw in the plan occurred to me. *King can't see me in the shaft, but he can see Emery. My gosh, Emery has a mask on! King will think he's me!* Then it hit me, like a ton of bricks. *Emery came into the lobby after the security cameras were down, and he was alarmed when he realized he had forgotten to put the mask on. He wants King to think he is me. He wants them to come after him. He's trying to buy me time.* It was a brave, noble, and completely stupid act. If his ploy worked, they would shoot first and ask questions later.

Above me, the elevator doors opened. The click of high heels echoed through the shaft. Frantically, I leapt from the cable toward the elevator floor doors in front of me. My foot caught the frame's ledge, and with my arms, I braced myself inside the frame. The elevator doors closed overhead as my right foot felt along the frame for a lever.

The elevator powered up.

I located the lever and pressed it down. Slowly, the doors before me began to open. The elevator above me dropped.

I dove through the slim opening just as the elevator plunged past me.

Lying on the floor, I took a couple of deep breaths to steady my racing heart before hopping to my feet. Down the center corridor, and down the corridors to my right and to my left, King's face suddenly appeared on every screen lining the walls.

"Hey, ninja, that was a dirty trick, sneaking your buddy in like that. Hoping we'd follow him around like dopes, huh?"

Focus, Cassidy, I reminded myself, *Think. Think.* Ignoring King, I visualized the blueprint and the location of the stairwell. *It's at the end of the right hall*, I decided, pivoting right and sprinting. King continued to talk.

"Wow, you're fast, ninja. Keep coming, fast, fast, fast as you can."

I picked up speed. In a split second, I was at the stairwell. King caught up with me.

"HOW DID YOU DO THAT?" he screamed from the monitor behind me as I opened the stairwell door.

Walking through, I met King's face. *Of course there would be monitors in the stairwell.*

His weasel face twisted in rage. "Hope you're not attached to your buddy. Heart is probably blowing his brains out now!"

I flew up the four flights of stairs. As I burst through the stairwell door to the top floor, I came face-to-face with Mr. Diamond, Mr. Club, and two large semi- automatic gun barrels. Suddenly, darkness engulfed us. I didn't waste a moment. The flash from the first round of ammunition tore through the blackness. Two swift kicks later, the thugs were down and the lights came back on, revealing white walls riddled with bullets and two unconscious henchmen sprawled on the floor. As I gathered their weapons, King went into hysterics on the screens.

"What do you think you're going to do with those? You plan on making me into Swiss cheese? I'm ready for you! This has only been a warm up!"

King abruptly stopped yelling. With the weapons in my arms, I looked up at the screen to see if he had keeled over from a burst blood vessel. I wasn't so lucky. He had muted the sound as he talked into a walkie-talkie. His lips twisted up into a smile. Switching the sound back on, he informed, "Heart's got the kid, ninja." His brows knitted in thought. "What are you doin' with that kid, anyway?" he asked himself more than me.

In that quiet second, relief washed over my rage. *Emery is alive.*

King's brow reformed into an enlightened expression, like he'd just figured out a challenging riddle. His expression wasn't triumphant. I don't think this was a riddle he cared for.

"Phillips. How'd he—" King violently shook his head, like he was trying to dislodge a thought. "It's Phillips who sent you, didn't he? Is he on his way? Is he? ANSWER MEEEE!" King practically foamed at the mouth.

Stunned, I stared up at the monitor, thinking, *King is afraid of Emery's dad.*

King's face contorted into mockery. "He's going to go berserk when he knows I've got his kid." He laughed, snorting like a pig.

Shaking my head to dislodge King's insanity, I focused on crossing this bridge. I glanced down the hall lined with glass-knobbed doors. *Maybe King has Dad and Professor Phillips gagged and tied up in a room down this hall. If he does, and I can locate them before any more henchmen show up, I can leave them with the guns while I rescue Emery.* This was the best I could come up with on the fly. I sniffed the air, picking up a faint trace of Dad. *He's here*, I thought excitedly, listening for movement. Though I didn't hear any, I decided not to rely on hearing alone and to check room by room.

With the guns in my arms, I began kicking in doors. They may have been unlocked, but kicking was less time-consuming.

After observing me kick in two doors, King asked, "What are you looking for, moron? I'll save you time. It's not anywhere near you."

I kicked in another door.

"Hey, how about a game of *Hot and Cold*?"

Another door flew open.

"Cold."

Another.

"Still cold."

King burst into laughter as I kicked in the next one. "Cold, but getting a wee bit warmer. Ninja, this *is* a stupid game, because before you get close to hot, you'll already be dead."

I kicked in another door. The room, like all the rest, was unoccupied.

"How stupid are you? No one is down there. The party is up here, and we are having a good time! Hey, moron, while you were messin' with doors, Heart brought the kid up here, right under your idiot nose. You've disappointed me. I thought you were better than this."

So did I. Bending into the empty room, I dropped the guns on the floor and closed the door.

King peeled into laughter. "You really are a hair- brain. Why go get rid of good guns like that? Don't need them, huh? Well, come and get me, ninja, but you won't make it through this next round. If you've got an ounce of brain, you'll turn and run with your tail between your legs."

I ran, but not away. Rounding the corner to the central corridor to King's office, I skidded to a stop.

Midway down the hall, dressed in identical black robes, stood three ninjas. With hands behind their backs, they stood, barefoot, side by side, like stone statues. Their faces revealed no emotion, but their dark eyes were fearless. They didn't wear hoods. They had nothing to hide. They were the real deal.

"Ninja, meet my ninjas...Tick, tick, tick...tick... Time is up."

Twenty-Two

Time is Up

My blood ran cold.

As I stared into the ninjas' still faces, fear gripped me. King's office doors were no more than a hundred feet away, but they may as well have been a hundred million. There would be no bulldozing these men.

Their penetrating dark eyes rested on me. I felt they could see under the polyester costume and through the purple paint, taking in my true face. They weren't fooled. They knew I was no match.

Where are you, Beast? I appealed, only feeling paralyzing fear. *These men are going to kill me. I'm so sorry, Dad.*

On the monitor, King addressed someone in his office. "So, what do you think, Mr. News? Good stuff, huh? Better than anything you bozos put on TV… What? No comment? Heart, why don't you teach him some manners after the show? On second thought, your program has been cancelled, Mr. News. When this is over, Heart's taking you off the air." He chuckled. "Get it? Off the air? Come on, Mr. News, admit it's funny."

As if a lit match had dropped into a barrel of gasoline, rage exploded in me. I could feel fury blast from the soles of my feet to the roots of my hair, consuming me completely. The blaze burned in my core, melting away fear and doubt. No barrier would keep me from my dad, especially not this human one.

My eyes narrowed to slits on the ninjas, waiting for them to make their move.

I am not an animal, but I will defeat these men.

The ninjas, who had appeared to be made of stone, closed their eyes and slightly bowed. Then their eyes opened, revealing controlled fierceness. They moved their hands from behind their backs, revealing weapons. The first ninja held nunchucks. Like a magician with a deck of cards, the second ninja fanned out small throwing stars, five in each hand. The third pulled a long, thin staff from his back.

The ninjas appeared to have a fighting order. The third ninja stepped forward. Raising the staff in the air, he twirled it wildly like a baton, abruptly thrusting it to the ground, catapulting toward me. Not expecting his speed, my eyes didn't track him quickly enough. His foot struck me on the side of the head. Stumbling back, my body righted itself instantly, and my eyes adjusted to his speed, tracking him as he leaped toward me. As he brought the end of the staff down toward my skull, my right hand darted up, caught the staff, and flung the ninja toward the floor. The ninja stopped his fall with the staff, flipping up onto his feet. Without pausing, he twisted toward me and dropped low, jabbing the end of the staff up toward my jaw. I swiftly moved to the side, narrowly avoiding having my head skewered.

"What happened? Did you see?" King asked his forced audience in surprise. "They moved so fast, I couldn't make out a thing."

The ninja swung the staff over his shoulder and lunged toward me, plunging the end of the staff toward my temple. My right hand shot up and blocked the staff inches from impact. Cupping the staff's end in my palm, I propelled it away from me. The force caused the staff to shoot through the air, harpooning the wall. The ninja stared in disbelief at the staff for a split second— the split second I needed to perform his twist and kick, planting my foot on the side of his head. His body spun in a full circle, his legs buckled, and he fell motionless to the floor.

"What? NO, YOU IDIOT!" King howled.

Something tore into my left arm. Looking down, I saw one of the stars lodged deep in my flesh. The pain intensified my focus as the next nine stars soared toward me. Like a deadly game of dodgeball, my body contorted to avoid contact. Eight stars zoomed past. The ninth headed for my face. As I bent backwards, my right hand shot up in the air, pinching the star dead center before it embedded in my cheek. Springing upright, I pirouetted, and with a snap of my wrist sent the star flying back at the second ninja. It grazed his shoulder and continued its flight, sinking into King's office door.

Without delay, the ninja charged at me, with the other ninja close behind. My star stunt had changed the "taking turns" strategy. The leading ninja leaped toward me in a perfect jump-kick. Imprinting, my body duplicated the jump-kick with more speed and precision. My heel made contact first, ramming into the side of his nose. I could feel the cartilage give way under my foot. Flying backwards, the ninja hit the floor, his bloody nose pushed to the side of his face.

A nunchuck struck the top of my head. I felt and heard my skull crack. In excruciating pain, I fell to the floor. My vision blurred, and sound diminished. King's words echoed through me: *Tick, tick, tick...tick...Time is up.*

No, it's not! Attempting to lift my aching skull, I saw a blurred object rapidly dropping at me. The end of the nunchuck closed in, and before I could react, the ninja jammed it viciously against my throat, crushing my windpipe. I gasped for air that could not enter. The pressure continued, the ninja putting his full weight against the nunchuck. A burning sensation gripped my heart as it beat faster, then slowed.

The pain faded, and my limbs tingled. Warmth spread throughout my body. The blurred brightness softened, creating a soothing glow, dimming to darkness. My last heartbeat thumped in my ear, dissolving into absolute silence.

Above me, a brilliant light appeared made of white fire. The licking flames, alive, spoke my name. My soul responded to the gentle, familiar voice, and gravity lost its hold. Light as a feather, my soul lifted, floating peacefully upward. Closer now, the flames began to move together. Excitement and serenity, two contrasting emotions, worked harmoniously within me as the flames took shape.

Suddenly, I felt a tugging at my core. Like a magnetic force, gravity grabbed me, pulling me rapidly down. The light became distant, then disappeared altogether. In a thud, my soul reunited with my body.

Pain returned, though bearable now, and so did sound. I heard a voice, but it wasn't God's. He wouldn't say the kinds of words I was hearing.

After releasing a string of victorious cuss words, King shouted, "I WON, YOU STUPID, DEAD NINJA!"

Rapidly, the pain subsided, and my heartbeats became strong and even, though air didn't yet flow into my lungs, due to the obstruction still pressing into my throat. My eyes flew open, startling the ninja who still leaned on the nunchuck. My hands darted up and gripped the nunchuck. The ninja stared into my eyes as I slowly lifted him and the nunchuck from my throat, my windpipe miraculously reforming with the ease of pressure. Taking a deep, glorious breath, I thrust the ninja over me, curling up my legs under him so my feet planted on his gut. Exhaling, I straightened my legs, launching the ninja. He flew thirty feet down the hall, slamming against King's office doors, rattling them.

Whole again, I sprung to my feet. As I faced the ninja slumped on the floor, he stared up at me in awe.

"WHAT!" King shouted, infuriated. "You're dead! You're dead! Get back down!"

The ninja slowly lifted himself from the floor and cautiously moved toward me, keeping his eyes lowered. Woozy and bloodied, the other ninjas joined him, the three assembling together. I positioned myself, waiting for their move. To my astonishment, the paid killers dropped their heads in reverence. I understood they were paying homage to the purple-faced ninja who had proven himself undefeatable by rising from the dead.

The miracle totally escaped King. "Kill him! Kill him! Kill him!" he screamed, ironically. "I'm paying you good money! KILL HIM!"

Raising his head, the first ninja's eyes lifted up to the monitor. "King-san, keep your money."

Bowing low to me, all three ninjas turned their backs to King and walked past me down the long corridor, side by side, to the elevator.

"Where do you think you're going?" King screamed. "COWARDS!"

As King ranted at the ninjas who had just left his employment, I gathered the throwing stars. Biting my lip, I quickly yanked out the one sunk in my arm. Within seconds, I felt the wound close. Pushing my robe aside, I stuck the stars in my back jeans pockets.

Tuning in to the office, I heard a henchman move into position behind the door. I knew I only had seconds before he started firing. Pulling the staff out of the wall, I ran, catapulting feet-first toward the doors. The doors burst in when my feet struck them, knocking Mr. Spade down. His machine gun skidded across the floor. Landing on my feet, I gave him a good wallop with the staff, knocking him unconscious.

Turning toward the room, my heart leapt as I looked into my dad's eyes. In the center of the open space, he sat in a chair to the left of Professor Phillips, with Emery to her right. Dad and the professor stared at me with astonished uncertainty. Emery smiled proudly. Our only obstacles now to a happy ending were the guns held to Dad's and Emery's heads by none other than Selma Heart and Detective Paul Reed, the crooked cop.

Perched on a platform in his cushy chair, King glowered at me. Security monitors filled the wall behind him, revealing every inch of the building, except the elevator shaft, and, of course, the lobby. On the stairwell monitor, Detective Conlin, Detective Drammeh, and ten uniformed officers with guns drawn cautiously weaved their way up.

Fixing my eyes on Miss Heart and Detective Reed, I pulled the stars out of my pockets, fanning them in my hands as the ninja had done. It would all go without a hitch if the people I came to rescue sat perfectly still.

In one swift motion, the stars glided one after another through the air, hitting their intended targets. The stars plunged into Miss Heart's and Detective Reed's hands and forearms. As they cried out in agonizing pain, Dad and Emery grabbed their guns.

Having seized Detective Reed's gun, Emery held it on the two henchmen. "On the floor," he ordered.

With injured arms and hands held carefully to her chest, Selma stood, sizing Emery up. Following her cue, Detective Reed also ignored the command.

Emery aided her analysis by pulling the hammer back.

The smile played on her lips as she slowly lowered herself to the floor. Though in tremendous pain, she didn't show it except for a wince here and there. Detective Reed wasn't so tough, crying out the entire, excruciating way down.

Behind me, Dad ordered King, "You, too, on the floor."

I smiled to myself.

"Down on the floor," Dad demanded again, a threatening edge in his voice.

Turning around to see why King resisted, I looked to see that Dad held the gun on me, not King. I gaped under the hood, my eyes moving from the barrel up to his face. His crystal blue eyes narrowed on me dangerously. I froze, unable to move a limb in the unfathomable situation.

"No!" Emery shouted behind me. "Mr. Jones, lower the gun. He's with us."

Speak, I instructed my unwilling vocal cords, *If Dad hears your voice, he'll put the gun down. Speak!* But no sound came forward. Immobile, bewildered, afraid, and despairing, my eyes filled with tears.

Dad's expression changed to disbelief. His lips began to form my name. Abruptly dropping his eyes, he slightly shook his head. I understood the gesture. He was dislodging the impossible thought. His eyes shot back up to mine, more resolute than before, and he pulled the hammer back.

"Down, now, or I shoot."

"No! Mr. Jones, you don't understand."

Suddenly, Professor Phillips filled in the gap between me and the gun. Facing my dad, she said, calmly, "Drake, lower the weapon."

"Serena, what are you doing? Get out of the way," Dad demanded.

Her right arm moved forward. "Drake, this is not an enemy." Her arm moved down. I knew then that she had placed her hand on the gun, lowering it herself. Turning toward me, she whispered urgently, "Go, my dear. King is escaping from the roof."

Whipping around to King's perch, I saw a staircase that had been revealed next to his command center. Through the secret doorway, I heard the sound of helicopter propellers warming up.

~~~

By the time I reached the rooftop, the little weasel was halfway to the helicopter. Scanning the roof, I noticed a long, thick metal chain coiled up next to the roof's guardrail. Leaping to the chain, I lifted the heavy end, twirling it over my head like a lasso. As the chain spun faster, I released more of it until about ten feet whirled over me. Taking aim, I released the chain. It flew through the air, hitting the spinning propellers and snapping them in two.

King stopped dead in his tracks. His body convulsed in rage. "LOUSY, STUPID NINJA!" he howled at the night, shaking his fists in the air. Jerking around to me, his pointy teeth poked out from his curled lip. "Great! Just great, ninja. Now we're trapped up here," he snarled.

Stunned, I stared at him. After everything he'd witnessed me do, I expected him to be quivering in a corner. At least, that was what a sane villain would have done when face-to-face with his assumed assassin. A sane villain wouldn't reprimand the assassin.

Pompously, he walked toward me, face twisted into a friendly expression. "Hey, ninja, let's work somethin' out here. A guy like you doesn't care who signs the paycheck. Guys like you are always on the lookout for a better opportunity, right?" Crookedly smiling, he lifted his elbows and flipped his palms up. "Well, here I am. Opportunity...Hey, I'll cover whatever this hit will cost you tonight. Heck, I'll double it! Work for me. I need a guy with your talent. First order of business is getting me off this roof. A smart guy like you already has a plan, right?"

Crossing my arms, I shook my head slowly. I didn't know if it was the money that made him feel indestructible, or the madness.

Undeterred, King continued to persuade. "Don't you get it, ninja? I'm your golden goose. Get us outta here, and you'll have riches beyond your imagination." Raising his hands to the diamond beacon above us, he cried passionately, "All of this will be yours, too. Give me your allegiance, and the world will be at our feet!"

Huh? I thought. *Wasn't there another serpent who tempted in a similar way? Sorry, you slimy snake, I'll have to pass.* Turning to the guard rail, I looked down. The way the floor-to-ceiling windows slanted, the side of the building appeared like a long, steep slide. Shrugging to myself, I thought, *Well, why not? It'll be the ride of my life, but after everything else, sliding three hundred feet is minor. What's the worst that can happen? I'll die...again.*

Hopping up to the top of the guardrail, I sat, dangling my legs, and prepared to go down.

King grabbed my forearm. "Don't leave me here," he pleaded in stunned disbelief. "Take me with you."

Looking down at him, I pulled my arm from his grasp.

His face twisted into fury. Grabbing my forearm again, he sank his pointy teeth into it, like a spoiled child throwing a temper tantrum.

Yanking my arm from his rabid mouth, I swatted his face, sending him reeling backwards. Quickly recovering, he ran at me, eyes wide, as I lifted my backside off the rail. His cussing followed me down the painfully bumpy descent. I hadn't taken the metal window frames into account.

As I slid past the second floor, I pushed off the cold glass, landing on my feet to the right of King Pharmaceutical's main entrance. Slipping into the shadows, I observed the police cars, ambulances, and media collected out front, a circus waiting for a circus. I wanted to hang around and watch King and his henchmen escorted out of his fortress in handcuffs, but I knew I had to get moving if Mom was going to find me peacefully sleeping in bed when she came in to tell me the good news.

"See you soon, Dad," I whispered, turning on my heels and heading homeward.

Twenty-Three

Homecoming

"Cassy, Dad's coming home!"

Nate's announcement reverberated through my head, which felt made of lead—or maybe it felt mushy, I couldn't figure out which.

Dropping my forearm over my eyes, I cheered in a groan, "Yay." When my pathetic cheer got no response, I realized the announcer had already left, his feet bounding down the stairs. Peeking out from behind my arm, I saw that *3:35* glowed on the alarm clock next to me. No wonder I was having trouble shaking myself out of this stupor. I had only made it to bed a little over an hour ago.

The front door opened, and a full-hearted cheer broke out. Suddenly in the here-and-now, I popped out of bed, squealing, "Dad's home." Flying out of my room to the staircase, I watched the heartwarming scene below. My teary-eyed father tightly embraced my joyfully weeping mother, and Chazz wrapped his arms around their legs. Dad's left arm released Mom to pull Nate into the family hug. At the open front door, Detective Conlin watched the reunion with a tear in his eye, and Ben leaned against the stair banister, grinning from ear to ear, enjoying the picture-perfect moment. There was only one thing missing.

Bounding down the stairs, I paused to hug Ben. The last time I'd seen him, he had been gagged and blindfolded. Throwing my arms around his neck, I thought, *I know what you did, brave Ben. I'll never forget it.*

In my ear, Ben whispered, choking up, "I know, I'm happy, too. Go see your dad."

Releasing his neck, I smiled up at him. Ben returned my smile with his sunny one, the worry lines gone from his forehead. His eyes welled with happy tears. "Go," he urged, playfully shoving me. "Before I start bawling."

Not needing to be told a second time, I ran into my dad's arms, which had just opened up for me. After a tight embrace, Dad cupped my face in his hands, searching my eyes.

Hoping my eyes looked innocent, I smiled up at him. "I love you, Daddy."

The concern on his face gave way to the loving expression I knew so well, the way my dad usually looked at me. Kissing the bandage on my forehead, he said, "I love you, too, sweetheart."

Detective Conlin cleared his throat. "Well, Jones family, this has been a long night for you. Drake, my friend—" He extended his hand toward Dad.

Dad grabbed his hand. "Bob, I can't thank you enough."

Stepping over to him, Mom gave the detective a quick hug. "Thank you, Bob. Forgive me for not trusting you."

He smiled regretfully. "No need to apologize. Reed snookered us all." The detective ran his fingers through his thin hair. "He really tangled up this investigation. It's going to be quite a mess to clean up. Thank heavens Emery left the map in Drake's printer, or we wouldn't have had any clue where to look for him. If he hadn't, things would have worked out a lot differently."

Interesting, I thought. *Emery left directions. He must not have been convinced the detectives were bad. Either way, it would have worked out. We had everything under control by the time the police arrived.* As if a cloud passed, I saw my predicament in a new light. If Formula 10X hadn't changed me, everything would have still happened just the same.

Professor Phillips would have still been kidnapped, Emery would have still come to stay with us, Dad would have still gone to King Pharmaceutical and been kidnapped, and we wouldn't have had the happy ending we had now. My accident had saved all of them.

Detective Conlin gripped Dad's shoulder. "Drake, get some rest, and I'll see you at the station later this morning. I'm going home myself for a few hours, since King and his crew have declined to talk until their lawyers show up. Fine with me. I could use some sleep before jumping into that circus."

As the detective turned to leave, Ben spoke up. "Wait up, Bob, I have something for you in my car."

A smile froze on my face to cover the panic.

Ben hugged Dad. "Good to see you, man. What I'm about to tell the good detective, you and I will talk about later, okay?" Patting Dad's back, Ben informed Detective Conlin, "I've got the kidnappers' guns in my car."

Everyone gasped.

Shocked, Dad began, "Ben, wh—"

Pointing at him and grinning, Ben repeated, "*Later*, Drake." Turning to the detective, he added, "I don't think they've been wiped. You should be able to lift good prints."

I gulped.

As they walked out, the clever detective said to Ben, "I didn't take you for a cat guy."

Closing the door, Ben laughed. "Yeah, Bob, I don't own cats. I can hardly afford to feed myself."

Staring at the door, Dad said to himself, "What did that kid get himself involved in?"

Hugging him, Mom mimicked Ben. "*Later*, Drake." She kissed his cheek. "Let's get you to bed before you have to go back to the station." Waving her hand toward the stairs, she

246

added, "Everyone back to bed. We'll talk after Dad gets sleep."

Tromping up the stairs, Dad held Chazz. Nestling his nose in Dad's neck, he asked, yawning, "When do I have to get up for school?"

Dad kissed his ear. "No school today, son. You all get the day off." He looked back at Nate and me. "Remember to stay away from the windows. Those pesky reporters will be showing up soon." He chuckled. "It'll be a media zoo for us and the Phillipses for a day or so." At the top of the stairs, he asked me, "Cass, can Chazz bunk with you?"

"Sure," I said as Dad put my tired brother on his feet.

Bending over, he whispered in Chazz's ear. "When you wake up, I'll tell you about the ninja that saved your daddy's life."

"Okay," Chazz whispered back, nodding enthusiastically.

Wrestling a grin off my face, I wondered at what point Dad had decided I was a good ninja assassin. Go figure.

After another round of hugs, I took Chazz by the hand, leading him to my room.

As I flipped on the light switch in my room, Chazz cried, "My Spidey pillow! It's in Nate's room." He said this like the sky was falling.

"I'll get it, Chazz. You climb in my bed." Crossing the hall to Nate's room, I knocked on his door. There was no answer. Knocking again, I opened the door, "Nate, Ch—" The pillow hit me square in the face. I couldn't believe I didn't see that one coming.

Reclining on his bed, Nate impishly grinned at me. "Anything else?"

"No. Sweet dreams." I stuck my tongue out at him as I closed the door.

Stepping through my door, I froze. Sitting on the floor, Chazz held in his lap the ninja costume that I had piled against my wall, along with other clothing evidence. Wide-eyed, he examined the tear from the star dagger. I noticed next to him were muddy footprints, trailing from the window to the bed. That explained the gritty feeling at the bottom of my sheets.

Thinking fast, I asked lightly, "Now, how did Nate's costume get in here? Did you bring it in?"

He frowned. "Yeah."

The kid totally threw me off.

"Well, here's your pillow, Chazzy," I said too cheerfully. "Let's go to bed." Turning to the bed, I saw a purple stain where I had pressed my face against the fitted sheet. Placing Chazz's pillow quickly over the stain, I glanced at him to see if he had noticed. He hadn't. He was too busy examining the muddy footprints on the carpet. "Come on, Chazz, in bed."

Without looking at me, he walked past me and climbed into bed, turning to his side. After staring at his back for a moment, I climbed into bed, switching off the light on the nightstand. At a loss for words, I lay on my back, staring up at the ceiling.

Turning to me, Chazz rested his head on my shoulder. "Thank you, Cassy," he whispered.

I responded carefully, "You're welcome. I like it when you sleep in here, too." I tensed, waiting for a response.

"Night," he yawned, snuggling closer. Within seconds, he fell asleep.

Nestling my cheek in his hair, I continued staring at the ceiling, mulling over the night's events. Of all the troubling things that had happened, from bloodied gladiators to guns with my fingerprints, the thing most disturbing was returning from the dead. The dying didn't distress me, nor did what occurred afterward; it was being pulled back here that caused angst. *Does the quick healing make me immortal?* I wondered. *Will I be immortally fourteen? Gads!* The thought brought tears to my eyes.

Though the thought of being forever fourteen was horrid, even more tormenting was the idea that I would stay the same while everyone else aged and eventually left me.

The tears streaming down my face dampened Chazz's hair, but I couldn't bear moving away from him. In my grief, a heaviness spread through me, making me feel I was sinking through the mattress to the floor. Finally giving in to the heaviness, I began to drift off.

Somewhere between wake and sleep, a quiet, still voice from within whispered, *Though your destiny is like no other, it will not be an unhappy one. You will not be alone.*

I fell into a deep, peaceful sleep.

Twenty-Four

New Neighbors

L ater that morning, Dad filled in some missing pieces to the complex puzzle before returning to the police station to give his official statement. What he told us, he said, was for our ears only and was never to go beyond our kitchen. While Professor Phillips and Dad were held captive, she'd explained to him what had motivated her abduction. "Assassin" had led to her kidnapping, but Assassin wasn't a person, like I had assumed—it was a weapon.

Sixteen years earlier, Professor Phillips had headed a top-secret military program, developing a biological weapon called Assassin. If it had been successfully developed, Assassin would have been a virus that, when released, would pass rapidly from person to person, without displaying symptoms, until it made contact with its target's DNA. Designed to rapidly attack and destroy cells and tissue, the virus would liquefy the target's organs in less than an hour after exposure.

Professor Phillips had justified developing Assassin, believing that in the long run it would save lives, since the weapon only targeted certain individuals. However, her feelings about creating the weapon changed when she got wind of corruption in the program and feared Assassin would go to the highest bidder. The risk of developing a weapon of such magnitude was too great. In the wrong hands, Assassin could put the world at an evil individual's feet.

Professor Phillips left the program, and it shut down. She told Dad she had destroyed the program's research so no one else could pick up where she left off. From that point on, she had dedicated her profession to helping others, making up for what she called her "destructive past." She had successfully buried that past, until Arthur King resurrected it. His motivation in abducting her was obvious: he wanted to become "King of the World."

King didn't have to dig deep to turn up Professor Phillips's past. His father, Arthur King Senior, had also been involved in the program. Later that day, I Googled King's father and discovered that he had been killed in a private plane crash eleven years earlier. According to his brief bio, King Sr., a scientist and business tycoon, had founded King Pharmaceutical thirty years ago, among other successful corporations. His entire fortune had been left to his only heir: his son.

Another piece added to the puzzle was King's motivation for kidnapping Dad. When Dad took the phone call outside King's office in front of the photo wall, King assumed Dad had recognized one of the employee photos, Selma Heart, and had snapped a picture of it with the phone.

Dad never saw his masked abductors, but he mentioned they spoke Spanish. Professor Phillips believed these men had also abducted her for King, because the last thing she remembered was letting a South American janitor push a trash can on wheels into her lab, and the smell of chloroform. I would put ten bucks down that he had a cigarette hanging out of his mouth, puffing sweet-smelling smoke all over the lab before wheeling the professor out of the building in the trash can, while Miss Heart held the door wide open.

When Dad mentioned the "lucky break" of getting the guns, I felt like I was turning a shade of green. Though tormented by those prints, I consoled myself with the thought that since I had no criminal past and my fingerprints weren't in a police database, for now the prints from the guns would remain unidentified. At least, that's what I thought. It would have been nice to have someone to talk this over with—which brings me to Emery.

Tuesday afternoon, he had called our house. Nate picked up the call on the handset in the family room. After briefly talking with Nate, Emery asked for me. I took the handset from my twin, forcing a neutral expression. Neutral was hardly what I felt.

"Hi," I said into the receiver, eyeing Nate. He lounged on the sectional across from me, flipping through the TV Guide.

"Cassidy, I don't have much time. We won't be able to talk again for the next two or three days."

"Why?"

"I don't have time to explain. Do you remember my promise to you?"

How could I forget? "Yes."

"Good. Could you do one thing for me?"

I'd do anything for you! "Sure."

"Don't go to school for the remainder of the week."

Oops. Can't do that. "Sure. I'll tell Miriam 'hi' tomorrow *at* school."

Nate grinned down at the TV Guide when I said this.

There was a long pause. During this silence, I listened to Emery's steady breathing, longing to see him, longing to know what his mom could do for me. This was the mission now, right? Helping Cassidy.

"This is what I want you to do," he eventually began, "whenever your emotions begin to get the best of you, picture Robin in your head."

Now, that was just cruel and not at all what I hoped to hear. "Okay. Anything else?"

"Yes. Work off the excess energy late at night in your room. It will help you cope better the next day."

"Got it. Anything *more*?"

"I'm sorry…That's all for now."

"Too bad," I said, fighting back tears. "Um, I should go."

"Cassidy, don't forget my promise."

My eyes misted up. "I won't."

"Don't forget to visualize Robin. And working off the excess."

"Okay," I said, my voice breaking. Nate glanced up at me. "Take care, Emery."

"You have my cell phone number. Call if something urgent comes up."

My whole life is urgent, I thought desperately, but only said, "All right. Bye." I hung up, wanting to collapse into a hopeless heap. Instead, I just stared at the handset in my hand. *What am I going to do?*

"You okay, Cass?"

I looked up at my twin's concerned face. "Why wouldn't I be?" I asked, drumming up a smile. "Anything good on?"

He tossed me the TV Guide. "You choose." Looking away, he turned on the television. I had never felt so alone and scared.

~~~

For the next three days, my feelings and thoughts swung from one end of the pendulum to the other. One second I'd be hopeful, sure Professor Phillips would suddenly show up at my front door and tell me all would be well, and then the next I'd be convinced Emery was a no-good liar and that they had skipped town, leaving me to deal with this nightmare on my own. Even in my darkest moments, I resisted calling Emery. There was a reason he couldn't call me, and no matter what my emotions dictated, I instinctively knew the wisest thing to do was to be patient, to wait, no matter how excruciating waiting was.

So I trudged on, employing Emery's coping strategies and trying to ignore the fact that school life had become like living in a fishbowl. Between breaking Robin's nose and Dad's kidnapping, there was no under- the-radar for Cassidy Jones. Knowing the boy who had held a gun on two henchmen didn't help my desire to remain inconspicuous, either. Emery's heroism, coupled with his humbling of Dixon Pilchowski, had made him a legend at Queen Anne High School. I just wondered when I'd see this legend again.

Friday afternoon answered that question.

When Miriam and I turned onto our street Friday after school and I caught sight of the huge moving van parked in front of the rental, I knew Emery's word was golden. *It has to be them*, I thought, trying to mask my excitement. If Miriam caught wind Emery could possibly be our new neighbor, she would race me down the street. She'd had Emery Phillips on the brain since he "rescued" her.

Playing it cool as we walked at a painfully slow pace, I said, "Oh, look. New renters." At that moment, Dad crossed the street from our house. He paused at the front of the van, extending his hand to someone out of view. I was dying to listen in, but Miriam was talking.

"*Gosh*, I hope a super cute boy is moving in," she said at the end of her ramble, grabbing hold of her front gate. "We need some excitement around here."

"I'm going to talk to my dad," I told her quickly, ready to break into a run. "See ya tomorrow."

"Call me if there's a boy, especially if he's hot," she unabashedly called after me.

I raised my hand in acknowledgement, while tuning in to Dad's voice, catching the tail end of his sentence. "—great family neighborhood."

A deep masculine voice smoothly answered, "Yes, this is obviously a friendly neighborhood. I feel at home already." In his voice, I picked up a touch of sarcasm, though his easy cadence covered it well. "My work requires me to travel quite a bit, and after what we've been through, it will be a comfort to know such a wonderful family will be looking out for mine when I'm not here."

The talker shifted, moving into my view. With a gasp, I skidded to a stop, almost falling on my backside. A supersized Emery looked from Dad to me. That is, a supersized Emery who had lost a UFC fight. The guy's face showed evidence of having received some serious blows.

"Drake, is that your daughter?"

Turning, Dad looked at me standing in the middle of the street. He grinned. "Cassidy, come over. I'd like you to meet our new neighbor." He said this like I didn't have eyes.

Forcing a smile, I moved toward them. Emery was the spitting image of his father. They shared the same black hair and eyes, fair complexion, and lofty build. Of course, his father's features were more mature, with prominent cheekbones, a strong chin, broad shoulders, and muscular chest under the navy blue v-neck sweater. Breathtakingly handsome, the guy definitely crunched more than numbers. Even the bruises, gouged lower lip, and gauze bandage slanted across his forehead didn't take away from his looks, but did, however, suggest Mr. Phillips was involved in some risky "accounting" business.

His smile was friendly as I stopped by my dad's side. Both Dad and I had to crane our necks to look into his face. His assessing gaze settled on me, making my heart feel like it was attempting escape. It didn't pound because of the man's utter beauty or roughed-up appearance; it pounded because of the danger that radiated from him. Mysterious Mr. Phillips was just plain scary.

Clearly not sensing "danger," Dad made introductions, pleased as punch. "Cassidy, I would like you to meet Gavin Phillips, Emery's dad."

Again, did he think I was blind? Trying to look surprised, I untangled my tongue. "Nice to meet you, Mr. Phillips."

Smiling, he extended his hand, which I timidly took. "It's nice to finally meet you, Cassidy." He squeezed my hand. I wondered if this was like an eyewink, letting me know he was in on my little secret. "Emery has talked about you nonstop."

"He has?" I could feel the confusion on my face. *If Mr. Phillips knows, why would he single me out in front of Dad? Wouldn't the goal be not to bring attention to me?*

His eyes narrowed on my face, but his expression remained amiable. "You seem surprised by all this. Didn't Emery mention when you called last night that our application had been accepted for this rental?"

Huh? "That wasn't me, Mr. Phillips. I haven't talked to Emery since Tuesday."

His scrutiny deepened. "Not since Tuesday?"

What is this? A cross-examination? I asked myself, staring at him bewildered. Suddenly, it dawned on me that was exactly what this was. *He doesn't know*, I realized. *He's putting pieces together, comparing information. Why wouldn't his wife and son tell him about me?*

Knowing there wasn't time to speculate, only to throw this fox off my trail, I thought fast. "Not since Tuesday," I confirmed. "He called Nate, and I answered the phone." To my dismay, I blushed. I could feel Dad's eyes on my face, curiously observing me.

Mr. Phillips took note of the blush, too. Then he switched tactics. "Emery is eager to start school with you on Monday," he said, smiling.

Shocked, I asked, "With me?"

"Yes, Cassidy," he replied, studying my face. "I registered him this morning. You'll have five classes together."

"Gavin, why would Emery attend high school?" Dad inquired, puzzled.

Surprise crossed Mr. Phillips's face, but then his features relaxed. "I understand the confusion now. Please forgive me. I wasn't aware my son mentioned his academic achievements to you. He is usually very modest about them." The easy smile reappeared. "Allow me to explain what's behind the madness. Being with your family, Drake, and attending school with you, Cassidy, made Emery realize how much he's missed out. His mother and I wanted to give him a chance to recoup what he lost not being with kids his own age. When he mentioned the house across from yours was for rent, we recognized this as the perfect opportunity." He gestured, unenthused, toward his new home.

Something told me there was not a lot of "we" in the decision. "What about Stanford?" I asked quickly.

"Stanford is on hold, which I must admit, pleases me. Emery *is* only fifteen." He paused, and then continued carefully, "I hope, Cassidy, you and your brother will be sensitive to the situation and not mention to your classmates Emery's accomplishments. It is extremely important that he fits in."

"We won't," I assured him, hoping guilt wasn't etched on my face. If I had been aware of the extremes Emery planned to go, I would have absolved him of his promise. "Uh, Mr. Phillips, is he here now?"

"Yes, he's helping his mother set up her lab."

"Here?" I squeaked.

"Yes, my wife has moved her lab here," he confirmed, staring at me. "I know he would like to see you. Why don't I take you down?" He smiled at Dad. "Drake, if that's all right with you?"

"Of course. I'd like to say hello to Serena and Emery myself, but unfortunately, I'm due back at the station." Dad offered his hand to Mr. Phillips. "I'm looking forward to getting to know you, Gavin."

Firmly shaking Dad's hand, Mr. Phillips replied, "Thank you for everything. I won't forget what you've done for my family."

~~~

My stomach was a nervous twist, watching Dad back the Volvo out of our driveway and onto the street. After waving good-bye, my gaze wandered up to the bandage on Mr. Phillips's forehead.

"Would you like to know what happened?" he asked.

My eyes dropped to his, and I nodded like a terrified child.

He smiled. "Bar fight."

My eyes widened. "Really?"

He shook his head, laughing lightly. "No, nothing that exciting." He looked directly into my eyes. "I fell down airplane stairs on my way here."

"All that from stairs?" I asked doubtfully. All I could think was, *Couldn't he come up with something more original?*

His grin grew; his eyes sharpened. "We're talking fifteen metal steps."

258

I forced a smile. "I guess that would bang you up. Did you need stitches?"

He touched the bandage. "A few. That fall caused my unfortunate delay."

Something caused your delay, and it wasn't airplane stairs, I thought, recalling King saying, *"Phillips. How'd he—"* The sly fox standing before me had escaped some kind of snare.

"How did you hurt your head?" he continued casually, but the look on his face told me mine gave too much away.

I shrugged, looking away from him. "I fell, too."

"Cassidy," Emery called from his front porch.

At that moment, Mr. Phillips and his slippery tale were completely forgotten.

Spinning around, I took in my friend's wonderful face. Was he a sight for sore eyes! The feelings surging through me were those an ex-soldier would experience seeing a former comrade in arms. The battle Emery and I had fought together had been short-lived, but the camaraderie resulting from it apparently was not.

Beyond excited, I left Mr. Phillips in the dust, dashing to Emery. "I knew as soon as I saw the moving van," I exclaimed, throwing my arms around his neck. "I was beginning to wonder if I'd ever see you again."

Emery wrapped his arms around me, whispering, "I did promise."

I nodded my head happily against his shoulder. Then I realized the hug was going on a little too long and it wasn't feeling so much like camaraderie. *Uh-oh.*

"I'm so glad you're here," I said in one breath, pulling away. Emery abruptly released his hold, causing me to stumble backwards. I caught myself before I could fall down the porch steps. "I can't believe it," I added awkwardly, righting myself. Then I looked up at his too-big grin. My brows knitted. *Something is up.*

"We found out late last night this rental worked out," he explained, giving me a lovey-dovey look. "I didn't want to say anything to you without knowing first."

"Oh," I said, dragging out the syllables. Struggling to find more familiar ground, my eyes traveled from his face. It was then I noticed he wasn't wearing his standard ensemble. Instead, he wore a gray hoodie, baggy jeans, and Nike tennis shoes. "Cool new threads."

"A little more to your liking?"

My eyes shot up to his face, narrowing.

His grin widened. Shoving his glasses up his nose, he lifted his head to look over mine. "Dad, I'm taking Cassidy down to the lab."

"Sure, Son, and let your mom know I'm out front keeping an eye on the movers." Mr. Phillips's voice held a suspicious edge. I guessed by the way Emery smiled at him that he must be smiling, too. I didn't dare turn around to look, not after his son's flirtatious act.

~~~

Inside, I quickly took note. With a living room to the right of the foyer, a dining room to the left, and kitchen behind the stairs, the house's floor plan resembled ours. "It's like our house," I said, glancing up at Emery.

He shrugged. "Similar, except this house doesn't have the office and family room, and there are only three bedrooms upstairs."

I noticed he said "this house" and not "our house."

"It'll look nice when you decorate it."

His lips curved into his amused smile. I had really missed that smile. "You want to talk about decorating?"

"No," I said, socking his arm. "What the heck was that all about?"

"You're referring to our overzealous greeting?"

This time I wished he had not said "our."

"Oh, just tell me why," I demanded, blushing. "And tell me why your dad is so intense. And why he doesn't know about me."

"All right, but bear with me," he said, trying to sound serious. Serious is difficult to pull off when you're grinning. "I'll have to answer your petitions in reverse order."

My eyes rolled. *Brother.*

Emery held up three fingers. "He doesn't know about you because my mom doesn't want him to know." He lowered his third finger, holding up two. "The intensity is normal, but elevated because he's suspicious. He wasn't buying the I-want-to-be-with- my-peers line, which leads me into—" He lowered his middle finger, leaving his index finger upright. "This morning he insisted on being with me while registering at your school. When the counselor pulled up the enrollment for the classes I requested, he noticed your name on the class rosters. From there, he drew his own conclusions. I think you know what those conclusions are."

My cheeks heated up.

Encouraged by my reaction, Emery mercilessly added, "In retrospect, a love-struck teenage boy would have been the better way to go. Infatuation is much more believable—"

I shoved him. "Stop already! You've embarrassed me enough." He started laughing, and I smiled, saying, "Geez! Is this how you behave during downtime? You're like Nate, but with a bigger vocabulary." This made Emery laugh harder. I shoved him again. "Okay, go ahead and fake infatuation—just not around me. I swear if you ever give me that gooey look again, I'll totally start laughing."

"It took me awhile to get that look down," he claimed, giving me "the look."

I laughed and shook a finger. "Enough. There are important things to discuss here."

"You're right, Cassidy," he said, catching his laugh. "You're just so much fun."

"Yeah, to make fun *of*...But seriously, who beat up your dad?"

He became serious. "He opted out of discussing it."

Okay...Strange. "Why doesn't your mom want him to know about me?"

"She didn't say specifically."

"Didn't you ask?"

"No."

Mind-boggling. "Well, what if your dad doesn't fall for all this and demands that you tell him the truth?"

Emery smiled like I had just cracked a good joke. "My family doesn't work like yours. We don't ask, and we don't demand. However, in this instance, due to the outrageousness of the request, he did put me through the third degree. Trust me. It wasn't pleasant. But you'll be glad to know that I didn't buckle," he teased.

Glancing toward the closed front door, I briefly tuned in to Mr. Phillips out front directing the movers. His smooth tone was edged like a razor. *This is a weird way for a family to function, but in this case, I'm grateful for the weirdness,* I thought, looking back at Emery. "Thank you for being here and for everything you're giving up for me. Hopefully it will only be for a short while," I said, adding with fingers crossed. "Can she help me?"

His expression became solemn. "Let's talk about it with her."

Twenty-Five

Where is the Syringe?

Sitting next to Emery in a metal folding chair, I nervously scanned the basement. Exposed brick walls and a cement floor revealed the large, unfinished space with a washer, dryer, and other utilities. Black paper covered the two small windows. Dim light emanated from the bare single bulbs hanging from the ceiling and five floor lamps scattered throughout the room. The tables from the professor's university office were laid out similarly, with boxes piled high on top. One feature in the room made me especially nervous: a medical exam table.

"My dear, how are you handling the transmutation?" Professor Phillips asked conversationally.

My head whipped around to her desk. "I-is that what you call it?"

"That's what she calls it," Emery said, looking steadily at his mother. "She's merely asking how you're coping, Cassidy."

"Oh," I said, making a mental note to Google "transmutation." I had a feeling I wouldn't like the definition. "Well, I'm not doing too good, Professor Phillips," I admitted, and then paused, hesitant to ask the question my life hinged upon. "Can you, uh…help me?"

Her eyes had that strange glow. "How so?"

Stunned, I stared at her, having no idea how to respond.

Emery responded for me. "'*How so*,' Mom? Isn't it fairly obvious what Cassidy is asking you?"

"It is obvious," she granted him, "but does she comprehend the significance of her cellular transformation?"

"Mom, we've already discussed this."

"Yes, *we* have—thoroughly. However, the decision is Cassidy's, and I sense she is undecided."

Undecided about what? I asked myself, feeling the blankness on my face. I hadn't a clue what decision I had to make.

Professor Phillips leaned toward me. "I don't know if you understand how unprecedented your alterations are," she continued eagerly. "The scientific community thought such cellular mutations were impossible, but here you are. Remarkable."

As if suddenly able to decipher some strange language, I understood where Professor Phillips was leading me, and my blood went instantly hot. "You want me to stay like this," I accused her. Emery quickly touched my shoulder. I shook his hand off angrily. "So you can strap me to that table," I raged on, jerking a hand toward the exam table. My fingers then folded into a fist. "So you can study me—experiment on me like some kind of *animal*!" I slammed my fist into the edge of the desk. The wood splintered under it, and I could feel bones crack in my hand. Excruciating pain shot up my arm like a jolt of electricity, and I gritted my teeth to keep from crying out.

The room fell silent.

Drawing in a jagged breath, I looked down at my broken hand. The fingers were misaligned, shifted toward the thumb. The burning pain had subsided to a dull tingling by now. Leaning toward me, Emery lightly touched my

265

forearm. "Look at your fingers," he said softly as my hand reformed before our eyes.

"Incredible," Professor Phillips whispered in awe. Having risen to her feet, she observed the miraculous event, too.

Emery sat back in his chair, silently watching his mother. Though his expression was impartial, I could feel disapproval roll off him in waves.

Lifting my healed hand, I glared at her. "I will not be your lab rat," I said through my teeth. "And I am decided. If you can fix me, do it."

Her brown eyes widened, getting that deer-in- the-headlights look. "I would never—" she began in a devastated tone, lowering herself into her chair. Seated, she dropped her gaze to a seared notebook on her desk. It was the same notebook Emery had held in the lab: the remnants of Formula 10X. The professor stared mournfully at the destroyed data, continuing in a rueful tone, "Cassidy, forgive my insensitivity. I know how difficult and confusing this is for you, especially being so young." Her softened eyes moved up to me. The look in them was genuine. "I will do everything in my power to find a solution. You have my word."

I exhaled a relieved breath. *She may be a mad scientist, but she isn't an evil one*, I decided. I believed her word, like her son's, was true.

Leaning forward, she reached across the desk to me, and I took her small hands in mine. I felt as if I stared into the face of hope, only "hope" didn't look very hopeful.

"You are safe, my dear. I won't let anything harm you. Now, please—" She gently squeezed my fingers. "Don't be frightened by what I'm about to tell you… What you were exposed to that day was developed in part from previous research I did for the military."

A lump formed in my throat. I swallowed it down, choking out, "Assassin?"

Her thumbs stroked mine. "Yes, but do not be afraid," she repeated. "I was using my Assassin research to develop something good, something beneficial, not destructive. This particular work I kept to myself. Not even Emery was aware of it. How he connected the dots I do not know." After saying this last part, she lost herself momentarily in thought. During this brief silence, I realized the "he" was someone other than Emery. I assumed "he" must be Arthur King.

Pulling her thoughts back in line, the professor continued, "Emery has only just learned of my past, and that is why it was difficult for him to understand what had happened to you. If he'd known about Assassin, he would have concluded what I'm about to share with you.

"When the liquid compounds combined, I believe some type of retrovirus was created. When you inhaled, the virus entered your body, infecting you. Once the gas dissipated, so did the virus. Obviously, and I'm not sure why this is yet, the virus cannot be passed the way viruses normally are. These microbes appear satisfied with their host. I believe the only way to contract the virus is in the gas form you were exposed to.

"This virus has incorporated itself into your cells, mutating them, if you will. Now, this virus is not attacking your immune system. It behaves in quite the opposite way. Your cells have been enhanced and have developed the ability to spontaneously regenerate. Similar to the way a starfish grows back a lost arm, your cells have that ability now. The mutation has also evolved your interneurons, which is why you can perform incredible physical feats and why your senses are heightened. This is also why you can process information in your environment and integrate it into your memory."

"Emery calls this imprinting," I said numbly, pulling my hands from hers. Slouching back in my chair, I let it all sink in. *There are microbes reforming my cells, reforming me. Into what? Into another species?* Suddenly, I had a fairly good idea what "transmutation" meant. "Professor Phillips—"

"Serena, please."

"Serena," I tested her name. "Are you sure this is what's wrong with me?"

"I'm almost positive, given what I know about what you were exposed to, but I won't know for certain until I have a look at your blood."

"Blood?" I croaked.

"My dear, you aren't afraid to have your blood drawn, are you?" Glancing at Emery, she added, "Emery is quite good at it. You won't feel a thing."

I pointed at Emery. "You mean *he* is going to draw my blood?"

Emery looked like he was about to laugh. "After everything, Cassidy, you doubt I can painlessly insert a needle into your cubital vein?"

Despite the situation, I laughed. "Well, when you put it like *that*." Then I added, rolling my eyes, "My own personal lab technician. What a lucky girl."

Emery grinned.

"Yes, my dear, you are quite lucky," Serena agreed, and then added with a smile, "I've been told my syringe techniques are just short of torture." I gathered this was a little Serena-humor.

A lull in conversation occurred after Serena's "joke." I decided this was a good time for some Q&A. "Professor—I mean, Serena—there is something I'd like to ask you about," I said. "It's about how I can't die—"

"We don't know what you can or cannot do yet," she interrupted, clarifying. "You're scientifically uncharted territory. Your cells have been reformed and most likely will continue to evolve. I believe there will still be changes we will observe in you."

"Well, okay," I said, moving on before these disturbing words could take hold. "Anyway, I want to know if you think I might stop aging, that is, until you find an antidote or something."

Her expression became disturbed. "I don't like to venture in speculation like this, but if you need an opinion to comfort you, I would guess that you will continue to grow until your growth plates close. Again, this is only a guess." Leaning forward, she continued, solemnly looking into my eyes, "My dear, you must understand that in order for me to help you, I must develop a vaccine. Finding a cure for a retrovirus is nearly impossible because viruses tend to mutate rapidly. Even if I successfully developed a vaccine, the virus would most likely mutate into a form the vaccine would have no effect on."

"In other words," I said, imagining a prison door clanging shut and locking, "I'm like this forever."

"Cassidy, 'nearly impossible' isn't impossible. I'm limited in my own knowledge. However, I believe there is much more taking place in the greater scheme of things, and in that there is always hope."

I didn't see an answer in her explanation. "So, you're *hoping* you can cure me?"

"No, I believe eventually we will find an answer."

I wasn't sure what the difference was, but by the way she smiled, I guessed there was one.

She continued, "Together, we will pursue that answer. You will not be left alone in this, and Emery and I will keep you safe."

Like her son, she said this with such confidence, I couldn't help but believe her. "Thank you." I glanced at Emery's confident face. "What now?"

Serena sounded like she was reading from a typical daily agenda. "I will work here on a solution. During the week, Emery will attend school with you. Every other afternoon, you will come here, have your blood drawn, et cetera, et cetera—"

The *et ceteras* made me cringe.

"In the evenings and on the weekends, Emery and I will continue working."

I looked guiltily at Emery. "This sounds like a life sentence for all of us. You know, you don't need to do this. Neither of you do." Swallowing hard, I feared they'd take me up on the release.

Turning in his chair to face me, Emery looked me square in the eye. "This is my choice. No one has coerced me. It isn't like we'll be bound by chains, you know. We'll have our own lives. For me, this will be like a daily job, and afterward, when I'm off the clock, I'll continue my own pursuits."

Great, I'm a job. "Let me get this straight. You're giving up Stanford so you can babysit me?"

"No, I'll give up *being* at Stanford so I can 'babysit' you," he clarified, flashing a quick smile. "Next spring, I'll continue my education through correspondence."

Next spring? He is planning for the long haul. "You know, I don't think subjecting yourself to high school every day is necessary."

A grin tugged at Emery's mouth. "No, it's necessary."

I narrowed my eyes on him. "Why? Because I'm so unstable?"

The grin continued to tug. "I don't like the word 'unstable.' It makes me think of a chemical reaction." He paused reflectively, throwing on a thoughtful look. But his lips kept twitching. "Never mind. 'Unstable' works."

Emery got a nice jab in the arm, which, of course, cracked him up.

Serena cleared her throat, frowning at her son. "There is another thing we need to discuss, and that is the importance of keeping this among ourselves," she said, setting a new mood. The new mood had "bad vibe" written all over it. "I'm not so naïve to believe we will be able to keep others ignorant in the long run, but we must try for as long as possible. Cassidy, understand under normal circumstances, I wouldn't ask any individual to go against the good values they've been taught. However, in this situation, secrecy is imperative. It could mean life or death."

The way she looked into my eyes made my skin crawl.

"If what has happened to you should get out, there are depraved individuals who would stop at nothing to get possession of you. I shudder to think what Arthur King would do if he gained knowledge of you."

Thoroughly pulled into her foreboding, I did shudder. "But he'll be in jail."

Her expression was haunting. "I was not referring to the son," she clarified slowly. "I was referring to the father."

"But he's dead," I barely whispered.

"No. He is not."

Simultaneously, my skin crawled and chills ran up my spine. Wide-eyed, I stared at her in horror.

Patting my shoulder, Emery said in a dismissive tone, "Don't bite the bait. No one will know beyond us."

Now who's being naïve? "What about your dad? He's already suspicious."

Emery grinned. "I already told you *how* he is suspicious."

"This isn't a game," I reprimanded.

"No, it is not," Serena agreed, looking with disapproval at her son. "Emery, your father cannot know. You have no idea how knowledge of this would conflict him." With an expression of regret, she whispered to herself, "I fear he wouldn't make the right choice."

"Ridiculous," Emery muttered.

Shocked by his blatant disrespect, I gaped at him. Serena wasn't pleased herself, but still, she didn't treat him like a child who had stepped out of line. "Emery, do not allow your brilliance to blind you. Understand that there are many situations that you do not understand, and this is one such situation."

Emery looked at her with an expression my mom would call "saucy." After a few tense moments of staring one another down, Emery said to his mother, "Between your doomsaying and Dad's intensity, you're going to make Cassidy afraid of her own shadow."

Bobbing my head, I admitted, "My shadow is becoming a little scary."

Emery pealed into laughter again, and again, received a jab in the arm from me.

Scowling profusely, Serena switched scare tactics. "I must share a concern with you both. There was something missing from my lab that wasn't on the evidence list the police provided."

Clearing the residual effects of laughter from his throat, Emery asked, "What is it, Mom?"

"The towel saturated with Cassidy's blood."

The last remnants of Emery's grin disappeared. "Was the towel in the refrigerator?"

"Yes. In a Ziploc bag."

"Is this bad?" I asked, my heart in my mouth.

"It depends on who has the towel, or, more precisely, who has your DNA," Serena answered matter-of-factly.

Emery grabbed my hand. "Cassidy, don't worry," he reassured me, glancing at his mom. "Everything is fine."

Staring at Serena's smug face, I thought, *Sorry, Emery, my bets are on the mad scientist. This will not be fine.* But how could I say this to the boy who had snuffed out his bright future to babysit, protect, and appease a mutant girl?

I smiled gratefully. "Thanks, Emery. I believe it will be, too."

"Good, Cassidy, good." He grinned approvingly, patting my hand.

My smile broadened as I added to my previous thought, *But you, you riddle of a boy, you're the one I will trust. Don't let me down.*

After brief scrutiny, Emery turned to the professor and asked casually, "Mom, do you know which box the syringes are in?"

AND VULCAN'S GIFT

Prologue

Rory Michaels sat in a wingback chair studded with aged brass nails, staring morosely at the dying embers in his study's fireplace. The embers were remnants of a fire that had burned bright and vibrant, as he once had, too.

"I have lived too long," he whispered into the silence.

His gaze dropped to his hands folded neatly in his lap, displaying wrinkles and other imperfections marking his years. Examining them, he mused about the vastness of their experiences. With his hands, he had muscled a plow through hard, rocky ground; cupped the face of his young bride; and gripped an M-1 rifle, his finger easing the trigger back. They had held the heads of dying comrades on blood-soaked soil, cradled the fragile body of his newborn son, and meticulously mixed metal compounds that would one day lead to his fortune.

A single hand had swung a forging hammer, shaken the hands of presidents and world leaders, and helped carry the caskets of loved ones to open graves. And now a single hand had struck the face of a deceiver, a deceiver he had loved like his own. His palm still felt the sting.

Tormented, he reflected on the confrontation that had just transpired.

When the deceiver had entered his study half an hour earlier, Rory had a moment of doubt as he looked into the blue eyes that had always shone with kindness and affection. However, he had the facts, had them verified, and knew the insidious bloodline this one descended from. There was only one reason this person would be in their midst.

"Here you are, Rory." The deceiver had handed him a cut crystal snifter with a shot of brandy, smiling a smile that had once warmed his heart, as the brandy would do. Rory sipped the brandy, relishing the comforting burn in his throat. After the sip, he downed the shot. It was time to get this over with.

"Let me take that for you, Rory."

Releasing the snifter into the deceiver's hand, he silently watched the deceiver walk to the granite-topped bar and rinse the glass in the small bronze sink. Grabbing a dishtowel, the deceiver carefully dried the snifter. "What is it you'd like to discuss with me?"

Rory heard the steel cords in the deceiver's voice. He had never heard them before, and he wondered what other new discoveries he would make this evening.

The deceiver returned the glass to the shelf over the bar and slowly turned around. "I'm all ears."

Rory marveled at the transformation in the blue eyes, turned hard and cold like glass. "You have your grandfather's eyes," he observed, a bitter taste coming into his mouth. "His were edged with madness, too."

"He was a great man," the deceiver said, as though they were in agreement.

"He was a menace," Rory corrected harshly. "Do you understand the evil he planned to unleash with this so-called gift from Vulcan?"

"Perfectly, *dieb*."

"How dare you call me 'thief'!"

"That is generally what someone is called who takes something that doesn't belong to them," the deceiver replied in a lethal tone. "It is *mine*, and I want it *now*."

Rory let out a humorless laugh. "It is the Devil's, and that is where it has gone."

"You're lying. Not even you, oh righteous *dieb*, would destroy the recipe for ultimate power."

"Your eyes will never look upon it."

A slow, cruel smile curved the deceiver's mouth. "Over your dead body?"

With a burst of fury, Rory launched at the deceiver, striking a hand across the face he had once cherished. The deceiver took the blow, and turned eyes full of mocking hatred back on Rory. The lips held a cruel smile.

Rory felt ready to collapse. "Get out," he whispered hoarsely, returning to his chair.

"This isn't over," the deceiver vowed, moving toward the door.

"Yes, it is."

The smile widened. "Yes. It is." With this puzzling response, the deceiver stepped out of the room and pulled the door shut.

Coming out of his thoughts, Rory noticed that the last of the embers in the fireplace had burned out, being reduced to ashes. Contemplating the deceiver's last statement, he realized that he had underestimated the motivation of this individual. When he had called the meeting, he'd been sure this was a case of a lost sheep in need of a shepherd's staff to hook its neck and navigate it to the right path. He had anticipated repentance, but instead learned the sheep was a wolf in disguise.

With this sad realization, Rory's heart clenched with grief, and then it quite literally clenched.

Pain riveted through his chest. "Brandy," he wheezed, clawing wildly at his heart. "What poison is this?" Gasping for air, he fell forward and collapsed to the floor.

"My child," he panted, rolling in agony. "You've murdered me."

Acknowledgments

Many thanks to:

My husband, David, and our children, Julia, Audrey, Catherine, and Ethan, for their unwavering support and patience, which made this endeavor possible.

My mom, Lynne, for her encouragement and dedication to read every word I write.

David and Phaidra Campbell, Marianne Loeser, James Morgan, Lee Shoblom, Stacey Urhammer, Gunner Redd, Electra Redd, Wyoma Claire, and Dawn Litterell for reading drafts and providing feedback.

Annie, Audrey, Emma, Hazel, Josie, Julia, Katie, Paula, and Riley for being beta readers.

William Greenleaf for the superb editing and invaluable writing critiques.

Twin Art Design for the awesome book cover.

Last but never least, Cassidy's fans. I look forward to continuing her journey with you.

Elise Stokes lives in Washington State with her husband and their four children, where she is at work on Cassidy's next exciting adventure.

Visit: www.cassidyjonesadventures.com
www.facebook.com/Cassidy.Jones.Adventures.Series
www.twitter.com/CassidyJonesAdv

Books in the Cassidy Jones Adventures series:

Cassidy Jones and the Secret Formula

Cassidy Jones and Vulcan's Gift

Cassidy Jones and the Seventh Attendant

Cassidy Jones and the Luminous

Cassidy Jones and the Eternal Flame

74160773R00172

Made in the USA
Middletown, DE
20 May 2018